GHOST PIRATES
THE MERMAID CHRONICLES BOOK FOUR

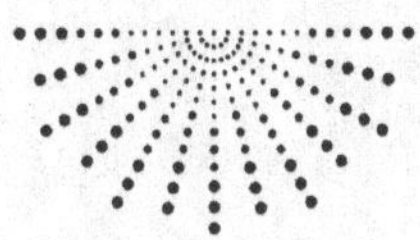

MARISA NOELLE

OTHER BOOKS BY MARISA NOELLE

The Shadow Keepers

The Unraveling of Luna Forester

The Unadjusteds Universe

The Unadjusteds Trilogy

The Unadjusteds

The Rise of The Altereds

The Reckoning

The Origin Stories

Silver Melody

Matt Lawson

Joe Rucker

Erica Swiftfield

Paige Starling

Hal Small

Kyle Lewis

Jacob Shea

Sawyer Watson

Addison Shields

President Bear

REVIEWS FOR THE MERMAID CHRONICLES

"If I could give this 10 stars, I would!" – Goodreads Reader

"Romeo & Juliet for today." - Amazon reader

"Romance, mermaids vs sharks - what more do you need? This is a thrilling read with great characters that you won't want to put down!" – SJ Willis, best-selling author of *Bite Risk*

"Packed with twists, could not stop reading!" – Louie Stowell, best-selling author of *Loki: A Bad God's Guide to Doing Good*

"Marisa Noelle does it again with her charming and gripping story of Cordelia and Wade as they navigate the tricky waters of love in a time of change and challenge." - Lynn Lipinski, author of *God of Internet* & *Bloodlines*, among many others

"A refreshing take on an emerging genre. I found this book so hard to put down. Lots of drama mixed with a dollop of romance and just a touch of the supernatural." – Melissa Welliver, author of *My Love Life and the Apocalypse*

"The premise is laced with conflict, and you'll cheer for Cordelia all the way through as she battle to overcome inherent differences and conflicts." - Author Stuart White, CEO of WriteMentor

"This is a brilliant series! I love it! It's like a mixture of Sirens the TV series and *Aquaman* and a *Romeo & Juliet* forbidden love story." - ARC reader

"Enchanting! Mesmerizing! Captivating! Heart-breaking!" - Book Blogger

"Deliciously romantic!" - Goodreads reader

"This series is so good, it got me out of my slump!" ARC reader

CONTENT WARNINGS

This book contains themes and references that some readers may find distressing, including, but not limited to:

- Violence
- Minor sexual content
- Death or dying
- Blood, gore, graphic injuries
- Mental illness, depression, alcoholism, anxiety
- Prejudice
- Swears or curses
- Murder
- War
- Monsters

GHOST PIRATES PLAYLIST

Mermaid - Train
Revenge - Danger Mouse
Anti-Hero - Taylor Swift
Titanium - David Guetta, Sia
Fight Song - Rachel Platten
Head Over Feet - Alanis Morissette
Leave a Light On - Tom Walker
I Try - Macy Gray
Love of my Life - Queen
Goodbye My Lover - James Blunt
Somewhere Over The Rainbow - Israel Kamakawiwo'ole
Don't Break The Heart - Tom Grennan
Cold Heart - Elton John, Dua Lipa
Believer - Imagine Dragons
Let Me Down Slowly - Alec Benjamin
When I Was older - Billie Eilish
Better Days - Dermot Kennedy

Be Careful - Tommee Profitt, Laney Jones
Lift Me Up - Rihanna

For Louise

RECAP OF BOOK 1 – SECRETS OF THE DEEP

On the approach of Cordelia Blue's eighteenth birthday, she decided it was time to break free from the shadows of her tragic past. The loss of her mother and twin brother in a devastating shark attack had haunted her for five long years, forcing her to abandon her once-promising swimming career. She even shied away from taking a simple bath.

With unwavering support from her best friends, Maya and Trent, Cordelia embarked on a journey to conquer her deepest fears head-on. Little did she know, this leap of faith would reveal a world of enchanting secrets lurking beneath the surface. As she dipped her toes into water for the first time since the attack, Cordelia unearthed her astonishing destiny—she was a mermaid, and her long-lost twin, Dylan, was alive too. Trapped in an aquatic realm, he was unable to shift into human form. Dylan entrusted Cordelia with a mystical pearl, a key to locating the elusive High Council— the sole authority capable of granting mermaids their precious legs once more. However, the mermaids weren't the only ones hunting for this gem. The selachii, shark shapeshifters cursed to the depths, yearned to regain their legs too. And would stop at nothing to find it.

Old flame, Wade Waters, swam back into Cordelia's life. Sparks flew, but lurking in the shadows were Wade's shady cousins, and Cordelia couldn't shake the feeling that he was harboring a deep, dark secret. And keeping her own secret concerning her mermaid lineage under wraps took a toll on their relationship.

When the pearl mysteriously vanished from Cordelia's grasp, she discovered Wade's secret—he was one of the selachii and had betrayed her. Worse yet, Trent, her loyal friend, fell victim to a brutal shark attack and was transformed into one of them.

With trust shattered and alliances uncertain, Cordelia turned to Maya and the ancient tome, *The Mermaid Chronicles*, which held the key to unraveling their intertwined destinies. Maya insisted that mermaids and selachii must unite to reclaim their lost glory. Cordelia delved into the book's secrets, uncovering a forgotten era of harmony between mermaids and selachii on the fabled island of Atlantis.

As Cordelia unmasked Zale, the leader of the selachii, as the thief behind the pearl's theft, she and Wade joined forces to retrieve the precious jewel, but almost cost them Wade's life. When Cordelia and Wade reunited, the pearl's secrets unraveled, whisking them away to another dimension to confront the enigmatic High Council.

The High Council, comprised of representatives from mermaids, selachii, dragon kings, and eelusionists, agreed to grant them legs once more. Yet, it came at a price—Cordelia and Wade were tasked with the monumental quest to unearth their lost homeland, the mythical Atlantis. The epic adventure had only just begun, and the fate of two worlds hung in the balance.

RECAP OF BOOK 2 – QUEST FOR ATLANTIS

When mermaids began mysteriously disappearing, stolen away by humans for display or sinister experiments, the hidden realm of mermaids and selachii was unveiled. Cordelia, Wade, and their friends fought valiantly, rescuing one of their own from a science lab. Yet, the global onslaught continued, casting an ever-growing shadow over their existence.

Their mission was clear: unveil the enigma of the lost island of Atlantis—an aquatic sanctuary where all ocean shifters could find refuge. To unlock its secrets, the team embarked on a quest for the fabled, scattered jewels that held the key to Atlantis' portal. But their journey was fraught with peril.

Beneath the icy depths of Mount Rainier and the treacherous Puget Sound, Cordelia and Wade faced near-death encounters with ice demons. Gal, a formidable dragon king and council member, defied convention to save them. The

Power of the Sea surged through them, healing their wounds and bestowing incredible gifts—a Herculean strength for Wade and the untamed power of fire for Cordelia.

Tensions flared as Wade's ex, Stephanie, intruded on the mission, determined to win him back, fueled by his mother's approval. Cordelia grappled with doubt, their bond tested by misunderstandings and painful infidelities, fracturing their once-unbreakable unity.

Maya's life hung by a thread after a harrowing accident, compelling Dylan to transform her into a mermaid. But the toll of their perilous journey didn't end there—Cordelia's father faced certain death in the unfathomable Mariana Trench, only to be transformed into a selachii through a desperate ritual led by Wade.

Amidst near-tragedies and heartaches, Cordelia and Wade rekindled their love, poised to confront those who sought to tear them apart. Armed with the keys to Atlantis, they crossed dimensions into a magical realm. But a harrowing sight awaited them—an island in ruins, guarded by legions of dragon kings. A savage battle ensued, with Cordelia mastering her fiery abilities to vanquish the malevolent force, at the cost of her dear mentor, Gal.

As the Power of the Sea was plunged into the Fountain of Youth, the island blossomed anew. Amidst the rejuvenation, Cordelia made an astonishing discovery—a long-lost captive, her mother, believed dead for over five years, was alive and well.

In a joyous reunion, Cordelia found her family and a newfound sanctuary where all could walk on land, hidden from prying human eyes. Amidst the serenity, Wade proposed to Cordelia, promising a blissful future, until the pages of *The Mermaid Chronicles* started turning once again.

RECAP OF BOOK 3 – FIGHT FOR FREEDOM

A year after the discovery of the long-lost Atlantis and their showdown with the fierce dragon kings, Cordelia and Wade tied the knot, ascending to their rightful thrones as the rulers of the mystical island. Hidden away from the prying eyes and judgmental gazes of ordinary humans, Atlantis basked in tranquility, shielded by an enchanting veil that isolated it from the rest of the world.

As the brave folks of Atlantis cautiously reconnected with their mainland families, a shockwave of devastating news rocked their world. A cataclysmic nuclear war had erupted, and fingers were pointed squarely at none other than the merfolk and selachii.

This apocalyptic nightmare was set in motion when a wealthy baron's wife met a watery demise. With no ocean shifters around to perform the life-saving resuscitation ritual, the baron pointed the finger of blame at the mysterious Atlantis, threatening to unleash nuclear annihilation unless the world revealed the whereabouts of the elusive merfolk. But nobody had a clue where the merfolk had vanished to, and humanity paid the price with widespread devastation.

Venturing back to the mainland, Cordelia, Wade, and their loyal friends stumbled upon two distinct groups of surviving humans. There were those desperate for survival after the nuclear apocalypse and a faction hell-bent on extracting vengeance from the ocean shifters.

Wade and Trent fell into the clutches of a former mercenary turned captor, the enigmatic Sean Wilson. Meanwhile, Cordelia found herself face-to-face with her high-school rival, the determined Babette, who pledged to aid her in freeing Atlanteans from the clutches of hostile humans, and giving them hope surrounding the latest prophecy in *The Mermaid Chronicles*. While distracted, Wade's ex-girlfriend, the ever-jealous Stephanie, resurfaced as a formidable sea witch, swearing vengeance on Wade and Atlantis.

While Cordelia and her fearless squad embarked on a daring rescue mission to free Wade from the clutches of mercenaries, they crossed paths with Blaze, the last surviving dragon king and Gal's only son, Cordelia's late mentor. With Blaze's remarkable abilities and Cordelia's fiery powers, they launched a mission to free the ocean shifters from captivity. Their journey back to Atlantis, however, took a treacherous turn when Stephanie and Aquaria unleashed the dreaded Hound of the Ocean, a venomous sea monster with a lethal breath.

Simultaneously, Sean Wilson invaded Atlantis, leaving a trail of death and destruction in his wake, including the loss of crucial High Council members. As the situation spiraled out of control and their people faced annihilation, Cordelia's powers went haywire, forcing an uneasy alliance with Babette, her father, and their human army, and fulfilling the prophecy.

Just when all hope seemed lost, Cordelia's wedding ring revealed astonishing powers, creating an impenetrable force-field around the ocean shifters and saving them from the deadly breath of the Hound. But humans were still dying. After vanquishing Aquaria, Cordelia confronted the monstrous sea beast with her fire abilities. Entrusting the ring to Babette, it extended its protection to the humans too, truly uniting all three species. With Wade by her side and a glimmer of the Power of the Sea from Edward, a High Council member, they finally achieved victory, though Stephanie managed to slip away.

Back on Atlantis, Cordelia and Wade threw open their island's gates to the surviving humans, offering refuge from the radiation and nuclear chaos ravaging the mainland. Babette was entrusted with the guardianship of the Power of the Sea by the last surviving High Council member as he breathed his last, ensuring that humans would forever feel a part of Atlantis.

In a poignant ceremony honoring those lost in the attack and the venerable High Council, Stephanie unleashed her venomous snakes, poisoning Atlanteans. Jordan, Wade's devoted cousin, who had once been enamored with Stephanie, delivered the fatal blow, stabbing her through the heart and ending her reign of terror.

Only then did tranquility return to the island, with Cordelia dropping the bombshell that she was pregnant. But the pages of *The Mermaid Chronicles* never remain still for long.

N
W
E
S
San
Diego
Lake
Echomere
City
Palace
ATLANTIS

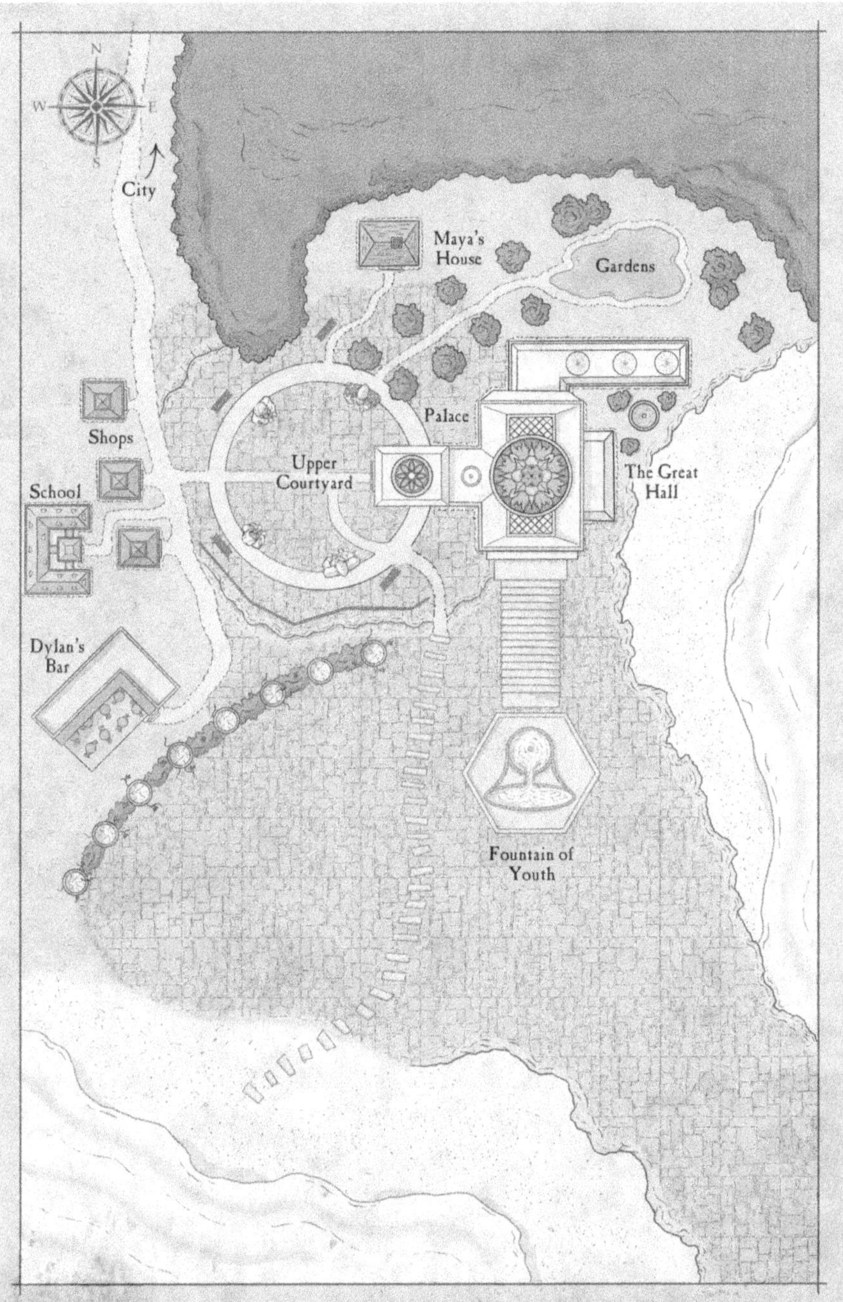

N
W E
S
City
Maya's
House
Gardens
Shops
Palace
Upper
Courtyard
The Great
Hall
School
Dylan's
Bar
Fountain of
Youth

PROLOGUE

ngelica cradled her nephew close, shushing him with meaningless platitudes as if he were conscious and could hear her soothing words. His ashray wounds were extensive. They covered such a vast span of his mottled skin that she couldn't say for sure if he would survive. Unlikely. She knew that deep down. But she refused to let the truth surface. Better to stuff it down deep with all the other pain. But pain had a limit. Loss could break a person. Grief was a physical thing. Guilt was another entity altogether. A nasty, dark, hard, growing *thing* made of nothing but meanness.

She squeezed her eyes shut against her morbid thoughts and sang to him, even though her voice trembled and didn't carry its usual timbre. What else could she do? An ashray wound was incurable. The ghostly rays attacked during the hours of darkness, burning human or orca flesh—it didn't make a difference to them—and left angry wounds that lasted for at least a year. For those who avoided infection, the pain alone was often unbearable, leading many to contemplate jumping off towering icebergs or drowning themselves in the sea. Her own sister...driven insane by the pain. But she wouldn't let that happen to her nephew, Frost. Not if it was the last thing she did.

The small ice shelf they rested on rocked with an unseen force. Angelica braced herself and held onto Frost, careful not to touch his wounds. As the ice shook beneath them, she cast a quick glance at the remainder of her resting clan. They were dotted among the icebergs, most of them with their orca tails still visible, but a few had transformed into their human forms. Not long ago, there were over fifty of them. Now their numbers were a mere twenty-five. The war. The ashrays. The dark mutterings of the deep.

A few acknowledged her panicked look, noted her trembling iceberg, and jumped into the frigid Antarctic water to come to her aid. Who knew what new monstrosity might arise? But before her clan reached her, a familiar head breached the surface of the water. Zale.

"You scared the shit out of me," Angelica said.

Treading water, Zale raised both palms. "I apologize."

Angelica relaxed back onto the ice but didn't lessen her hold on Frost.

"What do you want, Zale?" Angelica eyed the enormous selachii. His size was a new thing. All the time he'd spent with the Denizens of the Deep had finally paid off. According to him. Granting him not just their trust, but an extraordinary size. Megalodon size. No wonder the ice rattled when he swam. "I'm not in the mood."

"Is it not enough for me to enjoy your scintillating conversation?" He smirked.

"I've got other things on my mind."

His gaze fell to Frost, still unconscious on her lap. Zale shuddered. "Ashray, huh? Nasty fuckers."

"More than one." A wall of tears built behind her eyes, but it would do no good to shed them. "I don't know what to do. His wounds are so extensive. After my sister...I can't lose him, Zale."

Zale leaped out of the water and landed on the ice beside Angelica, rocking it again. His great white shark tail dangled in the water. He lifted both Angelica and Frost into his arms. "It's going to be okay."

She rested her head against his chest. "No, it's not, and it's all my fault."

His hand brushed the back of her head, a rare tender gesture, nothing he'd ever done during the nights they'd been intimate. "It's not your fault. You're only doing what you need to do to survive."

"Diving into uncharted territories? Taking him to dangerous or forbidden zones? Hunting the ashrays because all our food sources died after the war?"

"You're the clan leader. You must make difficult decisions."

"We've lost over twenty in five years," Angelica said, pulling back from him to look at his dark eyes.

His expression hardened. "You can blame the humans for that. And the mermaids. And the selachii."

"*You* are a selachii."

He shook his head. "Not anymore. I'm something else. Something bigger. Something better. Something far more powerful."

"What difference does that make?" Angelica glanced at Frost. His lips were blue. His skin was ice-white, even the mottled bits that made them so unique. The vitiligo that marked their human flesh when they weren't in their orca form. Distinct, beautiful, elegant. Yet on Frost, the markings were fading. A sign he was near death.

"I'm sorry." Zale lifted her chin with his finger so her eyes met his. "I know a way to help him."

"You do?" Angelica curled her fingers around his wrist, squeezed, trying to wring the answer out of him. "What is it?"

"Atlantis."

Angelica's heart sank. "Atlantis is a myth."

"I assure you, it is anything but a myth. It is entirely real."

"Then why aren't you there?"

"I have no interest in being there. Not yet."

"How can an island help Frost?" Angelica asked.

"Because the Fountain of Youth resides on Atlantis," Zale replied.

Hope pricked a thorn in Angelica's heart. "It's real?"

"It's real. And it can cure ashray wounds."

Angelica looked at Frost, at his frigid appearance, at the life leaching rapidly from him. "Tell me how to get there."

Zale grabbed the back of her neck, a gesture meant to intimidate, one she was more familiar with. "You must do something for me first."

Angelica raised her gaze from her dying nephew to meet the ice in Zale's eyes. "If it will save Frost."

Zale placed an object in her palm. A small hard thing with rough edges and glints of obsidian. A rock of some kind. "When you get to Atlantis, put it in the fountain."

"What is it?"

"Nothing you need to concern yourself with," Zale said. "All that's important is healing Frost. The rest will take care of itself." He slipped off the ice into the water, rocking the iceberg once more. "That is what you want, isn't it? To heal your nephew?"

Angelica nodded. Zale gave her directions to the hidden island, then slipped away beneath the frigid waves.

The rest of her clan surrounded her small ice shelf, casting her worried looks. Angelica kissed her nephew's forehead, then held the rock high in a tight fist. There wasn't a single member of the orcana who hadn't been wounded by an ashray. "To Atlantis. To heal all our wounds."

"To Atlantis!" They cheered back at her, smiles brimming with hope.

CHAPTER ONE

I blocked the punch, evaded the low sweep, and ducked under a threatening kick to my face. Each move was calculated, each strike met with precision. The shadows of my opponent danced around me, mirroring the intensity of the fight. No time to draw breath. Only time to react. The next kick connected with my stomach. Air left my lungs in a violent gust as darkness ebbed at the corner of my vision. I didn't feel pain, just a white-hot anger. But my fire would be no use here.

"Come on, Mom!" Gal called. "You can do it!"

Spinning, I caught myself on the stone balcony which overlooked the courtyard and ocean. The stone felt cold to my heated skin. I gripped the ledge as I struggled to breathe. Sweat poured down my face, ribboned down my spine, coated every inch of skin. Small sparks flickered on my fingers and streaked out the window. As I struggled to inflate my lungs, I watched the tiny flames head to the ocean and disappear under the water.

"Are you okay?" Ford put a hand on my back.

I faced my loyal and skilled bodyguard, the man who had saved my life multiple times. Not just mine, But Wade and Gal's too.

"I need a minute."

"Enemies don't give you a minute." He turned back to the practice mats.

A truth I knew all too well.

His words stirred anger in me. Before he could reach the middle of the room, I sprang, sweeping out both his legs. He landed flat on his back.

"Go, Mom!" Gal called.

I stood over Ford. "Never underestimate your opponent."

Ford's tough instructions were not only about physical prowess; they were about cultivating the mental strength needed to face any challenge life threw at us. The opportunity to learn from him was worth enduring the bruises and exhaustion. And I was glad to finally get one over on him.

He yanked my leg, and then I was beside him on the floor. "Never lose your concentration."

"Dammit," I muttered.

Ford launched to his feet; a neat little acrobatic maneuver that made him seem more elegant than a mermaid. He turned to Gal. "Your turn, buddy."

"I'll get him for you, Mom," he said.

Getting to my feet, I gave my son a high-five and made my way to the bench on the side of the room. Thirst crawled up my throat as sweat pooled at the small of my back. My entire body ached. But I wouldn't visit the fountain. If Gal had to endure the training sessions without being cured by the Fountain of Youth, then I would bear that with him.

Every morning, five days a week, before the sun crested the horizon, Gal and I wound our way through the palace to the turret and spent an hour battling it out with my personal bodyguard. Ford had been with Wade and me ever since we'd discovered Atlantis, and he'd never let us down.

I didn't need the training, not with my ability to conjure fire to my hands in less than a second, but Gal had no such powers to defend himself. He had insisted if we forced him to train for an hour before school every day, then I had to join him.

It became the one part of the day where I could momentarily free myself from overthinking. Sometimes. A time when I could concentrate on the rhythm of hits, the ducking, the blocking, the kicking. Breathe in the ocean's scent, the sweat in the room, the damp in the stone walls. Forget the book, the island, the unrest, the prophecies, and concentrate on defending myself, on teaching Gal how to defend himself.

I watched Gal as he warmed up. He jumped on the spot, swung his arms in both directions, performed a few deep lunges. Ford took out his leg, and he tumbled to the floor.

"Hey!" Gal protested. "I wasn't ready!"

Ford ruffled his auburn hair. "Do you think your opponent is going to play fair?"

Gal's shoulders slumped. "I guess not."

"Not so hard," I said to Ford.

Ford faced me. "I can't teach him to fight with feathers."

It was a comment I'd heard before. Several times. Almost daily.

"I know, I'm sorry. Carry on," I said, and braced myself as Gal readied himself to fight.

A mix of pride and concern surged through me as I watched my son. Each hit, thwack, punch, and kick reverberated off the stone walls and burrowed into my heart. I memorized each one, calculating how many new bruises Gal would incur. He'd been learning for more than two years. And even though he was getting better at blocking, bruises still littered his tanned skin on a permanent basis. But it was a small price to pay for his safety.

"We're going to start a martial arts competition, right?" Gal said, as he jabbed at Ford's chest. "And you can be the judge, and I'll win all the medals. Although it would be nice to have a worthy opponent. Maybe I can talk Ember into coming too—"

Ford swept out his legs, and Gal landed on his ass. Again. "Hey!"

"Less talking, more concentrating," Ford said. "Unless you plan to bore your opponent to death."

"Hey!" Gal said again, launching to his feet and running at Ford. Effortlessly, Ford held out a hand and caught Gal's fist in his palm. Gal swung, but he couldn't reach the wall of Ford's burly chest.

"No fair," Gal said.

"Think outside the box," Ford said.

I watched my son, urging him to think things through. Not that you had much time to think during a fight for your life, but these scenarios must become second nature to him. He was The Prince of Atlantis. There would always be challenges. Enemies. Prophecies.

Glugging on my water bottle, I attempted to push the anxious thoughts away, but with the brightening day, they stuck to me faster and harder. It wouldn't be long until Gal was at school for the day. Gone for seven hours. Out of my sight. Out of my protection. Anything could happen.

Gal stopped swinging at Ford. He looked up at the muscled man with an inquisitive expression, took a deep breath and, ran up his legs. With his hand still caught in Ford's palm, he flipped over the bigger man's arm, twisting out of his grasp. He landed with a triumphant smile, and thank God, wasn't foolish enough to gloat. He threw himself back into the fight, both arms jabbing.

"Good boy," Ford said.

"See, Mom?" Gal turned to me. "No one is going to sneak up on me! Whatever that book dishes out, I got it covered."

I wanted to smile at my son's enthusiasm. He was such a typical boy; all restless energy and endless stamina, an innate instinct to wrestle and fight. The smile that formed on my lips took effort, made my cheeks ache with practiced agony. I prayed he couldn't tell the difference between my real smiles and my forced ones, but deep down, I knew he was smarter than that.

"You've definitely got it covered," Ford said. "Hell, you should be *my* bodyguard."

"Yes!" Gal punched an arm in the air. "Best job ever!"

"No!" I launched to my feet.

They both stared at me.

My fears swelled, and I struggled to find the right words to convey my concerns without appearing overbearing. I swallowed my fear and gathered my thoughts. "The Prince of Atlantis must rule the island."

Gal rolled his eyes. I didn't blame him. Truthfully, I didn't care what he wanted to do. I wanted him to pursue his dreams, do what made him happy, and if he didn't want to be Prince, then I would find a way to make that possible. But at that moment, I couldn't think of another reason to explain why the idea of him fighting for his career wasn't an option I could get on board with.

"It's because of the fountain, isn't it?" Gal muttered. "I never get to do anything fun."

I winced. "You're here, aren't you? Having fun?"

"You know what I mean," Gal said, and slumped onto the bench. "What's the point of training if I'm not allowed to fight for real?"

So many thoughts tumbled through my brain, I didn't know which one to focus on first.

Ford raised an eyebrow at me, then lowered his voice. "How much have you told him about the book? Does he really need to know the details?"

"He is the *prince*," I said, my tone sharper than I intended. "There will always be threats. And I may not always be there to protect him."

"That's not your job."

"Of course it is," I said. "That's my *only* job."

"Cordelia—"

I raised a palm. "I don't want to hear it, Ford. Train my son. Make him indestructible. That's all I want from you."

"Cordelia—"

I glared at him. "Ford."

"Okay, okay." He raised both hands and took a step back. "I'm only asking because I care."

"I know." I went to my son and kneeled by him. "Why would you want to fight for your job?"

He looked at me with his big blue eyes. Wade's eyes. As mesmerizing as the ocean. "Because I want to help people. Protect people. Like Ford does for you and Dad. Or Rob leading the army. Protecting people is good."

I took both of his hands in mine. "It is. It's very good. I love that you see that. But we also must protect ourselves."

A little frown appeared above the bridge of his nose. I had the urge to kiss it away, but he was at the age where my kisses weren't so welcome anymore.

"But why am I the only one who has to train?"

"Because you are the prince."

"But I'm no different to Ember or Una or any other person here."

I sighed. "You know that's not true. You are being forced to grow up quicker than I would have liked. But some realities we must face, no matter how old or young you are. Your life will always be in danger—"

"I know. You don't need to remind me."

"I'm sorry. I am. I want you to be happy." I rested my forehead against his and squeezed his hands. "I love you, Gal."

"I love you too, Mom."

"Let's go get ready for school."

He stood, grabbed his water bottle, and headed out the

door, calling a 'thank you' to Ford on his way. I looked over my shoulder, held Ford's eyes. He nodded. I couldn't bring myself to smile. But I knew he understood my fears. That I didn't have to voice them aloud. He knew me almost as well as Wade. And that if anything happened to either my son or my husband, I wouldn't survive it.

CHAPTER TWO

As we prepared for the day ahead and I noted the new bruises on Gal, a tangle of emotions swirled within me. The fear of losing those I loved was a constant burden, and I worried the morbid thoughts and images that intruded my head had begun to consume me. Knowing I had to be strong for my family and my island, I kept them locked within, hoping they wouldn't fester or explode at the most inopportune moment. But I was walking a dangerous precipice, aware I couldn't continue to shoulder my fear alone, but unable to give voice to their true depths.

I sensed enemies closing in. We'd been too long in a period of peace. I spent hours attempting to predict how and when the next threat would arrive. Some might call it an obsession. But how could protecting your family be anything else? I loved them. I would do anything for them. Every move I made was calculated to protect us all.

When we entered the royal suite, Gal pulled off his T-shirt and threw it on the floor, then his shorts, leaving a trail of clothes to the shower. Wade was just climbing out of bed, and he grabbed Gal as he ran by and wrestled him onto his lap. Wade threw him on the bed and tickled him until Gal's face turned purple.

"Mercy!" Gal cried through his giggles.

"There is no mercy in the royal suite," Wade said, refusing to relent.

Gal wriggled and flailed, then connected his fist with Wade's jaw. Wade ducked out of the way, a hand holding his jaw, as Gal's face fell. "I'm so sorry, Dad."

Feigning hurt, Wade lunged for another attack. "You think a little seven-year-old punch is going to keep your old man down, huh? Do I need to remind you that the Power of the Sea gave me the ability of Herculean strength?"

Gal giggled. "But you still whine like a baby."

"Ohh, that's it, you're going to get it." Wade chased him out of the bedroom and into the bathroom. A moment later, I heard the water running and their light voices in easy conversation.

I plucked Gal's discarded clothing from the floor and shivered against a sudden chill. Here at the palace, Atlantis was usually warm, even during the night, with only rare storms bringing rain or frost. With a frown, I peered out the window, hoping to spot an impending storm, only to find a blue sky and an ocean sparkling like diamonds. The tug in my chest had me leaning further out the window. The water called to me. It wanted me. And I wanted it. But it couldn't have me. Not now. It was too dangerous.

"Hey." Wade circled his arms around my waist and kissed the back of my shoulder. "I missed you."

I smiled. "I was only gone an hour."

"But your side of the bed got cold."

"It is cold today," I said, scanning the horizon once more. A familiar edgy feeling crept up my spine. A sensation that accompanied me through most days. Nothing had happened so far. Nothing bad. But today was a new day. Perhaps the looming threat I'd been sensing would materialize today.

Wade's arms tightened around me, and his lips brushed against my shoulder. "Maybe we should go back to bed..."

"Gal is here."

"You know how long his showers last. We've got at least ten minutes."

I turned to face my husband, pressed my lips against his. "Not today."

"It's been a while."

"I'm sorry."

"No need to apologize, Cordelia Blue. I just want to know what's on your mind."

So many things. Where would I start? "I haven't been sleeping well."

Wade ran his fingers through my hair, gripped the back of my neck, and massaged the tension I stored there. "Why don't you go back to bed? I can walk Gal to school."

"No."

"No?"

"No, I like to walk him to school. You know that."

Wade took a step back, analyzed me with those scrutinizing blue eyes. "Cordelia—"

"Don't."

He rested both hands on his hips. He wore only a pair of

shorts, and his muscled torso beckoned for my touch. Perhaps I could distract him, but I was tired, and Gal would be stepping out of the shower any minute.

"He's seven years old," Wade said.

"So you keep reminding me."

"He can walk to school on his own."

"I didn't walk to school on my own when I was seven."

He pointed at the window. "You can see the school from here."

"I like to know he gets there safely."

Wade chewed on his lip, stared at me with those damn blue eyes. "How are you going to get over this?"

"Get over what?"

"Cordelia..." He took a step closer. "You know this isn't healthy, right?"

"Gal is out of my sight for seven hours a day. Excuse me if I want to make sure the *Prince of Atlantis* gets there in one piece."

"We all want to make sure he's safe," Wade said quietly. "This isn't about him. This is about you."

Tears stung my eyes for a second time that day. "If something happened to him..."

Wade rushed to my side, held both my hands. "Nothing is going to happen to him."

I gaped at him. "Have you forgotten he's the only person on this island who the Fountain of Youth can't cure?"

"He's not the only one. The humans—"

"So not the point."

"We spent twenty years on the mainland without the Fountain of Youth and we were just fine," Wade said.

"Were we?" I jabbed a finger into his solid chest. "Zale almost killed you. And me. Don't forget the ashrays. The battle for the pearl. The war with the dragon kings. The ice demons. Both of us almost died. So don't even begin to tell me we haven't become reliant on the fountain."

Wade huffed, then spun a small circle. "You know you can't be with Gal every minute of every day, right? You do know that?"

I dipped my chin. "I do."

"He's going to get older. He's going to take risks, and you're not always going to be there."

I winced. The medley of images assaulting my brain created a physical pain in my chest.

Wade closed the gap between us and rested his hand on my hip. "Tell me what to do to help you."

"I don't know," I whispered, allowing one miserable tear to track down my cheek.

"The book will tell us if there is anything wrong."

The Mermaid Chronicles. A book about mermaid and selachii history. Filled with ancient legends and future prophecies. Only the four members of the High Council could read the ancient language, and Maya, my best friend, possessed the capability to interpret each statement with uncanny accuracy. If it weren't for her and her daily reassurances, I'm sure I wouldn't be living in the palace, but in a hospital. Maybe the one had Babette established.

I looked Wade in the eyes. "I have the ability to blow up this island—"

"Cordy—"

"Not my point." I took a breath. "I'm the most powerful

person on this island." I looked at my hands, at my fingertips where my flames liked to play. "I'm the best choice to keep our son safe."

Wade turned a sad smile on me. "He doesn't need you to do that."

"Maybe not today. But someday."

"How can you live like that?"

"How can I not?"

"We wanted more children." Wade cradled me in his arms. "We wanted a long Atlantean life. We wanted...happiness."

"I'm sorry I let you down." I allowed another tear to escape.

"You haven't let me down." Wade kissed the shell of my ear. "But I wish I knew what to do to take your pain away."

"He will die before us. Even if he lives to old age."

Wade rested his chin on my head, squeezed me tighter. "I know."

The Fountain of Youth slowed the ageing process. If Gal couldn't reap the benefits, he would live a normal human life span. And I refused to live longer than him.

"You must drink, Cordy. I won't lose you both," Wade said, his voice catching.

I clung to him. I didn't allow myself to cry, but I tried to absorb as much of his strength as I could.

"I love you," Wade said.

"I love you," I echoed.

"Aw, you guys," Gal said, dripping wet from the shower. "You need to get a room."

With Wade's laughter echoing through the room, he playfully ruffled Gal's damp hair, coaxing a smile onto my lips. Wrapping my arms around Gal, I held him close, tightening my embrace when he squirmed.

"Hugs are for mugs," Gal said mischievously, twirling around the room with a glint in his eyes.

"Guess I'm a mug then," Wade chuckled, sweeping me into his arms once more. "Can't resist a good hug with your mom."

Gal darted off to his room to get dressed, pulling a mock gagging expression as he fled. Seizing the opportunity, Wade leaned in for a deep kiss, his longing for a passionate response palpable. I felt his desire for me to open up, to meet his kiss with an intensity of my own, but I couldn't get in the zone.

In the blink of an eye, Gal reappeared, dressed in a T-shirt and a pair of shorts. No shoes. I shot him a pointed look, a silent reminder of our discussions about foot safety. With an eyeroll, he snatched his sandals and carried them across the room.

"Come on, or we'll be late for school." I put a hand on the back of his neck and guided him toward the door.

As we passed by the open window, I shivered in a gust of frigid air. A single snowflake drifted into the room. I frowned. There had never been snow in the city before.

CHAPTER THREE

The cold chased us along the passageways, through the great hall where the Power of the Sea swirled gently atop its pillar, and into the casual dining room. As we entered the room, I spotted my mother closing the windows and my sister rubbing warmth into her bare arms. Ice clung to the windows; beautiful etchings of frost that I hadn't seen since the year Dad and I had spent Christmas skiing in Big Bear. Snow. Hot chocolate. Warm fires. Fond memories. Mostly.

The frigid air hung in the room like an awkward silence. Most of the people seated around the long table wore cardigans or sweatshirts over the typical Atlantean T-shirts and summer dresses.

My mother regained her seat next to my father. Raina, my sister, sat with her son Ember, Gal's cousin and best friend. Dylan's seat was absent. Not unusual. I couldn't remember the last time he'd joined us for a meal. He preferred to stay in his small apartment over the bar he managed, often eating on the go, or when Babette was around to remind him.

"Morning!" Gal said, zipping around the table and hugging every member of our family. Apart from Ember. Six- and seven-year-old boys were too cool for physical affection, apparently. So they performed a complicated handshake with a few fist bumps and high fives. They reminded me so much of Dylan and Trent when they were younger, and I couldn't keep the sudden smile from forming.

"I made waffles," Dad said, waving his fork in the air. One of Gal's favorite breakfasts. Mine too, when hunger managed to break through.

"Thanks, Gramps." Gal chucked his sandals behind his chair and proceeded to drown a couple of waffles in a gallon of maple syrup.

"Go easy on that." Wade lifted the syrup jug out of range. "Or you'll be bouncing off the walls all morning."

"Bouncing is my jam," Gal said, earning himself a ripple of laughter.

"I'll walk him to school if you like," Mom said, glancing in my direction.

I waved her suggestion away. "I got it covered."

"Or I can," Raina said. "You're still in your training kit, and you and Wade have that meeting with the senate this morning."

I swallowed a mouthful of waffle, a stubborn morsel hitching in my throat. It took a few tries to drag it down my esophagus. "I've got time. School's only across the courtyard."

"Seriously," Raina persisted, pointing at Ember. "I'm going there anyway."

"I'll take them both," I said. "I like the ceremony of it."

I had never discussed my anxiety concerning my son's safety with my family. Not because I doubted their support; they would all do anything for me. But because by voicing my fears I was afraid they would come true. And then whatever happened would be my fault. By keeping silent, by locking my fears inside, not only would I not jinx any potentially dangerous situation, but I could limit the amount of worry my family directed toward me. I didn't want them to know I was not okay. That anxiety and PTSD ruled most of my day, dominated my decision making, and suppressed the happiness that used to come so easily. I had caused them enough worry. There had been too much tragedy in our past. Since the nuclear war on the mainland and the battle with the Hound of the Ocean, we had lived peacefully on Atlantis for seven years. I refused to be the reason that changed.

"I need to catch up with Maya anyway," I said.

Wade put a hand on my knee. "She checks the book every day. She'll tell us if there's anything we need to know."

I glanced out the window at the smattering of snowflakes pirouetting across the courtyard. "I'm surprised she's not here already."

"There's going to be some long lines at the shops," Mom said, following my gaze to the window. "Lowest temperature we've had since we've been here."

"What about during the storm when Stephanie...?" Raina glanced at the kids and cut herself off. Ember and Gal knew of the battle with the Hound of the Ocean and the sea witches Aquaria and Stephanie, but they didn't need reminding of the lurking darkness, or the people we'd lost.

Wade's mother. It was during that time Raina had found us. Found Atlantis. And I was reunited with a sister I never knew I had.

Instead of history lessons, my focus was on preparing Gal for prophecies that appeared in *The Mermaid Chronicles*, without replacing his dreams with nightmares. It was a fine balance, and I wasn't sure I was succeeding. Many a night he'd call for me, roused by haunting visions. I would slip into his bed, clutching him close, both of us sweating, both of us clinging to each other. I'd stroke his hair and whisper into his ear, weaving pleasant images into his mind. We never spoke of the nightmares in the morning, as if we had an unspoken pact.

"Not even then," Mom said quietly. "We had rain, thunder, and lightning, but not snow."

"Like on the mountain in the north?" Gal asked me. "When am I going to learn how to ski? Please, Mom?"

I recalled the trip to Big Bear Dad and I had taken. Years ago. Just the two of us. When we thought my mother and brother were dead. It only took a week for us to realize we weren't built for snow, or the cold, or for tumbling down a ski slope, or for the plethora of broken limbs the ridiculous hobby boasted.

"We'll see," I replied with my standard response and pretended his disappointment didn't cause my chest to tighten. Better him alive and disappointed than the alternatives.

Dad balled his napkin and threw it at Gal, who caught it in his fist. "Trust me, you do not want to go skiing. Surfing is way cooler."

Gal gave me a sideways glance. "Mom won't let me do that either."

I placed my elbows on the table and massaged the headache pulsing at my temples. "I said you could learn to surf. *When* you are *old* enough."

"Una is learning, and she's two years younger than me," Gal said, grabbing the syrup jug once more.

"Her father is an expert," I snapped. Seven years old was far too young to learn to surf. Not with the enormous waves that swelled in the ocean surrounding our island.

I knew full well Trent was more than capable of teaching Gal how to surf. But what he couldn't control, what no one could control, were the dangers that lurked in the ocean's depths. I would not send my son to battle monsters he wasn't yet prepared for. Especially when I couldn't join him. I hadn't been in the ocean for over a year. I wouldn't. I couldn't. Even when the craving became too much to bear.

A silence thicker than the frigid air wound around the table. The clink of silverware scrapping against crockery grated on my nerves. No one spoke. Wade didn't even dare to touch me with a reassuring hand, but I felt the pity rolling off him in waves.

"I'll walk to school with you, Cordy," Dad said quietly. I didn't miss the intention in his voice. He wanted to have one of his well-meaning chats. "I could use a walk."

I lurched to my feet, balled my napkin, and threw it onto my plate. "I am twenty-seven years old. I am perfectly capable of walking my son to school all by myself." I turned to Gal. "It's time to go."

He rose without protest, settled his knife and fork on his plate, and put his sandals on without me having to ask.

As we left the breakfast table, he slipped his hand into mine and gave it a gentle squeeze. That small gesture almost broke me, almost released the dam of emotion I'd built a fragile wall around over the last seven years. Tears sprung to my eyes. Why were tears always springing to my eyes? Why couldn't I get through one damn day without feeling like I was going to drown in a well of emotions?

"It's going to be okay, Mom," Gal said as we approached the steps leading to the courtyard.

"You don't know that," I whispered. "Nobody does. And that's why I'm always so scared."

"But we've got each other, right?" He looked up at me with his bright blue eyes. Wade's eyes. Full of understanding and love. "That's what's important."

My throat thickened. How was I supposed to reply to that? "You are the best person I know."

Dropping my hand, Gal grinned, then clicked both fingers. "Even better than dad. Ka-ching! I'm the man."

Even though my heart ached with love, with the fierce need to hold him tight and never let go, I couldn't help but laugh.

Gal ran down the steps, taking them almost three at a time. A lone figure halfway down held out his arms and prevented Gal from tumbling head over feet. I breathed a sigh of relief as I approached the pair.

"Daniel," I said to Wade's father when I reached them. "It's been a while. Almost a year, I think. Have you any news?"

"I've been in remote waters. My crew was forced to the Antarctic. Fish are scarcer than ever." He searched my face. Daniel was a man of few words. He had no small chat to speak of and he never minced his words. "You look stressed."

"Thanks."

"Is Wade okay? Marina?"

"Everyone is fine."

Daniel visibly relaxed. He'd lost his wife during the battle with the Hound of the Ocean. And even though he spent more time on his fishing vessel than he did on Atlantis with his children, his first question upon returning was always about their welfare.

His eyes swept over my face once more. "*You* are not fine."

I sighed. "I'm tired of everyone telling me how to parent my child."

"He is the Prince of Atlantis."

"Exactly."

"There will be trials."

A shudder ran down my spine. Daniel had abdicated the Atlantean throne to Wade. He'd shown no interest in ruling. Or in his supposed subjects. And yet he nailed the situation like he could interpret *The Mermaid Chronicles*.

I stepped closer, one eye on Daniel, one eye on my son. "Do you know something?"

Daniel shook his head. "You know I'm not one for the traditional ways. The prophecies...but Gal is a prince. There will be ordeals..."

My heart boomed in my chest. My throat dried out. Nothing had changed since Gal and I had left breakfast, and yet Daniel's words seemed to confirm every fear I'd ever imagined.

I reached for Daniel's arm, squeezed my fingers around him tight. I couldn't remember the last time we'd made physical contact. "Thank you for understanding."

"It's one of the reasons I abdicated." He took off his hat and held it in both hands, looked at his feet. "I couldn't imagine carrying that responsibility. And if that makes me a lesser person. A weaker mortal, well, I've made my peace with that."

The proverbial lightbulb went off in my head. Daniel had always been against a union between Wade and me. All those years ago I had thought it was because Wade was a selachii and I a mermaid. And it *was* largely because of that. But Daniel Waters was far more intelligent and astute than I'd given him credit for. He'd foreseen that a union between mermaids and selachii had the potential to cause unrest among his subjects. That uniting us, if it didn't end in all-out war, would bring nothing but years of restlessness and unease.

Atlanteans had given sanctuary to humans seven years ago after nuclear war decimated the mainland. The time had not passed easily. Despite humans finding their place on the island, one thing set them apart from us. The Fountain of Youth did not work for them. No matter how many times I tried to explain that my own son was more like them than Wade and me, despite the onyx merfolk tail he sported in the water, they remained steadfast in their resentment that mermaids and selachii had a miracle cure, while they, who suffered cancers and tumors from the fallout of the war, did not.

"I have misjudged you," I said.

"That seems to be the standard between you and me." Daniel took my hand, skirted a glance at Gal playing on the lower steps. "Keep him close."

"Always."

A snowflake fell on his shoulder. "Why is it so cold here?"

"I have no idea." My lips tingled with tension. "But I'm going to find out."

CHAPTER FOUR

"*H*ey!" Looking for the source of the shout, I pivoted on the ball of my foot. Flames flickered on my fingertips, readying to deal with a threat.

"It's just Maya and Una," Gal said, blowing on my fingers.

I shook the flames out of my hands and forced myself to drop my shoulders. Maya was emerging from one of the palace tunnels, her eldest child, Una, skipping at her side. Trent and Maya lived in a house in the palace gardens. Being members of the senate and the High Council, respectively, it was important they kept a proximate distance from the royal family. Plus, although the other three High Council members could interpret the ancient language of *The Mermaid Chronicles* and the prophecies which appeared, Maya had the uncanny ability to understand their cryptic intentions and kept the book in her house most of the time.

"Wait up," Maya called, clutching the swell of her pregnant belly. Baby number four. How easy it was for her to conceive, to give birth, to parent, to be a family. The Summers family were full of smiles, sunshine, and rainbows, despite what she read in the book.

Una reached us first, a devilish smile causing the dimples on her cheeks to flare. "Today is the best day."

"I bet it is," I said, and pressed a kiss to her cheek. "Happy birthday, Una."

"Five is the best age," Una declared with a swagger.

"Until you turn seven," Gal said, waving a stick in the air like it was a sword from ancient times.

"Five *is* the best age," I said. At that age, parents were immortal, there was nothing worse than a scraped knee or overeating on sugar. Possibilities were endless. Reality was still years away. There were times I wished I was five again. But then I wouldn't have Wade, or Gal, or any of the other friends I cherished.

Gal poked me with his stick. "You said seven was the best number when it was my birthday."

I waved a hand. "They're all the best numbers."

Una giggled behind her hand. Gal rolled his eyes. He was getting good at that.

Maya joined us, beads of sweat prickling her forehead despite the plummeting temperatures. "Thanks for waiting."

"Why is it cold?" I asked.

Maya looked at the sky, scanned the beach and the steel-blue ocean. "There's nothing in the book."

"You checked it this morning?"

Maya frowned, huffed out a breath. "I checked it before I went to bed last night."

I clenched my jaw. "Things can change overnight."

"Not that drastically."

We started walking toward the school. Una skipped alongside Gal, full of chatter about her birthday party that afternoon. She slipped her hand into Gal's, who turned to me with a horror-stricken look. He stared at their joined hands, then at me, clearly hoping I would rescue him. Over the years, Maya and I had dreamed of our children ending up together. It's not a match we would ever force on them, but the idea of us being bonded in blood as well as friendship appealed to us both.

"Be nice," I whispered to Gal.

Another eyeroll. But at least he didn't let go of Una's hand.

We turned out of the palace courtyard to find the streets lined with dense clumps of people. The shops had barely opened and yet it seemed the entire population of the island had amassed to discuss the weather and buy warmer clothes.

"Something's not right," I said, avoiding the curious looks.

"It's just a cold turn," Maya said.

"It hasn't been this cold in eight years."

"It's always cold on the mountain." Maya wrapped her cardigan tighter around herself, the material not quite fitting around her belly. "Even Atlantis has seasons."

I stopped walking, touched her arm to make her face me. "Is that true?"

Sighing, Maya held onto a marble pillar for support as we rounded a corner. "Cordy, I would never lie to you."

"There's been snow on Atlantis before?"

Maya tilted her head. "It has happened."

"What aren't you telling me?"

"Nothing." Maya's eyes flashed a warning. "You know I would tell you the moment there was the tiniest piece of new information in the book. You know that, Cordy."

I did know that. And yet I couldn't help feeling we were missing something. That Maya was missing something. If I knew how to read the book, I'd be with it now. I'd probably never let it out of my sight. But I couldn't read it, and so I had to rely on the interpretation of my best friend.

"Something's not right." I heard Daniel's words in my head. He'd reaffirmed the concerns I carried. I was not crazy. I was not imagining things. Something was coming.

"We can check the book together, right after we drop the kids at school," Maya said.

"We have the senate meeting."

"Right after that, then."

"It might be too late by then."

Una and Gal skipped toward the school gates. Other parents waved and chatted and remarked on the cold. It wouldn't do for them to see Maya and me at odds, and yet I couldn't hide the worry I felt.

Maya touched my arm. "Take a breath, Cordy."

I stared at my best friend. "Don't tell me what to do."

"I care about you. I'm worried about you."

"Just check the fucking book, Maya. That's your job."

"And I do it to the best of my ability every day."

"Maybe your best isn't enough."

Maya flinched as if I'd slapped her. "That's why we have the other members of the High Council. So that we can discuss whatever appears in the book together. You need to trust us, Cordy."

I shook my head. "I don't trust anyone but myself."

Una ran back to me and tugged on my sleeve. As she eyed the crowd, she pulled me to her level and whispered in my ear. "You don't need to worry, Cordy. My mom is the mostest, importantest person on the island. She'll keep us all safe."

My heart clenched, thinking of how much innocence she and Gal had already lost growing up with the parents they had. But there was nothing I could do to change that.

Una reeled back, a guilty look on her face, then dropped into a full curtsey. "I'm mean, after you, of course."

"Of course." I winked at her. "But you're right, Una. Your mom really is the most important person on this island."

She beamed at me, took Gal's hand again, and dragged him through the school gates.

"She has a rather inflated opinion of me," Maya said.

I took her hand, squeezed lightly. "It's not inflated."

"Thanks for that," Maya said. "She thinks the world of you too."

"She's at that age. Princesses and rainbows and unicorns and all that."

"She's already got herself married off to Gal. Incorporated a whole color theme of black and gold to complement his tail."

We smiled at each other.

"Walk with me to the meeting?" Maya asked as she moved both hands under her belly.

I pointed at my training gear. "I need a quick shower first.

And I want to catch up with Miss Swan, see what the kids are doing today."

Maya searched my face. I didn't know what she was hoping to find. "They're going to be fine."

"I like to double check."

"At the risk of inflaming your anger again," Maya said. "Gal will have to go into the ocean at some point."

"He almost drowned."

"It's been over a year."

I dipped my chin. "I have nightmares."

"I know."

"I need more time," I said.

Maya pressed her thumb into my palm. "That's okay. But try not to stifle his progress."

Her words wormed into my heart, causing a deep ache. The thought of Gal in the ocean on his own...I couldn't stop the intrusive images flooding my mind. There were too many. Too many dangers. Our enemies were out there somewhere.

I turned away from Maya and headed toward Gal's teacher, then called over my shoulder. "I'll see you at the meeting."

I approached Miss Swan as she was closing the gate. She smiled, waiting for me to reach her. Most of the other parents had dispersed.

"What's on the agenda today?" I asked.

"Maths, creative writing, a spelling test, and a water polo match in the teaching pool."

"No ocean?"

She shook her head. "No ocean. We'd always inform you about a day trip."

I nodded and turned away, trying to get a glimpse of Gal through the classroom windows. There. Chatting to Ember, performing their secret handshake. I hadn't seen Raina arrive with Ember. Perhaps I had upset her too.

As I walked away from the school, a familiar tightness in my chest bloomed. I made it to the courtyard before my vision blurred and my breath caught. A panic attack. The one event I could count on occurring on a daily basis.

I waved an unsteady path through the marble pillars and ended up by the memorial statues of the old High Council. Gal, my son's namesake, cast forever in stone, his wings spread protectively. His knowing eyes penetrated my soul. I felt the disappointment rolling off him. I was not the person he knew. Not anymore. I was only a shadow of my former self. I knew that. But I was powerless to stop it.

CHAPTER FIVE

I entered the weekly assembly of the High Council and the senate only to find myself immediately immersed in a heated debate. Babette's voice reverberated off the stone walls as I pushed the heavy wooden door shut behind me.

"I am the only human representative at this meeting." She stood with her hands resting defiantly on her hips, a stark contrast to the seated figures around her. Ford was the exception, absorbed in kindling a fire in the hearth. A ripple of unease threaded through the faces of the gathered people. Marina, Wade's sister, cast a nervous glance at the frosted windows. "It's not enough. There is too much whispering, too much divide. The humans need more support."

"Did we not battle the Hound of the Ocean together?" I asked.

Babette waved my words away. "You know we did."

"Did we not vanquish Stephanie and Aquaria together?" I said.

Babette glared at me. "Yes. But that was eight years ago."

"Were you, Babette, a human, not joined with Wade and I as a united three? To help represent the mermaids, the selachii, and the humans?"

"You don't need to recite history," Babette snapped. "I was there. I'm simply saying the humans aren't content. We have a problem. And personally, I don't blame them."

Blaze raised an eyebrow at Babette. Steam poured from his nostrils, a sure sign the dragon king was peeved. "My son and I are the only two dragon kings left in existence, and you don't hear me whining about fair representation."

Babette whirled on him. "There are only two of you, and yet you are a member of the High Council. That's a rather uneven representation."

"The humans constitute less than ten percent of the island," Wade said. "And so having you, a human, on the council *is* fair representation."

Babette flicked a hand at us. "Not when I have to fight against all of you with your tails and your powers and your magic elixirs. Five of you here are selachii." Her gaze fell over Ford, Jordan, Marina, Trent, and Wade. "Three mermaids." Now her eyes fell on my mother, Maya, and me. "One dragon king, and me."

Wade stood, a frown etching his face. "But that's the point, Babette. You're not fighting *against* us. You're uniting *with* us."

Babette shook her head. "That's not how they feel."

"If you're having secret meetings with the humans, that is very dangerous," I said.

"We're not having secret meetings," Babette said. "But I

can't prevent people from approaching me with their concerns."

"Tell them to come to us," Wade said. "We will hear what anyone has to say, and we'll do our best to help."

Babette threw her hands in the air. "They don't trust you, not without the—"

"Fountain," my mother said. "They want the fountain."

"Yes," Babette confirmed. "They don't understand why you haven't found a way to make it work for the humans too."

All eyes fell on Maya. She'd spent the last eight years studying *The Mermaid Chronicles*, delving deep into the history of ocean shapeshifters. Her translated version, available in the palace library and soon accessible through the island's Wi-Fi, omitted only the classified prophecies reserved for the High Council's eyes only. There was no reason to start a panic. Not that there was anything to panic about.

"There is nothing in the book," Maya said. "You can read it. You know that, Babette."

"Do you not think making the fountain work for everyone has been my number one goal?" My voice turned to steel. "How can they consider themselves so apart from us when it doesn't work for my own son?"

Babette pressed her lips together, then said, "It's not the same."

I glared at her. "Like hell it isn't."

"Like hell it is," Babette replied. "You look at me like I stole its power from your son."

It definitely felt that way. But I knew it was impossible. "Of course not. That would make you a...traitor."

Maya inhaled sharply, but Babette didn't flinch. Verbal sparring wasn't new to us.

"I am the only human the fountain works for, and they don't trust me because of it," Babette said. "Not really. If it wasn't for the hospital I established or the trips to the mainland to look for survivors, I'm not sure they'd tolerate me."

"We might be getting a little off track," Mom said, standing between us. Everyone knew it was never a good idea to leave Babette and me alone in a discussion.

"An excellent point," I said. "I didn't come here today to discuss the complaints of the humans, who I might add we opened our island to as a sanctuary when they did nothing but want to hurt us, and we continue to do so when you bring back more survivors." I looked at Babette but didn't give her time to comment. "I want to discuss why there's snow in the air." I glanced at Marina, who was already dressed to enter the water. She spent more hours in the ocean than she did on land. "Anything in the water?"

She stood and shook her head. My father had taught her everything he knew about marine biology, and the two of them had been documenting the wildlife around the island. "Fish numbers are still low."

"Your father said as much," I said. "He reported he is forced to venture further and further south, and even then, fish are scarce."

"It's to be expected with the radiation leaking into the water," Trent said, his voice low. He'd lost both his parents during the war.

"It will recover eventually," Marina said.

"Any other ideas about what's causing the cold?" Wade said.

Maya tapped *The Mermaid Chronicles* propped on her knees. "It's nothing to worry about. We're getting a visit from an orca clan. They bring the cold with them."

"There are orca shifters?" Blaze asked.

"The orcana. And yes, but there's not many of them. They're a reclusive clan, stick mostly to their own kind," Maya said, tucking her blonde curls behind her ears. "But they need our help. The fountain, specifically."

"See? Just another species that the fountain works for," Babette muttered.

I ignored Babette and asked Maya, "That's all?"

Maya nodded. I forced my shoulders down, faking my relief. Since I'd woken to snow that morning, I couldn't shake the idea that something bad was coming. And Maya's words didn't change that.

"Well, I think we can all relax a little bit," Mom said. "Bundle up and prepare to greet our new visitors."

"And we can get back to talking about the humans," Babette said.

"We'll call a meeting," Wade said. "Anyone with any grievances can visit Cordy and me, and the senate and High Council any time this week. We will hear of their problems, and then discuss a plan to deal with them."

And that's why my husband was the king. His unwavering neutrality, immune to personal biases, both awed me and made me feel inadequate. Why was I not capable of the same? Wade claimed he cherished my fiery personality, my stubbornness, my determination, that my ability to wield fire matched the love in my heart. Yet I yearned for his level-headed diplomacy.

My mother skimmed through the calendar, reminding us of our weekly duties and availability for visitors. As she talked, I stood and walked by the windows lining the great hall. The sky had clouded over, a blanket of white that shrouded our island in an icy embrace. Snowflakes drifted in the air. The ocean turned a stormy blue. I shivered, despite the extra layers I wore, and the fire Ford had built in the hearth. There was ice in my core. Something woolen sweaters and warm fires would never thaw.

LATER THAT AFTERNOON, Maya, Raina, and I walked to the school to collect the kids and take them to Una's birthday party. After the meeting, we'd spent the afternoon blowing up balloons and hanging streamers in the courtyard. Trent was planning on entertaining the kids with a few magic tricks, but by the time we arrived in the courtyard, a thick, velvety blanket of snow had descended, transforming the island into a winter wonderland of sparkling crystals and pristine white. The kids' only desire was to build snowmen and have snowball fights.

"Wow," Una said, her breath forming delicate puffs of mist in the chilly air. She gazed at the landscape, her eyes wide.

"I know, right?" Gal lifted a handful of snow and let it fall through his fingers, each flake glimmering briefly before settling on the ground.

A group of children nearby squealed, their laughter echoing through the wintry air.

Ember ran to Raina. "Mom, can we build a snowman?" Raina's nod was all they needed. The trio dashed away, leaving trails of footprints in the untouched snow.

Maya lowered herself to the edge of the fountain, which mysteriously hadn't frozen over, despite the low temperatures. Bundled in a thick coat, I stood in the middle of the beautiful landscape, my breath pluming as I surveyed the snow.

"We'll have to take them indoors soon, before they catch cold," I said. I had managed to wrestle Gal into socks and sneakers, and a warm sweatshirt, but he still wore shorts and I had yet to obtain a coat for him.

"Agreed," Maya said. "I'm freezing my pregnant ass off."

"I thought I missed snow," Raina said, her teeth audibly chattering. "But it's only been twenty minutes and I am *so done.*"

I forced a chuckle, my thoughts swirling like the surrounding snowflakes. Despite the enchantment of the snow and laughter from the newfound ice rink, an uneasy feeling persisted.

Superstitious thinking. Wade had suggested therapy. Maybe it was time to consider it. But the memories I had of baring my soul after the death of my brother and mother left a hollow feeling in my stomach. Talking about my loss never took away my grief, and so I had resisted the idea of professional help. But anxiety was a different beast. Perhaps there were techniques I could learn to ease my burdens.

"Right?" Maya crossed her arms, hugging herself tight.

"When exactly is this orca clan arriving?" I asked, my words punctuated by a shiver.

"The book doesn't say," Maya replied. "It's not into exact times and a twenty-four-hour clock."

The three of us retrieved the kids from under a pile of snow and herded them toward Dylan's bar. Gal jump-kicked a few snowmen on the way, raising a couple impressed eyebrows from Una and Ember.

"Teach me, teach me!" Una pulled on his sleeve.

"I don't know if you're ready." Gal said, pretending to be serious. "I had to train for six months before Ford showed me."

Her face fell.

"But as it's your birthday." Gal smiled. "I'll help you."

They approached the next snowman together. Gal lifted Una into the air, and she kicked its head off. She landed with a huge grin, making us all laugh. "I'll be able to join the Atlantean army too."

"I'm all for equal opportunities," Maya whispered to me. "But I'd really rather she didn't."

I squeezed her hand. "I know the feeling."

We arrived at Dylan's bar, shaking off the snow from our clothes and shoes. Gal ran to his uncle, who was waiting for him at the door.

"Uncle Dylan!" Gal shouted, hugging him.

"Hey, squirt," Dylan said, ruffling his hair. "You look like a snowman."

The two of them performed a complicated handshake with lots of fist bumps and high fives and clicking fingers that passed by in a blur.

Maya smiled as we entered the warmth of the bar. "He needs his own kid."

"If Babette would stay on the island long enough, maybe they would," I said.

"Well, she's bound to be around for a while now. She wants to take on the senate and the High Council, so that will take her some time."

"I hope we can figure this all out."

Maya leaned into me, cradling her belly. "We will. It's all going to be okay."

I glanced at her. "Is that something you know? Or something you feel?"

"There's nothing in the book," she said as we made our way past crowded tables. "If that's what you're asking. But you know I get feelings about this stuff."

The door opened, and Wade and Blaze entered the bar. The smell of saltwater and seaweed clung to their clothes, an indication of a recent dive in the ocean. Snow dusted their hair. Wade smiled at me as he approached, his blue eyes sparkling. But before he could reach me, Gal threw a huge hug around his waist, nearly knocking him over.

"Hey buddy," Wade said, picking him up and carrying him back to us. "Did you miss me?"

Gal nodded, his auburn hair tousled. "You missed all the fun in the snow."

"I think we're going to have plenty of time for that."

Trent poked his head up the stairs at the back of the bar. He wore a black cape and a top hat, and had a fake mustache glued to his upper lip. "Come on kids, it's time!"

Wade put Gal back on his feet, and the kids ran after

Trent. The party was taking place in the basement where Trent would perform his repertoire of magic tricks. One staircase down. If I sat facing it, I'd see Gal when he came up. Raina escorted the children downstairs. Within minutes, laughter filled the stairwell.

"I could use a drink," I said, making my way to the bar where Dylan was serving. He was my twin brother, but we looked nothing alike. While my eyes were blue and my hair red and curly, his eyes were green and he had dark brown hair. He blended into the water, I did not. Not that it mattered; neither of us had been in the ocean in months.

"I'm going to take the little ones downstairs." Maya moved to the stairs with her two youngest children.

"I'll catch you in a few."

She gave me a backward wave.

Wade worked his way around the room, greeting Atlanteans; humans, merfolk, and selachii with equal interest. He didn't wear his crown, but his stature and gestures carried an effortless regalness.

As I settled on the stool in front of my twin brother, I spied Babette in the small adjacent office, a frown taking over her face. "Hey."

"Hey, yourself."

Movement caught my eye from the staircase. It was a kid, but it wasn't Gal. I could relax. Trent had promised an entire hour of entertainment.

Dylan placed a glass of fruit wine in front of me, made from the grapes that grew over the columns in the courtyard.

"Thanks." I twirled the stem in my hand before taking a

sip. The instant hit of warmth soothed my throat and settled in my stomach.

Dylan poured himself a glass and downed half of it. Babette marched out of the office, slammed the door behind her, and pinned Dylan with a stormy look. She shouldered past him and started rummaging through a cupboard on the other side of the bar.

"What's her problem?" I whispered to him.

He shrugged, then pointed at his wineglass. "She doesn't like it when I drink."

"You drink every day."

"Exactly."

Dylan's alcohol problem had begun when he returned from the ocean over eight years ago. I've given up trying to get him to stop. Over the last couple of years, I'd learned the bad habit of self-medicating myself. But I never drank more than two. I needed my wits about me.

Wade joined me and sat next to me, took a small sip from my glass.

"Everything okay?" I asked.

"I think so. I'm trying to spread the word about the open office hours this week. Lots of people interested."

Babette reappeared with a duffel bag.

"Going somewhere?" I asked.

"Mainland," she replied.

I gaped at her.

"What?" she snapped.

"Wasn't it just this morning you were demanding more representation for the humans and wanting us to arrange meetings, etcetera, and now you're ditching them for another few months?"

Babette leveled her gaze at me. "You want me to leave the human survivors wandering around in a nuclear wasteland?"

"It's hardly a wasteland."

"Have you been?"

The comment stung. I had been. Once. Just after the war. And I had no intention of going back. I had no idea what it was like now. "Are there any survivors left? It's been eight years."

"I bring back a few every time," Babette replied.

Wade cleared his throat. "I think what Cordelia is trying to say is that perhaps this isn't the best time. There is tension on the island, and your disappearance could make things worse."

"That's not my problem."

I counted to ten before responding. "It is *entirely* your problem."

"Babette," Wade said. "You are a member of the High Council. It is your job to help oversee the welfare of the inhabitants of the island. Not to mention protect the Power of the Sea." I still couldn't get my head around that last job. The Power of the Sea was a magical orb that powered our island, making the Fountain of Youth function, expanding Atlantis to accommodate new arrivals, ensuring there was enough land for everyone. It controlled the success of our crops, and so much more, and she was going to turn her back on it again? "You have responsibilities here."

"I have responsibilities out there too." Babette pointed toward the door.

"For fuck's sake, Bette," Dylan said. "Just listen to them."

Babette ignored him. "If I can find more survivors and bring them here, then we can elect more humans to the senate, then the people here will feel more represented and at ease with who makes the decisions. Perhaps that will appease them when the fountain doesn't work. So, yes, I'm helping my people, I'm helping your people, and I'm helping you. Okay? And if you're so worried about the Power of the Sea, I'll take it with me."

A laugh burst out of me. "Don't be ridiculous."

"You know it must stay on the island," Wade said. "But you are welcome to take a portion if you think it might help."

"You're letting her go?" I asked my husband.

"I'm not going to stop her. I just want her to think about her responsibilities."

I jabbed a finger into the counter. "You came storming into that meeting this morning, all guns blazing, and now you're going to pack up and leave?"

"I'll only be gone a couple months," she said. "You can ease things over during that time. And I'll help when I'm back." She shot a glance at Dylan. "It's not like I have a reason to stay."

I took a sip of my wine and swallowed deeply.

Dylan raised both hands. "Don't get me involved in this."

"Maybe if you were more available, I'd stick around," Babette said to him.

Dylan pointed at his chest. "So this is about me now? The fountain doesn't work on humans and you're blaming *me*?"

Babette rolled her eyes. "Don't be an idiot. Of course I'm

not blaming you for the fountain. But I am blaming you for your lack of commitment."

"Hey, I'm here every day." Dylan swept his hands around the bar, indicating the customers inside. "Severing my people, chatting, offering advice, making friends. It's you who are gone more than you're here."

"And I wonder why that is," Babette said.

"You can take me or leave me as I am," Dylan said. "I'm not changing for anyone."

"That's really mature," Babette snapped.

"Likewise," Dylan shot back.

"Guys," I said, casting a look around the room. A few heads had turned. "Can we chill?"

"Because you're so good at that," Babette said to me.

I took a breath, thought of my husband, and swore to myself I'd be as diplomatic as possible, even though this was Babette I was talking to. "This doesn't need to turn into an argument, okay? Babette, if you need to go, then go. Do what you need to do. Find more humans, get space from my brother, and hopefully by the time you get back, Wade and I will have smoothed things over with the humans. Okay?"

She gave me a curt nod.

"Dylan?" I asked.

"Bette's decisions are nothing to do with me," he said.

"You could come with me," Babette said.

"I have the bar," Dylan replied.

"Someone else can run the bar for a couple of months," Babette said.

There was a familiarity in their tone. They'd obviously had this discussion before.

"Not enough room for the booze on the boat," Dylan said.

Babette's lips pressed together. She hoisted the bag off the bar, turned her back, and marched away.

Wade slipped off his stool. "I'll go after her."

Better him than me. I no longer had my anger under control. My fingers were warming, a sign they might produce their flames.

"I'll see you at home," I said to Wade. He kissed me and then went after Babette.

After checking the stairs, I turned to my brother. "Really, Dylan?"

"What?" He feigned innocence.

"Why are you trying to provoke her?"

"Why do you?"

"I don't," I said. He gave me a knowing smile. "We just rub each other the wrong way."

"She's still leaving."

"I'm sorry."

He tilted his head. "It is what it is."

"Maybe if you—"

Dylan put a hand over my mouth. "Stop right there. I love you, Cordy, but I do not need your well-meaning advice. We are twenty-seven years old. I think I know how to be an adult."

"Do you? Because I'm not sure I do."

He laughed, then took in my expression. "You okay?"

"Define 'okay.'" I drained the rest of my glass.

CHAPTER SIX

ylan topped off our glasses with a practiced hand as I surveyed the dimly lit room. Darkness pressed in at the windows, earlier than usual. Several patrons had left, leaving the rest huddled by the fire. Atlantis had no heating system; the fountain would have to conjure one if the snowfall persisted.

"'Okay' is a relative term." Dylan swirled his drink. "It means something different to everyone."

"I hear that," I replied, clinking my glass against his before taking a sip. "I'm sorry I ever gave you a hard time about drinking."

Dylan chuckled softly. "I get it. You care. And you were right to. It's not healthy."

"But we have the fountain to cure our livers."

"But not addiction."

"Or anxiety."

"Is that the problem?" he asked.

"I guess," I said. "Atlantis isn't what I thought it would be."

"It's not all rainbows and unicorns."

"Was I really that naïve?"

Smiling, Dylan ran a cloth across the counter. "You had dreams. Ambitions. Nothing wrong with that."

"And I stand by them." I gazed at the flickering firelight reflected on my wine glass. "But I think finding the island, dealing with Stephanie and the hound...it took more out of me than I realized."

"And your grief over my death, clearly." Dylan winked.

"You're alive. And I'm thankful for that every day. But I still carry the pain I experienced when I thought you were dead."

"I get that."

"And now I have Gal to worry about." As I mentioned my son, my thoughts drifted to the dragon king he was named after. Blaze's father, Ember's grandfather. He had been a mentor to me in a foreign world. He had guided me when I needed it, motivated me, and saved my life. He'd died protecting me.

"So not rainbows and unicorns, but monsters and prophecies," Dylan said.

"Exactly."

"But you can't worry about what the future might bring." Sympathy lined Dylan's eyes.

"Tell that to my brain." I eyed the bottles lining the top shelf, the polished glasses above our heads, the mirrored splash back where I could see reflected patrons huddled by the fire. "So why do you drink?"

"Still trying to bury the past."

Dylan had spent five years away from the family when he was thirteen. After a murderous selachii attacked him and my mother, the merpeople had saved him, but he was unable to shapeshift into human form. He was trapped in the ocean. And because I had avoided water at all costs, I never knew he was alive. For five fucking years.

"Well, I'm trying to bury the future."

"How's that working for you?"

"It's not. Have you read *The Mermaid Chronicles*? All those creatures..." I shuddered. "We haven't met a fraction of them."

"And we probably never will."

I shook my head. "*Probably* isn't a word I'm going to make any bets on."

"What's the alternative?" Dylan poured a shot of something stronger into our wine.

"I end up in a room with padded walls. Preferably with Gal so I know nothing can hurt him." I took a long slug of wine, glanced at Dylan. "I know. I know I can't wrap him in cotton wool, but I still want to."

"He's tougher than you think."

"He's seven."

"He's still tougher than you think."

I looked into my brother's pain-streaked eyes. "How do you think he would have coped if he'd been there during the battle with the hound?"

"He wasn't."

"But there could be something coming equally evil."

Dylan rested both arms on the bar. "What can I do?"

"That's just it," I said. "There's nothing anyone *can* do."

"You two are looking rather serious," Maya said as she slid onto a stool next to me.

I spun around. How had I missed her coming back up the stairs? Where was Gal?

"Relax." Maya put a hand on my arm. "Trent's got them all sitting by the fire. It was cold in the basement."

I looked at the fire, at the ten or so children sitting near the hearth, at Trent handing out hot chocolates with his youngest cradled in his lap. Gal was a little closer to the fire than I would have liked, but we'd talked about fire safety many times, given my unusual power, and I trusted him to be sensible. Mostly.

Ember sat between his parents, huffing and puffing, obviously trying to expel a fiery breath. Blaze had told me most dragon kings came out of the womb breathing fire, but Ember had yet to master the ability. A fact the other kids loved to tease him about.

"I love how close they all are," Maya said, as Dylan slid her an elderflower cordial. I don't think I'd seen her drink anything else in the last five years. She was always pregnant.

Gal stood in front of the fire in the middle of the seawolf rug, an ugly thing with an oversized head and wickedly sharp teeth. Apparently, they'd become extinct centuries ago. The Hound of the Ocean was larger, but there was something about a seawolf that gave me chills.

Gal performed a few jump kicks and a routine Ford had taught him. When the other kids applauded, he took an exaggerated bow.

"He does love to show off," I said.

"He's allowed. He's the prince," Maya said.

Mini Cordelia, the first child born on Atlantis and named after me, picked him up and spun him around the room. She planted a kiss on his cheek, making him blush. She was only a year older than Gal and was clearly ready for a little puppy love.

"And breaking hearts everywhere he goes," Maya added.

"Help!" A piercing cry from outside interrupted our conversation, clearly audible even though the windows were closed tight against the snow. "Help!"

I jumped to my feet.

"What was that?" Maya asked, sliding off the stool.

Dylan rushed around the bar and headed to the door. "I don't know, but I'm going to find out."

I locked eyes with Gal. He stood in the middle of the seawolf rug, his fists raised. Without saying a word, we both moved at the same time, running for the front door.

"Help!"

"What is it, Mom?" Gal asked as we met by the door.

Dylan flung it open, and a rush of cold air and snow swept inside. I'd left my jacket on my stool, and the drop in temperate sent a skin of goosebumps coating my arms. A violent wind tunneled outside, kicking up snow and obscuring our view. It shrieked and howled, slammed against the windows, and tried to wrestle Dylan's hand off the door handle. Ghostly screams echoed off the dark courtyard, as if the wind were bringing prophecies instead of *The Mermaid Chronicles*.

"I don't know."

I didn't tell him to stay behind. No matter what faced us

outside, Gal was safer by my side. I could protect him with my fire power. No one inside the bar had my kind of ability.

I threw Maya a glance over my shoulder as I darted through the door. She shot me a reassuring nod, letting me know she'd look after the rest of the kids. And hopefully check *The Mermaid Chronicles* for new information.

Dylan, Gal, and I rushed outside, joining half the patrons of the bar.

"Help!" The cry came again, more desperate this time.

We followed the sound, making our way through the snow-covered courtyard. A tall woman with drenched long hair stumbled toward us in the dark. As she neared the lanterns lining the roof of the bar, I saw she was carrying something large. A boy. Maybe eleven or twelve. Unconscious. "Please, help."

"The fountain," Gal said, turning to run across the courtyard.

I grabbed his wrist. "We'll go together."

I met the woman in the snow. "This way."

Together, we dashed across the courtyard, slipping on the ice. I went down once. Fire burst from my fingertips, instantly melting the snow under my feet into a puddle. The stranger raised an eyebrow, but continued to follow Dylan and Gal toward the fountain. The wind slapped at my cheeks, whipped my hair, and tore at my clothes, slowing my progress. I was tempted to melt all the snow with my fire, but I had a feeling it would quickly be replaced.

As we approached the flowing fountain, the weather calmed. The woman laid the boy along the stone wall, then turned to me, panic tightening her eyes. "It's my nephew. Ashray wounds."

Gal was already standing in the fountain. Shivering and with his lips trembling, he reached for one of the half coconut shells we used as cups for anyone in need. He filled the shell with healing water and brought it to the boy's lips.

The boy's skin was pallid, his lips an alarming shade of blue. Infected ashray wounds covered much of his exposed skin, including his face. But underneath the wounds, his skin bore a patchwork of lighter and darker hues. The same as the woman's. This must be the orca clan. Their human skin showing what shifter they represented when not transformed.

Dylan helped Gal pour the liquid between the boy's lips. Most of it dribbled down his cheek.

The woman kneeled in front of him, stroked the boy's dark hair with a soothing hand. She dipped the other into the fountain and allowed droplets to fall from her fingers and onto his lips, her fingernails completely white. "Please, please, *please*."

I sensed movement at my back. Turning, I spotted several dark shapes. Maybe twenty people. As they neared, I noted their skin matched the woman's and the boy's. The orca clan. Orcana.

"Yes!" Gal's voice.

I turned back to the fountain. The boy's eyes fluttered, then opened. His irises were a bright, otherworldly white, and as he blinked, his ashray wounds disappeared, revealing beautifully pronounced markings that seemed to swirl and dance with life, creating a dizzying effect. "Where am I?" he muttered.

"Oh, thank Cascadia!" the woman said, and wrapped her arms around the boy. I hadn't heard the god's name evoked for some time. Cascadia, Vorago, and Tempest were the three water deities who created our land—according to legend—but with the last few centuries of ocean shifter history taking place on the mainland, their names had almost been forgotten.

The orca clan surrounded the fountain, their smiles wide, their whisperings joyful. They were similarly attired, with minimal amounts of clothing, all black, typical when a shifter clan spent more of their time in water than land.

"It really works."

"The Fountain of Youth."

The woman helped the boy to sit up, then stood. "Thank you."

"It's not me," I said. "It's the fountain."

She wiped a frozen tear away from her mottled cheek. "All the same."

"You must be cold," Dylan said. "Let's get you inside."

The woman smiled. "We're used to the cold."

"Well, we Atlanteans are not. Let's get you some food at least. All of you." I gestured to her people.

"Thank you, that would be kind. My name is Angelica." She held my gaze with her icy eyes. Everything about her was beautiful. From her flowing dark hair to her towering height and the delicate shadings of her skin. Along with intricate tattoos that raced along both arms; she carried a regalness I could never hope for.

"Cordelia." I offered my hand. Angelica shook it, leaving a frosty touch.

"I'm Gal," Gal said, offering his own hand. "This is my uncle, Dylan. And that's my mom. She's the queen."

Angelica's white eyes widened fractionally. "I guessed as much. Your hair. The fire on your fingers. You must hate the snow."

"Let's just say I'm not used to it," I said as I led her and her clan toward the bar. "Have you traveled far?"

"From Antarctica," she replied. "The ashrays have increased. So many of us are wounded. We didn't know where else to go."

"Please, you must all drink from the fountain. Heal your wounds. Recover here on Atlantis. It's always been a sanctuary for ocean shifters."

As they circled the fountain, most of the clan dipped shells into the water. Angelica included. And once they had drunk, their shoulders dropped, their wounds disappeared, and their beautiful markings swirled with life.

"Thank you for your hospitality," Angelica said. "And I apologize for the weather. We have a habit of bringing it with us."

"Please don't apologize," I said. "The kids are loving it." I indicated a few of the snowmen visible lining the path. They were adorned with scarves and hats, shells for eyes and carrots for noses. Adorable during the day, but in the dark night portrayed a ghoulish vibe.

When we reached the bar, Dylan thrust the door open to frantic activity. A couple of kids from the party were crying. Adults shouted and scurried around the large room. A couple ran down the stairs to the basement. Another person locked the back door. Several called for me.

"What is it?" I asked Maya.

Maya's eyes were tight. She clutched Una's hand while Trent held both their other two kids in his arms. "Mini Cordelia has gone missing."

"Missing?" I scanned the room. Nothing had changed. The fire, the comfortable couches, the seawolf rug, the polished wine glasses hanging above the bar. I'd only been gone twenty minutes. The last thing I saw her do was plant a kiss on Gal's cheek. "How can she have gone missing?"

"No one knows. One minute they were telling stories by the fire, the next she was gone. Someone said she went to get a glass of water. No one saw her leave. But the back door was unlocked and wide open."

I rushed to the bathrooms, all genders, checking every stall, and then searched the dark booths for any sign of Mini Cordelia. I ran down the stairs. The basement was empty, save for the balloons and streamers and a basket of candy. I ran back upstairs.

"Can I help?" Angelica asked.

I searched for Gal. How could I have left him alone?

CHAPTER SEVEN

I spotted Gal by the fire talking to the other kids. He placed a hand on Ember's shoulder, his arm around Una, clearly comforting them both. He was so like his father.

The rest of Angelica's clan squeezed into the bar. Some were asking questions, looking for a description of the missing girl. Dylan made a vat of mulled wine for them all. For everyone. Something was needed to chase away the chills and anxiety.

Wade appeared with Mini Cordelia's father, both of their faces tight, both of them covered in snow. Laura, the child's mother, paced behind one of the couches near the fire, repeating a description of her daughter and what she had been wearing.

"She knows better than to run off," Laura said.

"We're going to find her." Maya handed her a hot drink.

"We want to help." Angelica touched my arm, her fingers

leaving cold spots on my skin. Her nephew nodded beside her. "It's the least we can do."

"There's a child missing. Eight years old. Her name is Cordelia. Brown hair, brown skin, brown eyes. Dimples," I said. "We'll have to expand the search." I glanced at the windows, at the wind still howling through the open front door. She obviously wasn't inside, but how would we find her outside in this weather?

The island had expanded over the years to allow for new arrivals, and there were plenty of places for a child to get lost. The palace gardens, the surrounding city, the mountain in the north, the forests and farmland in the west. And all the villages in between. But she couldn't have gone far in twenty minutes. Make that thirty minutes. Most of the river channels had frozen over with the snow, so she had to be on foot. Could Atlanteans freeze? I wasn't sure. I prayed she'd remembered a coat.

Wade approached. "We're starting a search. It's dark outside. Adults only. Maya and Raina will take all the children to the school while the parents search. I've contacted Rob. He's gathering the army."

"I won't leave Gal," I said.

Wade glanced at Angelica, then leaned close so only I could hear. "This isn't the time, Cordy. We might need your power. And your undivided attention. Gal will be safe at the school, like he is every day."

I gritted my teeth and turned to Angelica. "We're starting a search party. If you want to help, please join a group." I pointed her to Rob, Babette's father, who had just walked through the front door.

She nodded and backed away.

"Who was that?" Wade asked.

"Angelica. The orca clan—"

"Convenient timing." Wade watched her progress through the bar and introduce herself to Rob.

I shook my head. "She's got nothing to do with it. Her nephew was injured. Fatally. Ashrays." Wade winced. "And most of her clan had wounds too. They came here for help."

"He's okay now?"

I nodded.

"And you trust her?"

"I don't know if I trust anyone," I said. "Apart from you. But I'm not sensing any negative vibes. And I'm not sending Gal to the school."

"Cordelia. We haven't got time to—"

"Dad!" Gal shouted and ran to us. "Mini Cordy is missing and Rob's here and the army and Ford said I could join him on the search party, and I think she might be in the tunnels, and this is so cool, but I hope she's okay—"

"Slow down there, buddy." Wade picked him up. "All the kids are going to the school. Maya and Aunt Raina will look after you."

Gal frowned. "But I've got skills!" He performed a couple of fast jabs, almost catching Wade on the chin. "I can take a bad guy down. I can help."

Wade ruffled his hair. "Not this time, buddy."

"But I don't want to go to school. I already went to school today."

"You can help Ember practice his fire," Wade replied.

"But I need to show you the tunnels. Where Mini Cordy might have gone."

"The tunnels under the city?" I asked. During the war with the humans, Ford had stumbled upon a network of subterranean passages beneath the island. The initial tunnel we came across connected the palace to the alley behind Dylan's bar. Most of the passageways originated from beneath the palace, serving as emergency escape routes during wartime. They branched in various directions, leading to concealed lakes, mountains, farms, forests, and villages. We once used a tunnel leading to an underground lake, which then led us to a waterfall on the island's eastern side, allowing us to escape a particularly intense battle and save my mother's life. Since then, Ford had been supervising a team tasked with excavating and securing the tunnels, but after eight years, only half of them had been restored to their former state. "Why would she go there?"

A guilty look flashed across Gal's face, and he sucked in his bottom lip.

"Gal?" Wade said. "If you know where she is, you need to tell us." Wade put him on his feet and we both crouched to his level.

"We were playing hide and seek," Gal said. "No one was supposed to leave the bar. But Mini Cordy loves playing in the tunnels. I think she may have gone there."

"Which tunnels?" I asked. "There are millions of them."

Gal cocked a shoulder. "The ones with the symbol."

Wade and I shared a look. We'd both been in the tunnels countless times, but I'd never seen any symbols.

"Which one, Gal?" Wade asked.

"I don't know. I can show you, though."

Wade looked at me. "I'll tell Rob. Wait for me, Cordy, and we'll go together."

While Wade went in search of Rob, I leaned down to talk to my son again. "Do you go into the tunnels?"

A second guilty look crossed his face.

"Gal! You know it's dangerous. They aren't all safe yet." I couldn't remember a time when he'd been out of my sight, but there were the senate and High Council meetings and he'd often been unavoidably entrusted into my father's or sister's care.

"I didn't tell you because I knew you'd worry."

"You got that right. The fact that you've gone behind my back and lied to me..." I took a breath. Now was not the time. And I couldn't take out my anxiety on my son.

"I'm sorry, Mom."

I sighed. "I know you are."

"There's something else."

I studied his face. Worry flashed through his eyes.

"What is it?"

"The tunnels were creaking the last time we were there. That's bad, right?"

"That doesn't sound good." I took his hand. "We need to go. Now." I rushed him through the backdoor and into the cold. But we didn't stay in the snow for long. We headed for the tunnel in the alley.

"Show me," I said.

Gal squeezed my hand. I wrenched the door to the tunnel open with a creak of rusty hinges. An immediate wave of musty air engulfed us as Gal and I began our descent down the worn stone stairs. The scent of ancient earth and dampness filled the air, mingling with the faint odor of old lantern oil. The tunnel had history, and it showed in its smells as well as its structure. This tunnel, one of the first to be improved, now boasted lanterns at regular intervals, their soft glow painting the path before us.

"If the snow lasts, we'll be using these tunnels a lot more," I said. Especially with the water channels frozen over. The rivers and streams and tributaries were our primary method of transport. There were no cars on the island. Merpeople and selachii could swim faster than most cars. We used boats to transport goods. Electric carts to move the goods from the water to the relevant premises. The air, as well as the water, remained pure and clean.

"I love the snow." Gal trailed his fingers along the rough stone wall, a small smile playing on his lips. "But I'm glad it's warmer down here."

Our steps echoed on the stone stairs as we descended, then we stepped onto packed earth. The walls were made of crumbling stone, the ceiling half-hearted efforts at molded arches mostly crumbling and raining dust. A draft followed us as we wound a path through the tunnel, chilling my cheeks and the back of my legs. We came to a crossroads. Straight ahead was well lit and led to the palace. The left turn was darker and a less used path, but still maintained.

"This way." Gal turned left.

The tunnel groaned. The draft sped past my cheeks, draining the heat from them. We looked at each other, remained rooted until the strange draft abated. Then I took Gal's hand, igniting the fingertips on the other to cast a warm, flickering light. The flames not only illuminated our path but also stirred the air, dispelling the chill and burning away the floating dust.

"How far is it?" I asked.

"Not sure." Gal trudged forward into the darkening passageway, his footsteps kicking up dust and debris. "It would be quicker if we could swim."

Stone and rocks shifted above us, sending a cascade of dirt and dust showering down. "We need to hurry," I urged, dropping his hand and igniting the flames on my remaining fingers.

Gal took a right turn, sending us into complete darkness. If it weren't for my flames, we'd be blind. Why hadn't I thought to bring a flashlight? No time, that's why. Mini Cordelia might be in danger.

We came to a fork. Gal took the right path, which descended sharply. The stench of mold increased until I had to breathe through my mouth. The air felt thick, a musty soup I had to physically drag into my lungs.

"You've been down here alone?" I whispered, the tunnel's atmosphere evoking a sense of caution. My flames flickered silently, leaving only the sound of our labored breaths and the faint drip of water.

"With Ember and Una. He wanted a safe place to practice his fire."

"This isn't a safe place."

"I know." We walked a few more yards, our footsteps and breaths the only sound. And the odd groan of the tunnel shifting under our feet. "I'm sorry."

"We'll talk about it later."

"I don't want to be in trouble."

I couldn't help the smile that warmed my lips. "You're not going to be in trouble. But we do need to talk about your safety and decision-making processes. Clearly the messages haven't sunk in." He *was* also only seven-years-old. There would never be a single conversation when it came to his wellbeing. His safety would be a topic we revisited again and again. It was a conversation I hated, because my nightmares would worsen for the next week or so, but he needed to be aware of the dangers, especially as he got older and craved more risk. The stories Wade told me about his escapades as an early teenager...I'd never be able to sleep if Gal ever attempted even half of what his father did.

"*Sounds* like I'm in trouble," he muttered, kicking at the ground. The tunnel rumbled and a large pebble rolled past his feet.

"Careful." I scanned the walls, the ceiling. Saw nothing but floating dust. We were okay for the moment. I redirected my attention back to my son. "Not as much trouble as Mini Cordelia will be if she is down here."

"I'll sneak her some treats while she's grounded."

I tapped his shoulder. "No sneaking anything anywhere, that's what's got you in trouble to begin with."

"So I *am* in trouble? See? I knew it." He smacked a fist into the opposite palm.

I shook my head. "I just want you to be safe. You almost drowned last year..."

"We don't talk about that."

"We can if you want," I said, bracing myself for his questions as we edged further into the darkness. "I know I'm not good at talking about the stuff that scares me...but if you have questions...that's okay, ask away."

He stopped walking, turned to face me. "I almost drowned." His expressions was one of utmost disgust; curled lips, a wrinkled nose, and fisted hands. "I'm a *merman* and I almost *drowned*. Ocean shifters aren't supposed to drown."

"I assure you; every ocean shifter is capable of drowning." Then I told him the story of how the Gal he was named after saved Wade and me and our friends when our boat had capsized and a storm threatened to drown us all. We wouldn't have survived without the protection of his enormous dragon king wings. "And the waves you faced that day; huge, enormous, way too big even for your dad."

Gal raised an eyebrow. "Really?"

"Really."

His eyes narrowed. "You're just trying to make me feel better."

He was too smart for his own good. "Did it work?"

"A little."

"Good. Because you're not going in the ocean for at least, oh, I don't know, another ten years."

"*Mooommmm!*"

"Kidding!" Sort of. A few loose stones skittered past our feet, propelled by an unseen force.

"I do actually want to learn how to surf."

A cold seat broke out over the back of my neck. All I could see were tsunamis. Which could morph into inescapable vortexes...which would lead to...I took a breath. "Let me think about it."

He studied me for a moment, then continued along the

depthless path, dirt meandering beneath our feet as the gradient steepened. The walls narrowed and the ceiling lowered until I had to duck. My hair was coated in dust and dirt.

I spread my arms, illuminating both sides of the narrow passage. Bugs climbed on the walls. Spiders roamed over thick webbing. The walls creaked as they shifted.

"You really think Mini Cordelia would come here alone?" I asked.

Gal shrugged. "She's brave. Like you."

My chest swelled. How wrong he was. But for some reason, I was a hero in my son's eyes.

"How much further?"

"Down here a bit," Gal replied.

I shivered. The tunnels had always been colder than the surface, but with the arrival of snow, they now felt downright frozen. Despite the flames on my fingers and the circle of heat they provided, goosebumps coated my skin. The drips of water turned to icicles. The walls were covered in ice. Gal slipped on a frozen puddle. I shook my flames out and grabbed his arms before he went down.

He crept closer to me as I reignited my flames, both of us more cautious.

"Cordelia?" I called, my voice echoing sharply off the stone.

An echo came back to me. Again and again. More times than it should.

"There it is," Gal said.

My heart raced. Had he spotted Cordelia in the shadows? I searched the darkness as far as my light would allow, but saw no other living shape. "There *what* is?"

He pointed to the wall a few feet ahead. "The symbol."

I extended my flames as we inched closer. Something within the wall caught the light and reflected a crimson hue onto our faces.

The tunnel groaned again, chunks of ice breaking off the walls, frigid rivulets of slushy dirt running along the ground. Amidst it all, a glowing symbol emerged. A crimson triangle, pointing upward and pulsating with varying shades of red, from dark blood to bright scarlet to a hint of rose.

"What is it, Mom?" Gal asked.

"I don't know."

I approached the glowing triangle. Cement and dirt drifted to the ground, rubble and dust fell from the ceiling.

"It's going to collapse," Gal said as he rubbed grit out of his eyes.

I held him close. "I got you."

I cradled Gal against me as I placed one hand against the glowing red symbol. The area beneath it trembled. Old cement and dust fell away until a large stone was revealed, and in its center, the glowing red triangle. With strained effort and emitting unusual vibrations, the stone shook itself free and landed at my feet, narrowly missing my toes. A bright red light filled the tunnel, and I had to shield my eyes.

Gal tugged my sleeve. "Mom. Look."

I opened my eyes to find a red orb floating in front of my face. Perhaps the size of a baseball, similar to the white pearl and keys we'd found on our journey to discover Atlantis. This orb seemed less solid, more like the Power of the Sea, and it throbbed with every hue of red imaginable. It hovered in the air, circled us both, moved close to my face, bringing an unusual but comforting warmth.

"I think it likes you," Gal said.

"But what is it?"

He extended his hand to touch it, and as soon as his fingers made contact, he recoiled and hissed. "It's hot."

The tunnel continued to shake and groan. Pebbles and rocks rained from the ceiling. The walls threatened to collapse. We didn't have much time.

"We need to get out of here," I said.

"We can't leave the orb here," Gal raised his voice over the shuddering and shaking. We clutched each other as shockwaves bucked the ground. "It's important."

Cautiously, I extended my flaming hand and curled my fingers around the glowing orb. It willingly nestled into my palm, and as soon as we made contact, the flames on my fingers surged a foot high.

"Cool!" Gal said.

"Not cool," I said, casting a quick glance back the way we'd come. Nothing but a circle of darkness. "We need to leave."

Turning to retrace our steps, we inched along the ascending path as the tunnel shuddered and tossed us to the ground. As I hauled Gal to his feet, the red orb followed our progress, circling my head, as if determined not to be left behind.

I extinguished my flames. The red orb gave us enough light to see by. We only took one step before the tunnel collapsed. I tried to shield my son from the falling debris, but couldn't prevent a sizeable chunk of stone lancing off his head before it crashed to the floor. Gal fell limp in my arms. The tunnel collapsed around us, filling the air with dampness and dust. Rocks and stones pelted my back, pushing me to the ground. I wrapped myself around my son, shielding him as best I could. While the whole time the red orb swirled around me and observed.

CHAPTER EIGHT

The world collapsed. Despite the immense power I commanded, and despite the countless dangers I had prepared for to ensure Gal's safety, there was nothing I could do as jagged stones and heavy dirt buried us alive.

I cocooned Gal within my embrace, his head nestled against my chest. The red orb floated above us as we were ensnared by the suffocating earth. If Wade were here, he would be able to shield us both. The increased strength the Power of the Sea had granted him afforded him the ability to withstand such blows. But I hadn't waited for him. I'd rushed ahead, spurred by mine and Gal's concern for Mini Cordelia's safety.

Was she down here with us? Was I responsible for burying her alive?

Silent tears streamed down my cheeks as the rocks cascaded around us, the red orb illuminating every detail. At least we weren't in complete darkness.

Dust, dirt, and debris infiltrated my senses, invading

my nostrils, filling my mouth and ears, and coating my hair and skin. Rocks and chunks of stone tumbled relentlessly. It all happened so fast, and yet it seemed to last forever. The roar of the collapsing tunnel thundered through my eardrums, making them vibrate painfully. I clutched Gal against me, willing him to wake up, but also wishing he would stay unconscious to spare him this trauma. A rock landed on my arm, pinning it to the rough ground and opening a large gash. Another landed on my ankle. A third on my back. More, until my son and I were completely covered.

"*Please, please, please, please,*" I whispered. "Please save my son."

The red orb bobbed in the air, untouched by falling debris. It swirled close to me, and the warmth it radiated mellowed my panic.

Finally, the tunnel stilled. One of my arms was pinned, as well as one of Gal's legs. A large gash cut across his forehead, but didn't look to be bleeding too profusely. By the light of the orb, I examined our new situation. We lay buried in rocks up to the tunnel's ceiling. I could make out a gap a foot wide near the top. No way could we fit through it, even if we weren't restrained and able to climb.

I tested my limbs, wincing as pain shot through me or when I encountered an obstruction. But even the lightest movement caused the rocks to shift, and I dreaded triggering another collapse. The red orb drew close to my face, as if offering a suggestion. Perhaps fire could provide a way out.

Carefully, I freed my arm from under Gal and raised my fingers as high as the constricting rocks allowed. I willed the flames onto my fingers, and within seconds, they were ablaze with ravenous flames. That was new.

I possessed the ability to wield immense fire, having used it to vanquish the dragon kings. I was capable of shooting fire from my palms and my eyes. But this felt different, more potent. Fueled by the presence of the new orb, the flames on my fingers roared a foot into the air.

It might be possible to burn my way out of the tunnel. To shoot fireballs at ceiling and rocks and walls until we set ourselves free. But I might also injure Gal in the process. Or cause a larger landslide. Knowing the Fountain of Youth didn't work for Gal, I wasn't prepared to take that risk.

I coughed, then sneezed, expelling some of the dust from my lungs and nose, but my chest remained tight.

"Mom?"

I looked at Gal. His eyelids fluttered open. "Right here, sweetheart."

"I hate it when you call me that."

A nervous laugh burbled out of my throat.

"What's so funny?"

"Nothing, I just love you."

"Love you too, Mom." He sighed. "Did we get the bad guys?"

"No bad guys down here."

He tried to sit up.

"Stay where you are. Your leg is pinned."

His eyes widened. "What happened?"

"The tunnel collapsed. You got a knock to the head. You feel okay?"

"It hurts. Like when Ember hit me with his baseball bat."

An accident that had caused Gal a concussion and a few nights' stay in the hospital.

"I know, buddy. Help will be here soon." If only the telepathy that merpeople and selachii shared was more extensive. It was usually used in water when speech was impossible and we swam within a few yards of each other. I'd never tested the distance, had no idea how far the range extended on land. I shouted my thoughts at Wade, hoping he might somehow hear us, that somehow, he knew we were trapped.

"Can't you blast us out of here?" Gal asked.

"That will probably do more harm than good."

"Your power is bigger now."

"It seems that way."

"Because of the orb?"

I glanced at the swirling red sphere. "Maybe."

"I'm really tied, Mom."

"I know, me too." I stroked his cheek.

"Think I'm going to take a little nap." His eyes fluttered closed.

"Gal? Gal?" I lifted his eyelids. His eyes rolled backward. "Gal? Stay awake. You must stay awake."

But it was no use; he had slipped into unconsciousness once more. A heavy drowsiness tugged at my own eyelids.

"Help!" I screamed. "Help! Wade! Someone! Please help!" I yelled until my throat grew hoarse, until the dry air took my voice.

The red orb watched, then it swirled away into the tunnel and left us in the darkness.

CHAPTER NINE

I stirred from a hazy slumber, jolted awake by the sound of shifting rock. I hadn't realized I'd fallen asleep. A sharp pain stretched across my chest, and my eyes stung from the dust. I coughed. Warm blood spotted the rock beneath my head.

"Cordelia?" The sound of my name reached me, muffled and distant. Or perhaps someone had found Mini Cordelia.

I checked on Gal. His eyes were closed, but his breaths were deep and even. Using two fingers, I measured his pulse at his throat. His heart rate seemed stable, but I wasn't a doctor. I was pretty sure he had a concussion, and I had no idea how to help him, what was happening beneath his skull, if his brain was swelling to a dangerous size.

I released a shallow breath, which caused another coughing fit. Panic swelled, blurring my vision, jittering through my limbs. I wished I had both hands free to cup my mouth and nose like my father had once taught me to do to abate a panic attack. But even if I could manage it, I wasn't sure the mere shallow breaths I was capable of would be sufficient to ease my nerves.

I coughed again. Another spot of blood on the rock. Breathing hurt my lungs, as if the air had turned to salt water, and I couldn't drag it past my throat.

"Cordelia!"

"Help!" I called back, but I had no voice. How would they find us? Agonizing, wracking coughs set my back and chest on fire. I checked for the appearance of my flames, thinking I may have set myself on fire, but there were no sparks or flickers in our enclosed area. Clearly, I had incurred an internal injury, was bleeding from the inside out. How long did I have? "Help!"

Gal squeezed my hand. I turned to look at him and found his glassy eyes fixed on my face.

"What's wrong?" he asked.

"We're trapped," I rasped as loud as my broken voice would allow.

"Pinky fingers in the air. You have to tell me the truth." It was our vow. And even though neither of us could raise a finger at the moment, I'd promised I'd never lie to him. Not about the big stuff, and not when he specifically asked. There was no point in hiding him from the danger of our lives; he had to live it.

"I need the fountain," I said.

"Cordelia?" The shout sounded closer.

"That sounds like dad," Gal said. "Dad?"

"Gal? Is that you?"

"Dad! We're here! We're stuck!" Gal looked at me. "It's Dad. He'll save us."

I nodded, but couldn't muster more words. A thick fatigue overcame me, and I laid my head against a rock while Gal shouted for his father.

As my eyelids drooped closed, a soothing red light filled the area. The red orb. It had come back.

"She needs help," Gal said. "Quick."

"Give this to her."

Cool water touched my lips, flowing into my parched mouth, down my throat. I groaned as the healing liquid soothed me. Wade had thought to bring a flask of the Fountain of Youth. It took only seconds to heal completely. I opened my eyes. There was no pain, no agony in my chest, no coughing blood into my palm. I was totally cured. If only it would work for Gal too.

Gal held the flask. In the opening above our heads, I spotted Wade, Ford, and Angelica.

"You found us," I said.

"You have Angelica to thank for that," Ford said. "She saw that weird red orb and thought it might be important. Insisted we follow it."

"I knew it would lead us to you," she said. "It's one of the elemental orbs. Fire, I believe. And as you are the fire mermaid, I thought...I hoped...it would lead us to you."

"We seem to have a connection," I said, staring at the whirring red light. "It makes my powers bigger."

Wade raised an eyebrow as he began to shift the rocks. "Like you need more fire power."

A relieved chuckle escaped my lips, and I clutched my son close. "We're going to be okay."

"I have a headache," Gal said.

"I know." I kissed his brow, wishing I could free my arm to hug him tight.

Wade, Ford, and Angelica worked quickly to release us from the rocks. The whole time, the red orb observed, staying close to me, warming my cheeks and body, and sometimes hovering near Gal.

"Did you find her?" I asked.

Wade shook his head. "Mini Cordelia is still missing."

"It's early yet. Hopefully, she just wandered off."

Wade's expression hardened and he exchanged a glance with Ford and Angelica.

"What is it?" I asked.

"It's been twelve hours," Wade replied.

"We've been here that long?" I asked.

Wade nodded. "And with the temperature dropping so low, I'm worried if she was stuck outside that she—" He shot a glance at our son.

"May not have survived," I whispered.

"I'm sorry," Angelica said. "I'm so sorry. The weather..."

"It's not your fault," I said.

"You can't be what you're not," Wade said. "You are connected to snow and ice. Wherever you go, you bring it. This is not on you."

"But if I'd never come...she'd be safe," Angelica said, her skin markings pulsing with sadness.

"That's not true," Wade said. "Your nephew would be dead. We wouldn't have found my wife and son. I owe you everything."

She dipped her head. "Sometimes the choices are too hard."

"And sometimes it isn't a choice at all," I said.

A few minutes later, the three of them created a gap wide enough for Gal and me to crawl through. While Wade braced his back against the ceiling to prevent a further collapse, Gal and I climbed back into civilization.

Wade picked Gal up and carried him out of the tunnel. I clutched Wade's arm, and Ford and Angelica followed, the strange red orb hovering between us.

"I'm sorry," I said.

Wade looked at me. "For what?"

"I didn't wait for you. I put our son in danger."

Wade sighed. "Cordelia Blue, I love you." I smiled at the use of my full name. My maiden name. "But what you don't seem to be able to get through that head of yours, as beautiful as it is, is that I trust you. I trust you and our love. I trust you with our son. I trust you to protect him, and me, and us, and our family, hell, our island too. Because I know you, I know how deeply you care. And I know you would never put our son in danger if you could avoid it. I understand you were worried about Mini Cordelia. You made a decision, one I respect, because you thought it was the right one. So no, there is no need to apologize to me. Gal is fine. You are fine. We're all okay."

"This time," I muttered.

He caught my chin with his free hand. "Every time."

"Are you guys gonna get all mushy and start kissing?" Gal asked, making us both laugh. God, I needed to laugh more.

A few minutes later, we arrived at the hospital where a couple of nurses admitted Gal to a bed and examined him for injuries. A concussion was confirmed, and he was hooked up to fluids for an overnight stay. Wade and I sat with him, the red orb casting a peaceful glow over the three of us.

As we watched our son sleep, I took Wade's hand in mine. "I don't know who I'd be without you."

"Cordelia?"

"Yes?"

"That's exactly how I feel about you."

"But I feel like I'm supposed to be this strong, independent, feminist woman who doesn't need a man and can rule an island on her own and make all the best decisions without ever having a panic attack—"

Wade pressed a finger against my lips, then pulled me onto his lap. "We are who we are. We live on a magical island with the Fountain of Youth. We have powers. We have faced evils no man, or woman, should ever face. I don't give a fuck about societal norms, or gender roles, or expectations, or fitting in, or whatever the hell normal is supposed to be. I can't exist without you. That doesn't make me weak. It doesn't make me less of a man. It just makes me irrevocably in love with you. Why the hell would I want to be alive without you by my side?"

Tears tracked down my face as I wrapped my arms around his neck.

"It's always been you and me," he said. "We were written in the stars, remember?"

I nodded.

"Fuck everything else."

"Fuck everything else," I repeated.

He kissed my cheek, then my ear, then his lips drifted over my neck. "Let's go home."

"But Gal—"

"Gal is perfectly safe in the hospital. Ford is keeping watch outside. Gal is out for the night. And if he wakes, someone can fetch us."

"I can't leave him," I said.

"I'm not asking you to," Wade said. "All I'm asking is for you to walk to the palace five minutes away and make love to your husband. Then we can come back."

"Think he'll be okay?"

Wade stood, lifting me in his arms. I wrapped my legs around his waist and clung to him. He cupped my cheek with his hand. "I know he'll be okay."

Wade placed me on my feet, and we left Gal's hospital room, stopping briefly to talk to Ford who was sitting outside his door.

"We need a moment," Wade said to him. "Can you keep an eye on the big guy?"

"Take more than one," Ford said. "You could both do with it."

I placed a hand on Ford's shoulder, thinking of our training session earlier that morning. It felt like a lifetime ago. "What would we do without you?"

"Get some rest, Cordelia." He cracked a grin. "I'm expecting you in the training room at 5:30 tomorrow morning."

I smiled. "Wouldn't miss it."

Wade led me out of the small hospital, across the snowy courtyard, and up the stone palace steps. The red orb tracked our movements, and when we reached the great hall, zipped into the vast room to float near the Power of the Sea.

"We need to find Maya and understand what that orb is all about," I said.

"Later," Wade said. "The orb appears to like you. To aid your powers. I think it can wait a few hours."

I gave the mysterious sphere one last glance before I followed Wade into the palace. Once we were in our bedroom, I didn't know what to do. I fiddled with the perfume bottles on my vanity table, glanced out the frosted windows, re-arranged the pillows on our bed. It had been so long since we'd made love. Because I'd been stuck in my own head.

Wade approached me from behind, circled his arms around my waist. "We don't have to, if you don't want to."

I turned in his arms, cupping his cheek, and watched his selachii eyes flash black. "I do want to."

He kissed me, his tongue parting my lips. I tangled my fingers in his hair, pulling him closer, desperate to feel the reassurance of his hard, solid body against me.

"I love you, Cordelia Blue," he whispered as he kissed the shell of my ear.

"Not as much as I love you."

"So not true," he laughed.

He lifted me into his arms and carried me to our bed. Gently laying me on the covers, he kneeled in front of me, his lips grazing my ankle, leaving delicate kisses along my burning skin. A needful longing stirred between my legs. A longing I hadn't allowed myself to feel in months. Now, I wanted this, I wanted him, and I wanted to forget everything else.

Wade kissed his way up my legs, his lips tracing the

inside of my knee and then my inner thigh, until he arrived at my heated core. But he wasn't willing to satisfy me yet. He seemed determined to tease, his kisses drifting higher, circling my navel through my clothing, before yanking my trousers and panties off. The cool air circled my need, and I gasped.

"I want you," I whispered, clutching him close.

"Not as much as I want you," he replied, making me laugh.

His fingers skated across my warm skin, lifting my shirt until it was over my head and tossed somewhere on the other side of the room. He unfastened my bra with one practiced hand and then lowered his lips to my already erect nipples. Now completely naked, I pushed myself against him, eagerly tugging at his trousers and shirt, impatient to feel him inside me. I'd forgotten how good this was. How incredible we were together.

When we were both naked, he held both my wrists above my head with one powerful hand and pressed his lips to my neck, to the soft part of my throat, to the valley between my breasts. He released my hands, moved lower, and used his tongue to trail down my stomach, around my navel, until he reached the moist, aching part of me.

I gasped as his tongue circled my clitoris, gently capturing it between his teeth and then sucking and tugging until I cried out his name. A wave of ecstasy surged over me, stronger than the fiercest ocean current. I arched against him, pulling him deeper into my heat.

He worked his way back up my body, kissing a line along my stomach and around my breasts. He took my bottom in his hands, gripped it tightly, then entered me without warning. I gasped as he filled me with his hard warmth. I circled my arms around his neck, then clutched his buttocks hard against me, drawing him deeper.

He thrust inside me. Powerful, quick strokes. I met each one with a circle of my hips. Both of us breathless. Both of us gasping. Both of us nipping at each other wherever we could find exposed skin.

As I crested a new wave, he tensed inside me, throbbing with his pleasure. He groaned in my ear as he pushed deeper. I held him against me, riding the wave, allowing the orgasm to consume me and block out everything else in my head.

I bucked against him, holding him as tight as I could manage. He thrust again and again, powerful strokes taking me to a new level, causing every muscle in my body to spasm.

When he peaked, he lifted his head and roared my name. A roar so loud I was sure the entire population of Atlantis could hear. But I didn't care, and screamed right along with him.

Wade collapsed in my arms, his head resting on my breasts, his length still inside me.

"Another child wouldn't be so bad, would it?" he asked.

It had been so long since we'd made love, I'd forgotten we had been using protection. Because of Gal. Because it took all my energy to protect him. How could I do that for two? But in that moment, I felt the rightness of it. Gal deserved a sibling. Wade deserved another child. I deserved a shot at having a happy family.

"No," I said. "It wouldn't be bad at all."

Wade fell asleep in my arms. When his breaths became deep and even, I eased myself out from under him. I walked across the room and grabbed some clothes from an armchair, then stood at the window. Since snow had appeared on Atlantis over twenty-four hours ago, the windows had already become double glazed, and radiators appeared in every room.

Leaving the warmth of the radiator, I dressed quickly and made my way outside into the chilly evening air. The sun had set, and the warm and welcoming lights of the hospital assured me Gal was still okay. Before I entered the building, I tipped my head back to look at the stars. I could use a shooting one right about now to make a wish upon. The night was cloudless, save for one large shape. Moving faster than it should. A cloud in the shape of a ship. I could even make out the mast and the image of a giant kraken figurehead at the bow.

Smiling, I shook my head. Creating shapes from clouds had been one of my treasured childhood pastimes. But that's all they were. Clouds.

CHAPTER TEN

The ship of clouds trailed behind me as I walked toward the hospital, a silent sentinel in the sky. I couldn't resist stealing one last glance at it before stepping inside the building, attempting to memorize its shape so I could tell Gal about it if he was awake. Perhaps we could concoct a story about a cloud ship sailing through the high skies, ferrying dreams to the lands they passed. Maybe there were other forgotten magical islands out there besides Atlantis.

Before I entered Gal's room, I approached Ford, who was sitting outside on a small stool at a rickety table engrossed in a game of cards with a deck that had seen better days. I noted the image of sharks on the back and couldn't help but smile.

"Remind me to buy you a new pack for Christmas," I said. "Maybe with images of mermaids this time."

He chuckled as he picked up the cards and began to shuffle. "Or perhaps with orca shifters?"

I raised a brow. "Someone caught your eye?"

"They're a decent bunch."

"They certainly seem that way. Do you know where Angelica is now?"

"Rob set them up in some of the guest houses until we understand how long they're staying."

"Any news on Mini Cordelia?"

Meeting my eyes, Ford shook his head. "The entire Atlantean army is scouring the island."

I glanced at my watch. "She's been missing for twenty-four hours. And she's only eight years old."

"I hear that."

My gaze shifted from Ford to Gal's bedroom door and then down the hallway. Gal would be safe here under Ford's protection. The doctors would keep an eye on him. I could join the search for the missing girl. But how much use would I be? Yes, I had my flames, larger now thanks to the red orb which had remained in the great hall, but unless there was a formidable enemy to be defeated, they wouldn't be much use. No imminent threat could be lurking in Atlantis without a prophecy appearing in *The Mermaid Chronicles*.

Ford put a hand on my arm. "You stay here, where you're needed. He'll be awake before long."

I nodded, then opened Gal's door and tiptoed into the room. He was fast asleep with the covers tucked to his chin, one leg hanging off the bed and revealing a filthy sole. He often removed his shoes as soon as he was out of my sight. Glowing green monitors beeped softly as they measured his heart rate. I curled up on the bed next to him, weaving my arms around him until his head lay against my chest. Together, we slept.

THE ENTICING aroma of coffee and pastries woke me. I opened my eyes to find Wade sitting on a chair by the bed, engaged in a hushed conversation with Gal as they ate pain au chocolate, spilling crumbs over the sheets.

"Is it morning already?" I asked.

Wade leaned over to place a gentle kiss on my cheek as he handed me a cup of coffee. His blue eyes turned selachii black as he whispered in my ear. "Thank you for last night."

I blushed. After eight years of marriage, he could still make me blush.

Gal gave me a side-eye. "Did you guys do mushy things?"

Wade laughed and ruffled his head. "None of your business, buddy."

I placed a hand on my stomach, contemplating the consequences of our passionate night, wondering if we might have conceived. Maybe a girl this time. It was time to address my anxiety.

Sipping my coffee, I turned to my son. "How are you feeling?"

"My head feels better," he said, rubbing his temples. "But you hogged all the covers."

I laughed and hugged him. Thank God he was okay. And then the memory of Mini Cordelia's disappearance flooded back. I looked at Wade. He seemed to understand what I was asking, for his face fell and he shook his head.

"Doctor will be around in an hour or two," Wade said to Gal. "And hopefully she can give you the all clear."

Ford poked his head into the room. "I've a hoard of anxious people here waiting to see if our fine young prince is able to receive visitors."

"Are their presents?" Gal asked, craning his neck to look beyond our burly bodyguard. "Last time I was in hospital, people brought me presents. Chocolate, and teddies, and those sweets I like from the little shop down the hill—"

Wade covered Gal's mouth with his hand. "I think the pastries are enough for now, buddy."

"Send them in," I said to Ford.

First, my parents entered, followed by my sister, Raina, with Ember tagging along. Dylan, Trent and Maya with all three of their kids. Una and Ember clambered onto the bed next to Gal and demanded a blow-by-blow account of his adventure in the tunnel.

As Dylan leaned in for a hug, I caught the smell of alcohol on his breath. His eyes were unfocused and the skin beneath bruised.

"You okay?" I asked him.

"Was worried about the little guy," he replied.

I squeezed his arm. "He's okay."

"Where's other Grandpa?" Gal asked.

"Back on the water," Wade replied.

"What about Cousin Jordan?"

"On one of the search teams looking for little Cordelia," Wade said.

Gal's face fell. "She hasn't been found yet?"

"Not yet, buddy," Wade replied.

"I hope she's not stuck under a rock like Mom and me were," Gal said.

"Everyone is looking," Trent said. "We'll find her soon enough."

"She's really good at hiding," Gal said.

"Well, when you're released, you can show us all her favorite hiding spots," Wade said.

"Will I get a medal when I find her?" Gal asked.

Everyone laughed. Apart from Maya. Despite the stage of her pregnancy, she stood ramrod straight, her expression hard, anxiety flashing through her eyes.

I caught her eye and she gestured for me to join her. I positioned a chair in the corner of the room for her to sit and then crouched at her level.

"What is it?" I asked.

"The pages are turning."

I froze. Tension lanced through my chest, and I struggled to find my voice. "What does it say?"

"I don't know yet," Maya replied, one hand resting on her swollen belly. "You know the book sometimes takes its time to settle on a prophecy. But I have a feeling something is happening."

"Something good or something bad?"

"We've had seven years of good."

I clutched her hand. I felt the warmth drain from my face.

"We can't panic yet," Maya said.

Anxiety surged through my limbs, making them tremble. I took a deep breath, squeezed my eyes closed, and had a strong talking to myself. I couldn't help anyone if I fell apart. "Does anyone else know?"

Maya shook her head. "I think Trent suspects, but I

haven't told him anything yet."

"Perhaps we should inform the rest of the High Council?"

"I will as soon as we've finished visiting Gal," she said. "Then we can all wait together."

"I hate waiting."

"It is the pits," Maya said as she cast a glance at her stomach.

"How much longer?"

"A week or two." She met my eyes. "Not the best timing, is it?"

"We don't know anything yet."

The appearance of the doctor prevented further conversation. She sent everyone outside while she checked Gal over. Wade and I stood by Gal's bed and awaited her assessment.

"He's doing well. He still has a concussion, so I'd like to keep him in for the rest of the day, just for observation, but if he's feeling okay by dinnertime, I don't see why he couldn't go home and have one of those delicious palace dinners."

"Yes." Gal pumped his fist.

"You need to rest for a few days." The doctor wagged her finger. "And I want you back here at the end of the week to check on your symptoms."

We spent the day with Gal while the rest of the island searched for Mini Cordelia. Wade sat on the edge of his bed, sometimes playing cards with the deck borrowed from Ford, other times regaling him with magical stories. They reminded me of the cloud ship I had seen the previous night.

Restless, I paced the small room, unable to fully engage in the lighthearted conversation as I stared at the snow outside.

The Mermaid Chronicles was about to deliver a new prophecy. I'd felt something building in my gut. Every day my anxiety and worry had increased until I felt like I was going to explode from the pressure. But now I understood why. I was sensing an event on the horizon. Now, it was almost here, but there was nothing I could do to prepare until I had more information.

It was just after five when Gal was released. He allowed Wade and me to take a hand each and steer him along the hallway and into the frigid air. With the arrival of the snow on Atlantis, the sun had been setting earlier, and now it lazed happily on its downward arc, almost touching the horizon.

Trent brought Una and Ember to meet us in the courtyard, and we allowed Gal a few minutes of gentle play to stretch his legs.

"What's that, Mom?" Gal pointed to the sky.

I followed his finger and spotted an unusual cloud formation. The shape of a ship sailing across the twilight. I frowned. It was exactly the same ship I'd seen the previous night. But that was impossible. Clouds didn't remain in one shape, they drifted and morphed and moved across the planet. There was no way that cloud could still exist.

Everyone in our small group gathered to gaze at the sky, captivated by the spectacle. "That's so cool," Una said.

"It is actually flying?" Ember asked.

I shot a glance at Wade and then drew Gal close to my side. "I don't know what that is."

Blaze and Raina joined us in the courtyard and we all watched the cloud ship descend. It glided through the sky, weaving through the other clouds, and passed by emerging stars, all in the space of a minute or two.

Angelica and her nephew came to watch. A small crowd gathered. My heart skipped a beat.

"What's it doing?" Wade said in my ear.

"The pages are turning again," I said.

Trent caught my comment. "Should we get the kids inside?"

"Ember!" Raina called. "Come back here, please."

"Aw, Mom, I want to see the ship." He hurled a snowball into the sky.

The ship loomed into existence. A tall ship of the old days hovered over the island, passing over the beach. The entire structure appeared to be made of...clouds?

"I see Mini Cordelia!" Una pointed at the ship.

Dread pooled in the pit of my stomach as the ship drew nearer.

"Everyone, get back!" Wade said as the ship drifted over our heads.

The ship brought with it a sinister presence, an aura of despair and hopelessness that seemed to infect the air around us. It carried the reek of death and misery. Its rigging appeared to be made from cobwebs and dust. Its mast from mold and rotting rope. Movement on board caught my eye. A group of...pirates. A motley crew. Nothing more than skeletal remains draped in tattered rags, clutching rusted muskets, with seaweed trailing behind them, staring at us with malevolent grins. And poor Mini Cordelia tied to the side of the ship. White spiders with hungry crimson eyes scuttled all over the vessel, spitting an unknown liquid and casting iridescent webbing. What was this monstrosity that had invaded our sacred island?

Mini Cordelia's terrified screams filled the air, but the ship itself seemed to pulse with an eerie life, despite its crew being unmistakably dead or unearthly. Her face was frozen in the shape of a horrified scream, her eyes squeezed shut, her fists clenched in a white-knuckle grip.

Gal wrestled free of my gasp. "I'll save you!" He lunged toward the menacing ship.

CHAPTER ELEVEN

Gal charged forward, wielding a stick in one hand and clutching a snowball in the other. He hurled the icy missile at the ship where it collided with a swarm of scurrying spiders. Webbing shot out, disintegrating the snowball in an instant.

"Get back here!" Wade yelled at our son, who was already several feet ahead and skidding on the ice straight toward the ship.

I readied my fiery powers, flames roaring to new heights, almost licking the belly of the rotting ship.

With his stick thrust high, Gal cast a look over his shoulder, locked eyes with me. "This is what I've been training for."

"Gal, no!"

While the adults all had their eyes glued to the overhead ship, Ember and Una wrestled free from their parents' grasp.

"I'll help you!" Ember shouted, charging forward without a weapon. He huffed as if trying to summon fire, but nothing emerged. Raina attempted to grab the back of his shirt, but Ember was too quick, darting and leaping over clumps of snow, his dragon wings beating furiously.

Una took advantage of the fact that both her parents were clutching her younger siblings tight. "Wait for me!" She skipped ahead.

"It's the ghost pirates," Frost whispered, his entire body trembling, his wide eyes fixed on the creaking ship.

"They're far worse than ashrays," Angelica said, winding her arms around Frost.

Wade chased after our son, his long strides quickly closing the gap between them. With flames flickering on my fingertips, I followed, but I wouldn't be able to grab him without burning him. Other adults dashed forward, desperately trying to reach their children.

"I'll ready the fountain," Maya called after us, running toward the healing water with her youngest in her arms.

White spiders with hungry red eyes descended from thick webbing, landing on our heads, faces, and arms—everywhere. As soon as they landed, they spat acid that burned my skin. Screams peeled through the courtyard. Some turned back to the fountain. A spider clung to my face, and I burned it off with one of my fiery fingertips.

Wade closed in on Gal, reached out to scoop him up, but a long, quivering whip lashed down from the ship's deck, cutting Wade's flesh. The wound parted, it steamed and hissed, causing pustules and boils to run the length of it. Poisonous. The whips were poisonous. Wade screamed, fell to his knees, and rolled in the snow, surrounded by scurrying spiders.

Blaze took to the air, his dragon king wings flapping frantically, his fiery breath heating the night sky. Gal reached the rigging, grabbed for a rope, and was immediately hauled into the air above my head. Ember and Una soon followed. Although the kids struggled and fought and kicked and bit, the pirates restrained them with their poisonous whips.

"It hurts!" Una yelled.

I cast a desperate glance at my husband behind me, writhing on the snow, Maya bringing him water from the fountain, and I charged ahead with little thought as to what I would do. Raising my palms, I shot my flames at the ship, sending enormous fireballs tearing through the sky. But nothing happened. The ship remained unscathed. It didn't burn. The stench of burned flesh and noxious poison filled the air, but the whole time the ship remained, silently drifting over the courtyard. The pirates grinned and lashed their whips at the crowd below, attacking anyone who dared to venture too close. The poison took quickly. Several adults lay crumpled on the ground.

Gal, Ember, and Una were secured aboard, their terrified shouts filling my heart with unbearable agony.

Raina screamed, ran at the ship, climbed the rotten ropes until a pirate struck her with a whip and sent her tumbling to the ground. She landed on her back, motionless.

"Raina!" I yelled at my sister. "Raina!"

All the adults in the courtyard fought. They threw spears at the pirates, attempted to climb the deadly webbing, swatted at poisonous spiders, tended to those who'd fallen. I saw Dylan running at the ship. My parents emerging from the palace. Rob and a troop of soldiers tearing along the beach.

Blaze covered the ship in flames. I continued to throw my fireballs, but when one went sailing by Mini Cordelia and singed her hair, I stopped and yelled at Blaze to cease fire. Flames did nothing to destroy the ship. I concentrated on the spiders skittering over the courtyard, blazing them with an intense heat, burning them out of existence.

Ignoring the screams of my fallen people, their blistering faces, their oozing skin, I screamed at the ship. "What do you want?"

A whip swung dangerously close to my head. I grabbed it and immediately recoiled, the poison instantly burning my skin. I held on for a second longer as the ship began to ascend into the night, and when I could bear it no more, I let go and fell to the blood-soaked snow. Dylan was on the ground beside me, battling murderous white spiders who snapped at his cheeks and crawled under his clothes. He kicked and screamed, pustules and boils sweeping over his skin. I sent a fireball in his direction, burning the spiders away, also burning his eyebrows off his face.

"Get to the fountain!" I yelled at him. He staggered to his feet and ran.

The ship creaked and groaned, the pirates chuckled and lashed their whips, and the children onboard screamed. I couldn't see what was happening to them, but their voices pierced my heart. Gal threatening the pirates, Una screaming, Ember calling for his father. The ship sped through the clouds, into the stars, and disappeared. Blaze trailed them as far as he could, then he dropped out of the sky and splashed into the water. Rob sent a rescue team to retrieve him.

Only then did I become aware of the courtyard once more. Angelica, Maya, Trent, and Wade were distributing shells of water from the fountain.

Angelica approached with a coconut shell. "You need to drink."

Wordlessly, I did as I was told, and my health was restored instantaneously, but it didn't erase the memory of the spider bites, of the poison leaking into my body, or the agony of the burn.

"I think you're in shock." Angelica led me to the edge of the fountain and made me sit. I could only stare. People whispered around me. Shadows of white spiders flickered in my peripheral vision.

Wade kneeled at my feet, sobbing into my lap. I ran my hands through his hair. Angelica left us alone.

"He's gone," I whispered. "He has a concussion…"

Wade clutched at my dress. "We have to get him back."

My eyes focused on one unmoving shape partially concealed by snow and blood. A human who'd fought bravely in the battle and had succumbed to their injuries without the healing aspects of the Fountain of Youth. Guilt lanced through my body. We would never be the same while the fountain treated us differently. I didn't blame them for their discontent. Not when they died like this. For my son.

Maya found me, tears streaming down her face, her two youngest children clutched to her chest. I wrapped my arms around her, but I could not cry. The worst had happened. The ache in my chest was far bigger than I had imagined it could be. It didn't allow for emotions. It didn't allow for tears. It only allowed for a suffocating numbness that clouded my thoughts and fatigued my body.

Angelica and her nephew came back to check on me. "Is there anything I can do?"

Wade looked up. "I heard Frost mention the ghost pirates, what...who are they?"

Angelica and Frost shared a look. Her clan gathered around her, their skin markings pulsing with tension.

"We know of a legend that's been passed down through our people for generations. The pirates were cursed to live a life of the undead," Angelica said, holding everyone's attention. Her voice rang out in the frigid air, ice crystals gathering on her breath. "And the only way they can power their ship is with the innocence of children."

I clutched Wade's hand. "What does that mean?"

Angelica cast a look at the worried parents in the courtyard, at Mini Cordelia's parents who had appeared.

"They feed off the children's innocence until there is nothing left to feed off. Until they are..."

"Dead," Frost finished. "Then they throw their bodies overboard. Nothing more than a dried husk is left."

An icy wind whipped through the courtyard, stealing everyone's breath.

Wade struggled to his feet. "We must check the book."

All eyes turned to Maya. After a brief nod, she led a weary procession up the palace steps and into the great hall. She sent Trent to retrieve *The Mermaid Chronicles* from their home, while the rest of us whispered and speculated. The new fire orb floated around the Power of the Sea in a gentle orbit, pulsing with life and color, as if it had a message to convey. It had certainly increased my power, but it had done little to help in the battle with the ghost pirates.

I pulled Angelica aside. "What more do you know of the pirates?"

"Only stories," she replied. "No one really believed them. But the legend goes that when they run out of innocent souls, they scour the land and gather as many children as they can."

"Do you know of a way to defeat them?" I asked.

She shook her head. "It was only a story, until today."

CHAPTER TWELVE

I stared past our frigid island and into the night. Thick clouds scudded across the sky and wind whipped the snow into violent flurries, as if the island itself sensed the absence of our prince and sought to mirror the turmoil within our hearts.

I glared at the sky, my thoughts angry and incomplete, daring the ship to return. In the great hall, the red orb hovered by my head, a silent sentinel, as if anticipating its role in our fate. My friends and family were scattered behind me, some draped across the furniture, others pacing across the tiled floor. Ford built a fire in the hearth, but it did little to warm the pervasive chill that gripped my soul. Angelica remained with her nephew, giving details of their legends to anyone who asked. Most regretted their questions.

Wade paced with a knuckle glued to his mouth.

The heavy wooden door creaked open and Trent entered carrying *The Mermaid Chronicles*. Maya settled in front of the fire and opened the ancient tome in her lap.

I remained by the window, frozen with indecision. While it was important to understand the prophecy and our adversaries, I still wasn't ready to confront it.

Ford and Blaze gathered around Maya. With Babette missing, the High Council had been reduced to three, the only three who could read the book and understand the prophecies. The room stilled. The Power of the Sea pulsed on top of its pillar. The red orb remained close to me as Maya flicked through the pages toward the back of the book where the prophecies appeared.

Blaze frowned. Ford gave me a quick glance, his expression unreadable, his eyes betraying nothing.

"What's taking so long?" Wade asked. "What does it say?"

Although not a member of the senate or High Council, Dylan remained. He poured himself a drink and gulped it down, his eyes fixed on the fire. I tiptoed closer to the huddled group.

"I don't understand," Maya confessed, her eyes never leaving the book.

"Neither do I," Ford said.

Steam emerged from Blaze's nostrils. "That doesn't make sense."

I stood in front of Maya. My courage had deserted me, but I also couldn't stay in this moment forever. "What does it say?"

Maya met my gaze, tears glistening in her eyes. "It says, *'The one who sees will not see.'*"

No one spoke. The fire in the hearth crackled and spat.

Dylan barked out a laugh. No one asked him what was funny.

Maya's shoulders shook and her hands trembled as she flicked the page back and forth.

"What does it mean?" I asked the obvious, even though I knew she had no answer.

She shook her head, her voice choked. "I don't know."

Maya had been the interpreter of *The Mermaid Chronicles* for the last nine years. Although members of the High Council were automatically able to read the ancient and forgotten language, she had a special affinity for the book, passed down to her through generations, that enabled her to understand the meaning behind the words. We had relied on her ability to do this each time a new prophecy appeared. But this time, she remained clueless.

"How can you not know?" Raina asked, wringing her hands. "That's what you do, isn't it? You have to know. We must get our children back."

"Go easy," Blaze said. "We'll figure it out."

"Will we?" I asked. "It says nothing about the ghost pirates. About the white venomous spiders that can kill with one bite, about the poisonous whips, about stolen innocence... our children ...*how* do we figure it out?"

Ford took the book from Maya. "*The one who sees will not see.*"

"I think it's safe to assume that Maya, or the book itself, has been blinded," Wade said. "We can't rely on you or your visions."

"I'm so sorry," Maya said.

Angelica stood with her hands laced in front of her. "It's not your fault, Maya."

Maya launched to her feet, holding her belly with one hand. "Of course it's my fault. It is my job to keep this island safe and everyone on it, to warn everyone of impending dangers...and I've...failed."

Trent circled his arms around her. "Angelica is right. It's not your fault."

"No one blames you," I said to my best friend.

She met my eyes. Hers were filled with tears. Mine remained stoically dry.

"How do we get our children back?" Raina asked, sinking into a chair.

"The history section," I said.

Dylan smirked. "We need to look to the future."

"No, I mean *The Mermaid Chronicles* is divided into three sections, right?" Maya nodded. "The history of mermaids and selachii, an encyclopedia of ocean creatures and shifters, as well as the prophecies. The history or reference section surely has something on ghost pirates."

"Yes!" Maya grabbed the book back from Ford. "I'm not keen on reading about past battles, but I'm sure the reference section will tell us what we need to know."

As Maya flicked through the pages, memories of another battle surfaced. Over seven years ago, when Wade's ex-girlfriend, Stephanie, had turned into a sea witch and tried to sell us out to a bunch of human mercenaries. She had mentioned the ghost pirates. I'm sure of it. She had brought the Hound of the Ocean to our waters and claimed she was powerful enough to evoke many more evil creatures. Had she unleashed the ghost pirates before her death? Was she still casting a shadow over our lives so many years later? Did it even matter where they came from? No. The important thing was learning their weakness and getting the kids back.

I turned to face the group. Three pairs of eyes were glued to a page in *The Mermaid Chronicles*.

"What does it say?" I asked.

"Read it out loud," Wade said.

"Shit," Ford muttered.

Maya's hands shook. "The ghost pirates are creatures of the undead cursed to remain unfulfilled and miserable for stealing treasure from Atlantis centuries ago. As we know, their whips are laced with poison, and venomous spiders on their ship are their allies. They are immortal in their undead form."

A collective gasp filled the room.

"Immortal?" Blazed whispered.

"Their form can be changed," Ford said quickly, his eyes scanning the page. "And then they will become mortal."

My stomach pooled with acid, for I sensed this battle would surpass any we had faced before. The prophecies had grown increasingly perilous, with more lives lost each time. I'd spent the last seven years feeling broken, worrying over the safety of my son, only to have him snatched from my grasp. Now that he was gone and we had to face evil once more...I didn't know if I could.

I had promised myself I would keep him safe. That I would never let him out of my sight, that I would ensure the places he went without me were protected. Of course there would be danger. It was unavoidable, but I'd thought if I tried hard enough, attempted to predict all the possible threats, prepared for every eventuality, kept him by my side as much as I could, then he would be safe. After all, I was the most powerful person on Atlantis. And yet my son had been taken practically out of my arms. Because I had trained him to be brave and to face anything, and he wanted to prove he could. This was all my fault.

Dylan took a swig of his drink. "Out with it then, how do we change their form?"

Maya chewed on her lip. "We must gather the elemental orbs, combine them, and throw them at the ship. Only then will the ship and pirates be susceptible to our weapons."

Everyone stared at the red orb floating by my head. Wade cautiously reached out to touch it, then yelped as it scorched his fingers.

Wade shook his hand. "This one clearly has a relationship with you."

"She is the fire mermaid," Maya said, flicking through the pages. "There are six orbs. Besides the Power of the Sea, there is Fire and Heat, Snow and Ice, Rock and Earth, Air and Flight, and Spirit and Soul. Each orb has a connection with an individual Atlantean. And when they are combined they create an unimaginable power. More powerful than the Power of the Sea, which obviously represents water."

"Babette," I muttered, irritated again that she had taken off for the mainland. Although the Power of the Sea helped all Atlanteans. It didn't spurn those it wasn't personally connected to, not like my fire orb.

"Where did you find your orb, Cordy?" Trent asked.

"In the tunnels," I said. "Gal and I were looking for Mini

Cordelia. We stumbled on a glowing symbol etched into a large stone. When we dug it out, the orb was released. And then the tunnel collapsed."

"Half of that tunnel system is still uncharted," Ford said.

"Do you think they're all down there?" Wade asked.

Maya closed the book and turned it around so we could see. We'd spent hours marveling over the images on the cover when it had first come into her possession. Two mermaids swimming around a symbol that we'd never understood.

Maya tapped a finger on the symbol. "This represents the six elemental orbs. They're here on Atlantis somewhere. And we already have two."

"Probably all embedded in the tunnel walls," Blaze said. "We need to find them."

"How do we do that without the entire system collapsing? Like it did on Cordy and Gal?" Wade asked. "It's fine for me, I have the strength to bear it, but it will take me years to excavate the tunnels on my own."

"We put the army on it," Ford said. "That will become their entire focus. We'll speed up the charting, revisit secured areas, and we'll make safe the new areas as we go."

"It could still take years," I said.

"We don't have a choice," Blaze said.

CHAPTER THIRTEEN

$\mathcal{N}$o matter how hard I stared at the sky, the ship did not return.

Wade lay on our bed, a pillow over his face. Slowly, he rose and flung the pillow across the room, where it careened into the vanity table and toppled a bottle of perfume. He pushed himself to his feet and walked across the room to where I stood by the window.

"I can't stay here," I said. "I need to do something."

"The army is in the tunnels now."

It had been hours since we'd left the great hall, and I'd half expected another orb to be found. No, not expected, hoped. But that would be too easy.

"I can't just sit around and wait."

Wade opened his arms.

"I can't right now." I stepped back. "I need to get out of here. I need to walk."

"I'll come with you."

I shook my head. "I need to be alone."

"Don't shut me out."

"I'm not trying to. I just need to think. To walk. To be on my own."

"What if I need to be with you?" The expression on his face almost broke me. But I was broken already. If I didn't protect myself, I'd never leave the room.

"I'm sorry. I'm not trying to hurt you." I walked away without another word, out of our suite, along the hushed marble halls, and into the courtyard. It was after midnight, and even colder without the sun. As cold as the fear I carried in my heart. But I didn't stop for a coat. I marched to the beach, needing to feel the salt spray on my skin, needing to be in the water, even though I hadn't transitioned to my mermaid form for over a year.

As I neared the water's edge, I threw off my dress, dug my feet into the snowy sand, and dove into the turbulent waves. The icy grasp of freezing water seized my lungs, but only for an instant. As soon as I transformed into my mermaid form, my scarlet tail flicking out behind me, I no longer felt the cold. Air came through my gills as I dove deep into the dark water. Visibility was poor, and part of me half expected to happen upon an ashray or a ghost pirate or something equally deadly, but sea life was sparse, as if the ocean sensed I needed to be on my own.

I swam without thinking, unsure how far I intended to go or even which direction. My powerful tail sliced through the relentless currents and at last I was home again. Why had I denied myself this for so long? Gal. He was young, too young to face the dangers of the ocean, and so I had prevented him from entering the water. I too had avoided the ocean, insistent that a shared abstinence would help somehow. I'd also avoided drinking from the fountain and shunned all the things he couldn't take part in. His sacrifice had become mine. It was only fair.

But what had I taught him? What examples had I set? To face danger bravely without a care for his own safety? That had never been my intention. And in spite of the predicament we faced with his abduction, I knew he would encounter worse in his lifetime.

I swam to the depths, and when the pressure became uncomfortable, when my gills stuttered, I swam deeper. Past any wading sea creatures or shifters whose telepathic thoughts I might stumble on. The water was mine. It wanted me, and I gave it what it wanted. I succumbed to my most primal need. But it did nothing to ease the agonizing burden of loss that gnawed at my heart. There were no answers here. The answers lay in the clouds and stars above my head. On a deadly ghost ship.

Turning my back on the water, I flicked my tail and sped back to my island. If finding four magical spheres was the only thing that was going to save my son, then I would find the elemental orbs.

I emerged from the water onto the snow-covered beach, not bothering to dry myself before I slipped my dress over my head. Shivering, I made my way along the beach path to the courtyard surrounded by marble columns and frozen vines, then to the back of Dylan's bar. Before I passed, I pressed my nose to the glass. At this late hour, there were no patrons inside, but a dying fire struggled for life in the hearth and

Dylan himself lay slumped asleep across his bar, his hand wrapped around a half empty glass.

I tiptoed by before the frigid air froze me in place. Hunching my shoulders against the cold, I located the entrance to the tunnels in the alley behind the bar. This part of the network was well maintained and secure, so I dashed down the steps, threw open the heavy wooden door, and ran through the familiar passages. I doubted the elemental orbs would be found in the areas already charted; they would have been unearthed by now. It seemed they wanted to be found. So I headed toward the uncharted area Gal had shown me, the tunnel that had collapsed on us.

When I arrived at the rockslide, I drew in a musty breath, took in the tiny space where we had laid huddled together for hours. As I climbed over the rocks, I traced my fingers over the cold ground, longing for any trace of Gal's warmth, but found none. I half wished I'd thought to bring my fire orb, not only to keep me warm, but to light my way.

I stumbled on, tripping over the coarse terrain, my flames flickering on my fingers. Muffled voices reached me, echoing off the clay walls. I couldn't tell what direction they came from. It was most likely Rob and the army searching for the orbs.

I heard a voice at my back and pivoted toward the source, my flames high, my palms ready to throw fireballs. In times of high stress and during intense battles, I had been known to shoot fire from my eyes. I felt the heat behind them now.

A wavering shadow materialized on the wall, and then Maya emerged into view, raising her hands in surrender, one clutching a flashlight. "Don't shoot."

I lowered my hands, but kept the flames flickering to give us both heat and light. "What are you doing here?"

A smile ghosted her lips. "I suspect the same as you."

"The orbs."

"Indeed."

"You don't trust the army?"

"Usually."

"But not when your child is involved."

"Exactly," she said. "I want her back. I want her back *now*."

"It's dangerous down here," I said. "And you're in no condition to go scourging through unstable tunnels."

She stood straighter, squared her shoulders, her pregnant belly swelling between us. "I'll do what needs to be done."

I gestured to the dark path ahead. Two heads were better than one. And I couldn't deny having my best friend with me helped push the shadows back a little further.

"Do you have any idea where to look?" she asked as she stepped around a wickedly sharp stalactite.

"The fire orb was found over there." I hiked my thumb toward the pile of rubble that had buried Gal and me. "I have no idea how spread out they are. Do you? Does the book?"

Maya shook her head, wiped cobwebs and dust from her face. "It didn't say. The combined orbs wield an unimaginable power. I guess the book doesn't want to make it easy for anyone who happens to be able to read it."

"I guess not."

"My guess is they would be far apart, spread out across the entire island."

"The island keeps growing."

"I know." She spat dust onto the ground. "We'll just have to keep looking."

Movement caught my attention—a spider crawling down the stone walls. A white spider with red eyes. Maya gasped. I set one of my flaming fingers to its body and it disintegrated immediately.

"Some of them escaped," I said.

"They're deadly without the fountain."

"Did you bring a flask with you?"

Maya shook her head. "No. You?"

"No. I wasn't thinking straight at the time. I didn't know I was going to come here."

"Your hair is wet."

"I went into the ocean."

Maya gave me a once over. "It's been a long time."

I sighed, checked the wall for spiders before I leaned against it. "Staying out of the water did absolutely nothing to protect Gal."

Maya tilted her head, her eyes brimmed with sympathy. "You're a wonderful mother."

My chin jerked in surprise. "I don't feel like a wonderful mother. He's been abducted by evil ghost pirates who want to steal his innocence to power their ship. And he was just released from the hospital. With a concussion."

"I'm aware."

"Good mothers don't allow that to happen."

"Prophecies and the threats to Atlantis have nothing to do with your ability to mother. Or mine. Or anyone else's on this island. Life is just life. We can't predict it. We can't foresee every potential danger, even with *The Mermaid*

Chronicles. We can't protect our children from every single threat, large or small. We can only do the best we can."

"But they're gone," I whispered.

She grasped my wrist, earning herself a burn from my flames. "And we're going to get them back."

The sting of tears welled behind my eyes. "You promise?"

She hugged me. "It's you and me."

I wiped my eyes with the back of my hand, took a breath, and stepped on another spider. Muffled shouts wound through the musty tunnel. Stones rained from the ceiling, showering us in dust.

"Come on," I said. "Before this tunnel collapses again."

Maya leaned against the wall, supporting her swollen belly with both arms. Sweat beaned on her upper lip and forehead, and pain flashed through her eyes.

"You okay?"

She nodded. "Back ache."

"I remember that well," I said. "We can go to the fountain."

She shook her head. "Pointless. It will make my aches and pains feel better for all of five minutes before they settle in again. I just need to get this baby out."

"You've got another couple of weeks."

Maya rolled her eyes. "Tell me about it." She turned her gaze to the darkness beyond. "Have you been this far before?"

"No," I said as we inched along the wall, one hand with five flickering flames leading the way. "Not this far."

Our pace was frustratingly slow. Between Maya's pregnant shuffle and the copious rivers of stone and dust cascading down the walls, we dare not risk a faster pace. If we upset the balance of the precarious tunnels, we'd be buried alive.

"It's so damp down here. I can barely breathe," Maya said.

"Sixty percent of Atlantis is water."

"Weird there are tunnels beneath a city that used to be submerged."

"They were secret exits for royalty," I said, remembering the section of *The Mermaid Chronicles* I'd read online. "They had to keep rebuilding them when they collapsed under the pressure."

"I remember now," she said as she leaned against a wall.

"We can't stop."

"Just give me a minute."

I shifted my weight from foot to foot, shot a fireball into the darkness, but only succeeded in burning through a thick layer of cobwebs. Hopefully, none belonging to the white spiders. I prayed that few of them had survived, and if any did, they hadn't made it down here to nest.

Maya gestured for me to start walking again. After several yards, we arrived at a fork in the tunnel. Both options were shrouded in darkness.

"Which way?" I asked.

"Left," she replied, and we inched into the shadows.

My feet sloshed through an inch of water. I ducked my head under the low ceiling. Movement scurried on the walls, but I couldn't make out what was down here with us.

"What's that?" Maya asked.

"What?"

She pointed down the tunnel. I made out a faint green glow. "The army?"

"I think we'd hear their voices if that was the army."

We stared at each other. Had we stumbled upon another orb so soon?

"Ow." Maya clutched her stomach.

"What is it?"

"Cramps."

"Cramps? What kind of cramps?"

She lifted her shoulder weakly. "I hope normal I-ate-something-bad cramps."

"You *hope*?" Her face glistened with sweat, her hair stuck to her skin, despite the coolness in the tunnel.

"I think the baby is coming."

"But you've got two more weeks," I said.

She laughed. "I don't think it cares."

I chewed on my lip as I placed my flames over her face to inspect her condition. "We need to get you out of here."

"I don't think there's time."

"I'll get help."

"There's no time for that either. It's my fourth child." She grabbed my arm, earning herself a second burn. "Please don't leave me."

The tunnel rumbled.

"I don't know how to deliver a baby."

"You can do it."

"Why the hell did you come down here if you were having contractions?"

She locked her eyes on me. "Because I want my daughter back."

There was nothing I could say to that.

"I'm going to need both hands," I said.

She nodded.

"It's going to be dark."

"Scary dark," she whispered, checking both ends of the tunnel, her flickering flashlight only reaching a couple of feet into the gloom. "I can't make it back." She fell into a squat, supporting her back against the wall. "It hurts, Cordy."

"Okay, okay." I made her crouch, use the crumbling wall to support herself, and hopefully gravity would do its thing. There could be venomous spiders down here. They could bite either of us, or the baby. And we were a long way from the fountain.

"Help!" I yelled. My voiced echoed back at me. Dust drifted down the walls. A few pebbles dropped from the ceiling. The ground shifted beneath my feet.

"Don't shout," Maya panted. "You'll bring the tunnel down."

CHAPTER FOURTEEN

There was no stopping the baby. Maya lay crumpled against the damp wall, her skin drenched in sweat. Pain twisted her features. Beside her, a feeble flashlight cast a futile light that barely pushed back the consuming darkness.

"I think it's coming," she groaned.

I extinguished the flames on my hands, instantly plunging us into darkness. The flashlight, a meager beacon, now illuminated only a tiny pocket of the tunnel, revealing Maya's hunched form. Kneeling in front of her, I nudged her knees apart and angled the fading beam between her legs. It wouldn't last much longer.

"I can see the head," I said.

Maya panted, clutching her belly, drawing her knees beneath her arms.

"I think you need to start pushing," I said.

She nodded, unable to speak. Sweat soaked her skin, her

hair clung to her face, her dress twisted around her limbs and hitched up to her waist. The ground shuddered. Loose dirt and dust rained down from the unstable ceiling.

Maya inhaled deeply, teeth gritted, and the baby's head emerged further.

"That's it!"

She flinched. "I think I saw a spider." Her gaze was fixed on the darkness. "One of those white ones."

"Don't think about that now," I said. "Concentrate on you and your baby."

A groan erupted from her, intensifying into a scream as her back arched, and she clawed at the ground, her nails digging deep lines into the dirt. The tunnel shuddered again. A large chunk of stone fell and landed near my ankle. We stared at each other.

"Push," I said.

She pushed, a scream brewing in her chest, pressing through her teeth. It turned into some kind of war cry as her back arched and she gripped the ground, tearing at the dirt.

The baby's head emerged. I placed a supportive hand beneath it, ready to guide it out. Maya pushed and screamed again. The body followed. I gathered the baby in my arms. Then the flashlight winked off.

Maya screamed. It echoed through the pitch-black tunnel.

"Are you okay?" I reached for her hand in the dark.

"I don't know. I think so. Is the baby okay?"

I placed the baby in one arm, gently clearing moisture from its nose and mouth with my fingers. Then I summoned the flames to one hand, brought them as close as I dared to the baby's face. Its eyes were closed. It sucked in a breath and then released a heartwarming gurgle.

"She's okay," I said.

"It's a she?" Maya tried to sit up. "I get two of each?"

"You get two of each," I said. "Sit back. Rest a minute."

Maya extended her arms. "I want to hold her."

I transferred the baby into her arms, keeping my flames alight on one hand. When I pulled back, I noted the pool of blood beneath Maya, blooming, widening, seeping into the ground.

"We should get you to the fountain," I said.

"Let me rest a minute." Maya cradled the baby to her chest.

The ground shook again. And the walls, and the ceiling. The tunnel creaked and groaned, screeched and roared, sending rocks tumbling to block the path behind us.

"Get up." I pulled Maya to her feet.

She leaned heavily against me, clutching her baby, her eyelids drooping, her pale skin chalky.

"We have to move."

Rocks fell. Chunks of the ceiling crashed to the ground. The entire passageway was collapsing. I supported Maya as best I could, urging her deeper into the darkness, venturing into uncharted territory that had remained untouched for centuries. With each step, a trickle of blood coursed down the back of her legs. Her movements grew sluggish, her breath shallow and labored.

"I'm so tired, Cordy."

"Just a little further," I said.

The falling rocks ceased behind us. The air was filled with thick dust and dampness. We both coughed and sneezed as we inched our way forward. The baby's cries pierced the air.

"I can't," Maya said.

"I know, hon, I know. But we can't stay here."

After a few more yards, Maya came to a halt at a fork in the tunnel. Both options looked equally foreboding.

Maya extended a hand and inched down the wall to the ground. She curled around her baby. "Just a minute."

I kept one hand alight. The baby cried into her mother's chest. Maya continued to bleed. We didn't have a minute.

"Help!" I screamed, cursing myself for finding myself in the same situation twice in two days. Soldiers had to be somewhere nearby; they had to hear us eventually. But eventually might be too late.

I stared at the hypnotizing flames on my hands. I could blast us out of the tunnel system, but I might cause a more catastrophic collapse, inadvertently burying us or the many soldiers searching for the orbs. And worse, I might bury an unearthed orb. I couldn't risk my power.

"Help!"

"Shhh," Maya whispered at me.

I looked at my best friend. At her damp blonde hair curled around her neck, at her milky white skin, at the child nestled in her arms. She was beautiful. I loved her. I would not let her die.

I raised my head, lifted my chin, and yelled at the ceiling. "Help!"

"Sit with me." Maya patted the ground.

"No." I leaned down, extinguished my flames, and curled my arms beneath her body. I wasn't as strong as Wade. The Power of the Sea had gifted me with flames, not strength, but I had been working out with Gal every morning for the last two years. I could handle my petite best friend and her baby.

Maya cradled her baby, and I carried her. Unable to rely on my flames, we were thrust into complete darkness. I couldn't discern up from down, front from back, and my sense of direction was utterly lost. But there were no other options. Using the uneven wall as a guide, I inched further into the passage, fervently hoping that no white spider would drop on us. I took the right fork this time. Every few seconds, I raised my chin and yelled for help.

Despite the frozen state of Atlantis and the icy air infiltrating the tunnels, sweat poured down my back, ran between my breasts, soaked my hairline, and gathered between my thighs. Maya burned a fever while I held her, and the baby continued to cry.

I dared not risk a faster pace. I couldn't see where I was going and scraped my back against the uneven wall as a guide.

I struggled along the path, Maya unconscious in my arms, the baby wailing, the darkness pressing in at my vision, creating shadows and flickers that weren't really there. The tackiness of Maya's seeping blood coated my arms, and the cloying tang of copper dwarfed the musty reek in the tunnel.

"Hold on," I told her. "I need you. I can't do this without you."

I didn't know how much further I managed. Hours seemed to pass, but it might have only been minutes. A light bloomed in the distance. My voice was hoarse from shouting, but I didn't stop calling for help.

A moment later, a flashlight burned my eyes.

"Who is that?" I asked.

The flashlight lowered. I spotted shapes in the darkness.

"The fountain, do you have a flask? Hurry!"

The dark shapes approached. Rob, the head of the army, came into view. My arms trembled as I held Maya. Someone took the baby from her grasp. Someone else poured water between her lips. She coughed, choked, and her eyelids fluttered open. Rob removed her from my arms and placed her gently on her feet.

My arms shook uncontrollably. Someone poured water into the baby's tiny mouth, and she quieted immediately.

Maya took in her surroundings, at the blood covering her clothes, at the army bathing us in light in one of the darkest tunnels I'd dared to venture. "What happened?"

"The baby came," I told her, and gestured for a soldier to place the infant in her arms.

"Coral," Maya whispered and kissed the baby's head.

"That's a beautiful name," I said.

"Congratulations," Rob said, before reaching for his radio. Even though an internal internet system had developed, a cell phone network was only in its initial stages. Raina, managing journalism and reporting for the island, wanted to make an online Atlantean newspaper that people could access with devices. Others had ideas for dating apps, shifter identification software, and various other functions. Until it was completed, we relied on telepathy and radios for further distances. He spoke into the walkie, something about Wade and Trent.

Maya turned to me. "Thank you. You saved our lives."

I hugged her. And then I cried.

Rob tapped my shoulder. "Wade and Trent are on their way. They've been worried."

Wade would be furious. It was the second time I'd been caught in a collapsing tunnel. But if I hadn't been there...

I nodded at Rob, then accepted a sip of healing water from another soldier.

"Is there any news?" I asked.

Their faces turned grim.

"What is it?" I asked.

"The ship came again," Rob said. "Five more children were taken."

My stomach hollowed out and I threw up what little contents I'd ingested.

"Five humans were killed. One Atlantean who didn't get to the fountain in time," Rob said. "A human child was taken. The humans are...unhappy."

I leaned against the wall, my mind reeling. Eight years ago, when Atlantis had extended sanctuary to humans after the devastating nuclear apocalypse, tensions had nearly ignited a civil war between the humans and ocean shifters. Grief had gripped them, and emotions were volatile, the politics unestablished, many had lost most or all their family members. We had avoided a war then, but the sticking factor remained that the Fountain of Youth continued not to work for humans, despite our efforts and their sacrifices. No one understood why, and it was a source of growing resentment.

There was nothing in the book. The Power of the Sea refused to reveal a solution.

Something had to change. And I desperately wished it wouldn't take a civil war for people to be satisfied. We'd all endured enough loss. There was no answer in death. And considering humans made less than ten percent of the population on our island, they would do well to mind their manners and maybe be a tiny bit fucking grateful that they had the option of living on a paradise island. The Fountain of Youth didn't exist on the mainland; you couldn't take it off the island, so I never understood their entitled attitude. It was the merpeople and selachii who had fought terrible battles with fantastical beasts and relied on the healing powers of the fountain. Why couldn't they understand that? Were they there when we fought the dragon kings to reclaim Atlantis, when I lost one of the most beloved people in my life? No. Were they there when I was in a submersible at the bottom of the ocean and it split apart and almost killed everyone inside? No. Were they there when I faced an electric ball of eels determined to kill me and my friends? No. Were they there when Zale took my mother and brother? No. And if the fountain didn't work for my own son, what the hell were they complaining about?

But I couldn't voice my thoughts, couldn't allow my prejudice to fester. I was a queen, a diplomat, a figure who was supposed to be welcoming to all. Wade and I, along with the senate and the High Council, needed to put a stop to the unrest. But how might we do that when our children were being stolen? It was a time when people needed to unite, not divide. But I had little choice. If I wanted to keep my island safe, and everyone who lived on it, I had to deal with it.

"Cordy!" Wade's voice broke through the amassed soldiers. Then Trent's, then they were both shouting for Maya and me.

Wade pushed through the gathered soldiers, ran to me, narrowly avoiding scraping his head on the low ceiling, and pulled me into his arms. I allowed him to embrace me. I leaned into the solid wall of his body. But it brought me no comfort. My best friend had almost died. I'd been on the verge of being buried alive in a tunnel. And my son was missing, his innocence draining with every passing moment.

Wade pulled back and held me at arm's length. He inspected my face with his bright blue eyes. Even in the tunnel, their ocean blueness shone. "What were you thinking, Cordy?" he asked softly, though it carried a hint of reproach.

"I was looking for the orbs. To get our son back. If I hadn't been here, Maya would dead."

He pulled me close once more, but I couldn't curl my body into his, even though it fit perfectly. A wall had gone up. My mission to find the orbs had failed. The realization that it could take years pressed down on my shoulders, filled my chest with a suffocating heaviness. My son was gone. How could I live in a world where my son was gone?

Wade cupped my face in his hands, brushed soft kisses against my cheeks, whispered that he loved me. Leading me out of the tunnels, we emerged beneath the palace, where he guided me to our suite. He placed a steaming cup of coffee in my trembling hands. The warmth of the beverage eased the tension in my face, but it did nothing to thaw the icy grip of sorrow in my heart.

Wade pulled a chair over and sat in front of me. "While you were gone, Blaze and Ford consulted with the Power of the Sea," he began, referring to the magical and potent orb that fueled our island, sometimes revealing visions within its swirling sphere. Not always. But sometimes. "The book has been blinded. That's why we didn't know about the ghost pirates."

"Shouldn't Maya have known?" I asked, my frustration seeping into my words. "Shouldn't there have been a prophecy to warn her she would be blinded?"

Wade rubbed his forehead. "You know the book can only tell us so much, or it risks altering our future into something worse."

"What could be worse than this?"

He sighed. "The humans are unhappy."

"Fuck the humans."

"Cordy—"

I arched an eyebrow at him. "I have other things on my mind."

"I know," he said. "But it's our duty to care for them."

I set my coffee down with more gentleness than I felt. "How do you do it?"

"Do what?"

I waved a hand. "Cater to their every whim. Deal with the politics of this island when your son has been kidnapped. How do you do it?"

"I don't have a choice."

"Yes, you do. You can get angry. You can shout and yell and do anything you want to do."

"But what good would it do me?" he said quietly.

I shook my head. "I'm not like you."

"And I love you for it."

"I can't sit here and listen to trivial human complaints while my son is missing."

He grabbed my hand. "I know."

Tears tracked down my cheeks. I had cried in the tunnel and I hadn't expected to cry now. But I was not in control of my emotions. The tears became desperate. My shoulders shook, my stomach heaved. Wade wrapped his arms around me and threaded his fingers through my hair. He didn't tell me everything was going to be okay. Neither of us were that foolish.

"I can't do this again," I gasped.

He didn't reply. We both knew we had little choice.

His arms tightened around me. "I can't lose you," he whispered in my ear.

Scooping me into his arms, Wade carried me to our bed and laid me on the covers.

"We should be out looking," I said.

"The entire island is looking." He lay beside me.

We lay side by side, holding hands, staring at the ceiling. We didn't sleep, just lay there, neither of us talking, sharing each other's pain.

Hours later, when Wade had succumbed to sleep and I could no longer bear the quiet, I rose from the bed. I pulled on some thick layers and furry boots and made my way outside. I didn't know what time it was, maybe a couple of hours before dawn.

I'd promised Wade I wouldn't go in the tunnels again on my own, so I descended the palace steps and made my way to the fountain in the central courtyard. It was snowing again. As if the snow could fool me into thinking everything looked blissful and pure, but there were still blood-stained tiles from the battle with the pirates under the fresh layer of whiteness. I sat on the edge of the fountain and trailed my fingers through icy water. If only the fountain would heal emotional wounds too. The humans weren't missing much. Babette had seen that a hospital was established and doctors and nurses trained. Wade and I had put our support behind it, and not just because the fountain didn't work for our son, but because we wanted to be as welcoming as possible. How could they not see that we'd tried?

"I think this is all my fault," a voice broke into my thoughts.

I looked up to see Angelica standing before me. She wore only a black vest top, black harem trousers, no shoes.

"Couldn't sleep?" I asked.

She rubbed her face. "I can't remember the last time I slept well. The last time I wasn't worried about Frost, the ashrays, our food source...sorry, you have enough on your mind."

"Sometimes it helps to hear about other people's problems."

"We were going to leave," Angelica said.

"So soon?" I asked. "You're welcome to stay." See, I could be welcoming. And I did genuinely like the orca clan.

"We brought winter with us." Angelic made a face. "I think you're all suited to the warmer weather."

"The snow would stop if you left?" I asked.

Angelica splayed a hand. "I believe so. I thought it best we leave you in peace, allow the warmer weather to reappear, allow you to weather this latest crisis. But one of our clan was taken in the night."

"I'm sorry."

Angelica dipped her head. "And I think it's all my fault."

CHAPTER FIFTEEN

$\mathcal{A}$ngelica's skin markings dimmed, nearly vanishing into the canvas of her complexion, and her lips tightened into a tense line. Suspicion crawled along my spine. Despite her being a newcomer to the island, it didn't occur to me that she could be responsible for the ghost pirates' sudden appearance. Absurd, I had assured Wade recently. But now doubt gnawed at me.

"What do you mean, *it's your fault?*" I demanded, my voice sharper than intended.

She edged toward me, but stopped when she caught my hard expression. "The ghost pirates. Your son. Maya being blind...everything."

I stood, my hands fisting at my sides. "Explain."

Her gaze flitted about, taking in the courtyard, the fountain's dancing waters, the beach beyond, and the flickering lights of Dylan's bar. Finally, her eyes met mine, laden with guilt and an unspoken burden. "Our arrival changed everything. We brought the winter. We changed Atlantis. If we hadn't come..."

Guilt. A universal sentiment nestled in the hearts of leaders, mothers, aunts, and anyone who cared too much. Anyone who had ever failed a loved one. Those who had tasted the bitterness of disappointment and failure, big or small. Looking at Angelica now, I sensed the crushing weight she carried. But she wasn't a villain. Or a threat. Angelica, as my instinct had suggested, was a friend, an ally, a harbinger of snow. "Our current predicaments have nothing to do with your arrival," I said, attempting to relax my shoulders.

She splayed a hand, several rings lining her fingers glinting in the lantern light. "But you had several years of peace before we arrived."

"There are real monsters in the world, but you are not one of them, Angelica." I approached her and stood with her by the fountain. "Atlantis has always had enemies. Wade and I have always had enemies. We've faced threats before. Yes, we've had several years of peace, but it was never going to last, whether you came to the island or not."

"I can't help feeling..." She fidgeted with her black harem pants, restlessly shifting her hands in her pockets, only to remove them again. Her skin markings pulsed from black to white, swirling with a unique iridescence. "I can't help feeling it's my fault."

Snow fell, landing on our heads, our eyelashes, our shoulders, covering the ground as if it could hide any number of evils.

"Maya mentioned that the last prophecy before she was

blinded spoke of your arrival, but there was nothing negative in the book. She was delighted at the thought," I said.

She pursed her lips, stared at the white luminescence of her toenails, then glanced at the fountain. "I don't claim to know how the book works, or the fountain, for that matter, but perhaps she was already blinded."

"That's why we have the High Council, to help her interpret the prophecies." I indicated the glow of light spilling out the windows of the great hall where the senate and council often gathered. "They have each other to lean on. It's not one person's responsibility."

"Like it's not just your job to protect Gal, but Wade's too."

"That's different."

"I feel the same way about Frost." An unspoken understanding passed between us. "Perhaps even more so. He's my nephew. If anything happens to him, it's not only me I'm failing, but my sister too."

"It's good you came here."

"I had no knowledge of the fountain, Atlantis, or you. A friend revealed everything when I needed it most."

"That's a good friend."

"I'm not so certain anymore."

"Why didn't you know of Atlantis?" I asked. "It's existed in the human world for years."

Angelica shrugged; the casual gesture somehow seemed elegant when performed by her. "We tend to be reclusive, rarely venturing beyond the southern waters, and we seldom encounter other ocean shifters. Maybe it's better that way." She sighed. "I still think we shouldn't have come."

"I sense a similarity in our thought processes."

"How so?"

"Over thinking."

Angelica chuckled. "I do have a habit of doing that. With the orcana numbers dwindling...it's fallen to me to shoulder the weight of our uncertain future."

"I can understand that burden."

A wisp of a smile touched her lips and her skin markings settled into a stable color. "We'd leave you in peace if it was an option," she said. "But we must remain until Storm is returned to us. And I'd like to show my appreciation for your generous hospitality by helping you get your children back too."

"We could use all the help we can get."

Angelica trailed me up the palace steps, through the vast welcoming foyers, and down the small staircase that led to the tunnels beneath the island.

"You've almost been buried alive twice," she said. "Do you have a plan?"

I turned to face her. "I know the army is looking. But I have to search for myself. And I promised Wade I wouldn't go into the tunnels alone again, so we'll have to join the army."

She nodded and followed me down the rest of the steps.

The tunnel yawned into a dimly lit foyer, where time had etched its history on the walls. A single lantern dangled from the ceiling, casting an amber glow that unveiled a meticulously drawn map of the labyrinthine passages sprawled across a cluttered desk. Rob stood behind the desk. A handful of soldiers were busy behind him, barking into walkies and running off to refill their flasks from the fountain.

Rob glanced up, concern etching lines into his features. "Is everything okay?"

"I've come to help with the search," I said. "I can't sit in my room any longer."

Rob keyed his radio and said, "Ford, you're needed at Tunnel HQ. Repeat. You're needed at Tunnel HQ."

"Received," came the muffled reply. "On my way."

Rob turned his attention back to me. "You'll be okay in Ford's company?"

"Yes, thank you," I replied. "Have you heard from Babette?"

"I managed to get in touch with her this morning," Rob said. "She's on her way back. With a boatload of survivors."

"She'll be needed."

"I made her aware."

"Thank you."

Ford appeared, took one look at me and his face softened. Sympathy. I was tired of seeing it on the faces of my friends. I needed action. Results. And my son.

"We want to help find the orbs," Angelica said.

"Very well," Ford replied. "But you must follow my instructions, is that clear? It's dangerous in the tunnels. We've had several collapses. Two of which you were in." He glanced at me. "We can't afford to lose the queen, or the leader of the orcana."

We both agreed.

"We'll be careful," I said.

"It's the least I can do..." Angelica shifted her gaze to the darkness of the tunnel at Ford's back, but didn't say more. Perhaps she'd been about to rehash the sentiments of guilt she had spoken of in the courtyard.

Someone handed Ford a refilled flask. "I'm not happy about how many times we've needed to use the flasks," Ford said. "It's become mandatory that everyone down here carry a flask of the fountain water with them."

"Do you have enough for the three of us?" Angelica asked.

Ford nodded. "Let's go."

Following him along a well-lit tunnel, lanterns and sconces affixed to dusty walls, thick cables snaking along the floor and ceiling, and sturdy supports at regular intervals, I asked, "Have you spotted any of those white spiders?"

"That's one of the reasons we have the flasks," Ford said.

I could send fireballs through the entire tunnel network, burning the dangerous arachnids into nonexistence, but it would have to wait until after the orbs were found. My power could collapse the entire system and I couldn't risk losing the orbs.

"I'm so sorry," Angelica whispered to me. I felt her eyes on my face, and again her need to say more. "Your son..."

Ford, ahead of us, made an effort to ignore our conversation.

"I can't go there right now," I said. "Let's concentrate on finding the orbs. Then we can think about the kids."

As we navigated the passageways, Ford elaborated on the measures they had taken to stabilize the tunnels and the lack of any signs of the elusive orbs. Flames flickered to life on my hands, and I quickly extinguished them. There was no need for them in these well-lit tunnels, but my emotions often had a different idea. In times of high stress, my powers became unpredictable, sometimes vanishing entirely, other times erupting uncontrollably. When I was pregnant with Gal, they had become so unpredictable that I had feared being near anyone. I had thought I'd gotten a handle on them, that I knew how to control my state of mind enough that my powers never put anyone in danger again, but now it seemed they had a mind of their own. I tucked my hands behind my back.

Ford drew to a halt at a fork in the tunnel. The right pathway was lit, the left dark.

I stepped into the darkness.

"We haven't secured that tunnel yet, Cordelia," Ford said.

"Then that's the place we should look," I replied.

Ford hesitated, holding his lantern high, jostling his weight from one foot to the other. "I promised Wade you would be safe."

"And there's no reason I won't be." Besides Wade, Ford was the strongest person on the island.

A faint tremor grumbled under our feet.

"It's not safe down there," Ford said.

"So we'll be careful," I said.

He examined my face. "You're probably going to go down there without me, aren't you?"

"I promised Wade I wouldn't be reckless." I promised him I'd stay alive for our son. But if any harm came to Gal...I couldn't finish the thought.

"We need to get the kids back," Angelica said, her arm brushing against mine.

Ford transferred his gaze to the orca shifter, then back to me.

"If I say run, we run, got it?"

"Got it," I replied.

"Of course," Angelica said.

With Ford in the lead, we ventured further into the eerie darkness; the lantern casting a feeble light that struggled to pierce the oppressive shadows. He kept his other hand resting on the flask.

We inched our way forward, slower than I would have liked, as the lantern pushed the shadows into the depths of the tunnel. The passage was no different to all the others. Damp clay walls, crumbling stone, dust and mildew. The reek of a place that hadn't felt air in centuries. Cobwebs, insects, the odd drip of water echoing through the system.

"It's creepy down here," Angelica said with a shiver. "I prefer the open spaces of the southern oceans."

"Keep your voices down," Ford said. "Even speaking can cause a collapse."

I glanced back, the distant light from the previous tunnel a mere speck. Ahead, a void of darkness beckoned.

Our progress slowed to a crawl. We happened upon an old collapse, stone and rock and cement piled to one side of the narrow tunnel. We skirted around it as the passageway descended. The ceiling lowered. The walls closed in around us. I had never been claustrophobic before. But I felt every inch of rock and water above my head, pressing down on me. The weight of it all.

I heard Angelica swallow. I heard Ford's measured breaths. I heard loose pebbles skitter under our feet and other indistinct sounds I couldn't identify. I smelled nothing but death.

Straining my eyes to peer into the darkness, I glimpsed something in the distance. Something glowed. Only for a fraction of a second. Perhaps I had imagined it.

"We should turn back," Ford said when we reached another pile of rocks. This one blocking the path.

"Not yet," I said and began to move the rocks out of the way.

With the three of us working together, we had the path cleared in half an hour. Ford whispered into his walkie, giving our location to HQ, but the connection was lost, and at the sound of Ford's deep voice, cement cascaded down the walls. He turned his walkie off and stuck it in his belt.

Another flash, a faint glow in the distance.

"We must turn back now." Ford gave me his non-negotiable face; his jaw set, and his brow furrowed, his body already leaning back the way we had come.

"I think I saw something," I said. "Just a little further."

He gave me a measured look, but knew better than to try to dissuade me. The three of us huddled together, inching forward step by step, barely daring to breathe.

The glow increased, a faint luminescence that seeped into the tunnel, eating away at the gloom.

"What is that?" Angelica whispered.

"I should call for backup," Ford said.

"We're too deep in the tunnels now," I said. "Just a few more feet to see what it was."

"Cordelia." A muscle ticked in Ford's jaw as he stared me down.

"We're so close," I whispered.

Angelica raised a hand, moving her thumb and forefinger so there was only a hair's gap between them.

Ford stood alert, his shoulders tense, legs poised for action, and his head tilted toward the darkness, listening intently.

"Ford—"

He raised a single finger. Something grumbled in the distance. We stood in silence for a full minute before he lowered his hand and indicated for us to follow him.

Without speaking, we began to move again, all three of us holding our breath. My pulse rushed in my ears, loud and throbbing and insistent. A flame sprung to life on my forefinger. As we drew closer to the mysterious glow, it brightened until we drew level with it.

Before us, embedded in the wall, was a radiant stone. A glowing green triangle with a horizontal line through its center pointing down.

"Is that what I think it is?" Angelica whispered, her voice softer than snow.

I nodded. "One of the orbs is behind that stone."

"Any idea which one?" Ford asked.

"It's green. It's probably nature. Earth," Angelica replied.

I pressed a hand against the glowing symbol, tracing its etching with my fingers.

"I'll go and inform Rob, then we can figure out how to release it," Ford said.

I rubbed at the edges of the stone with a finger, wearing away the cement, causing it to drift to the ground.

Ford grabbed my wrist. "One missing stone could cause

this entire tunnel to collapse. We have to do this the right way."

I glared at him. "We don't have time to secure the entire tunnel. We must have walked for at least a mile. We need the orbs now."

"It's not like we've found the others yet," Ford said, the sympathy in his eyes slicing through me once more. "We can take our time with this one."

I gritted my teeth. I wanted to scream at him like I was a little girl, demand he listen to me, but I knew he was right. He was here because of me, risking his life. And if anything happened, I knew he would die for me. I didn't want him to die.

"Fuck!" I yelled and threw my hands in the air.

"Shh," Ford whispered.

The three of us stood in silence for a moment, listening to each other breathe, staring between the glowing stone and the flames flickering on my fingers.

Ford indicated we should retreat.

"How long will it take to secure the tunnel?" I asked.

Ford grimaced. "Could take a week."

My frustration erupted, flames bursting from my hands, glancing off the walls, the ground, the ceiling, burning a path around the edges of the glowing stone. Heat blasted by my face, lifted my hair, burned the dust out of the air.

"I'm so sorry." I shook my flames out of existence. Why couldn't I control my own damn power? Why did I always make everything worse?

Ford glanced at the tunnel walls, the ceiling. A tremor

rippled under our feet. We braced ourselves, but nothing happened.

"I think we're okay," Ford whispered.

"I'm so sorry," I said again.

"I know you are," he said.

"Look." Angelica pointed at the wall.

The cement around the stone had burned away. The stone appeared to defy gravity, supported solely by the wall's willpower.

"We could..." Angelica stared at the glowing green symbol.

I shook my head. "Ford is right. It's too dangerous."

Ford rubbed his chin, the green glow reflected in his eyes. "I don't know. Perhaps we could...I feel like it wants to break free..." He placed his fingers around the stone.

I held my breath as Ford traced the stone's contours.

"Hold this." He passed me the lantern and I directed it at the stone.

Ford placed his fingers into the stone's grooves. "Are we in agreement?"

"Do it," Angelica said.

I nodded.

Biting his lip, Ford wiggled the stone. It slipped from the wall with unexpected ease, and a brilliant green light filled the passage. A glowing green orb emerged from the recess, swirling with all the hues of all the greens imaginable, from vibrant grass to delicate mint to deep pine and every shade in between. It was utterly breathtaking.

Ford secured the stone back into the wall as the green orb

circled us. It floated in the air, as if considering its surroundings, then seemed to perch on Ford's shoulder.

"I think it likes you," Angelica said.

"I think you were meant to find it," I said.

Ford's mouth fell open. "I'm to be the keeper of an orb?"

"It definitely seems that way." I smiled. "I can't think of anyone more deserving."

"Rock and Earth, right?" Angelica asked.

"I guess I do spend a lot of time in these tunnels."

"It's not about the tunnels," I said. "It's because you're stoic, reassuring, solid, reliable, steadfast—"

"You're in danger of inflating my ego," Ford said.

I laughed. "It's true. You are all those things. And you have a deep connection with the way Atlantis functions. It's only right that Rock and Earth should be yours."

"We're one step closer," Angelica said. "Now we only need three more."

CHAPTER SIXTEEN

The screams found us before we left the tunnel. When Ford, Angelica and I reached the rickety table that comprised the HQ for the orb search, Rob and the soldiers had disappeared. Yells and shouts thundered through the passageways, echoing off the damp clay walls. The ground shook, threatening to collapse under our feet.

"What's going on?" I asked.

We shared a glance. The green orb cast its serene hue over us, but it was useless without the other five.

With a silent and shared understanding, we dashed up the tunnel staircase, through the wide palace halls, and emerged at the top of the marble steps to find the courtyard had turned into a battleground.

The ghost pirate ship floated a few feet overhead, its skeletal crew illuminated by the moonlight, their luminous whips cracking ominously at anyone who dared approach. Spiders scuttled over the ship, making the inanimate vessel seem alive. From my higher vantage point, I counted over twenty Atlantean children on board, tied to the port and starboard sides. I searched for Gal, but saw no sign of him. He had a concussion, was already weak…too weak to survive?

Amidst the cacophony of children's screams, I recognized Una's piercing cry. She wailed desperately, crying for her mother and father.

The ship took no heed, was indifferent to the screaming children. It glinted with power, moving in a way no ship should be able to move.

Three more children were lifted into the air by those treacherous whips. Atlanteans fought in the courtyard, running from the lashing poison, slapping at the venomous spiders, hurling spears at the pirates. But their weapons proved futile, bouncing off the ship or passing straight through the ghostly crew.

I wrung my hands, evoking my flames, and aimed them at the sky. Huge fireballs tore from my fingers, shot from my eyes, and streaked toward the malevolent ship. In battle, my flames had the ability to understand their target. The fireballs surged toward the ship, appeared to engulf the pirates, but none of them reacted. None of them cared they were on fire. The ship glowed as if absorbing my power. My flames were useless. But I couldn't just stand there.

While I prepared to unleash my flames once more, desperate to find a target that would succumb to my power, Ford raced down the steps. The green orb followed him, creating large steppingstones from rapidly growing trees beneath his feet. He dashed along a path at the same height as the palace steps, the sprouting trees keeping pace with the ship. He glanced once over his shoulder, locked eyes with me, then ran along his wooden route all the way to the ship. A white whip lashed out of the ship, encircling his neck. Ford's eyes bulged and he grasped the noose, struggling to free himself. His body bucked and he kicked out, then fell loose, dangling from the end of the whip.

"Oh no." Angelica covered her mouth with her hands.

The fresh snow was ruined. The white courtyard turned red once more. Hundreds of Atlanteans hurled themselves at the ship, trying to get their children back, trying to prevent others from being taken. But it was no use. Everything they touched was poisonous. Many fell, unmoving. Not all made it to the fountain. I spotted Wade among the chaos, ducking under whips, calling for our son. My sister stood in the middle of the courtyard, her face thrust at the sky, screaming at the ship, demanding the pirates release her son.

Angelica took a step back, merging with the shadows. "Why is this happening?"

With my firepower useless, there was nothing I could do in this battle. There was nothing any of us could do. Yet my people continued to fight, both Atlanteans and humans. I dashed down the steps, screaming at people to get back. Angelica stayed nearby, bringing the fountain to as many fallen individuals as possible. One of them was Ford. I found him lying on the ground, his lips blue, his face swelling, his eyes about to dim. I wrestled the whip from around his neck and cast it aside, my hands searing with pain. Angelica provided us both with fountain water. Once Ford regained his health, he leaped to his feet and turned to charge at the ship once more, his companion orb hovering by his side.

I grabbed his wrist. "We have to pick our battles. Isn't that what you taught me?"

He nodded grimly, and together, we gathered our people, urging them to withdraw. Our chances of winning the fight against the pirates were hopeless until we found all the elemental orbs. Until that day, the best we could do was stay safe and watch our children be taken.

WE AMASSED in the great hall, the Power of the Sea swirling majestically upon its pedestal and the two smaller orbs floating nearby. Although everyone present had drunk from the fountain and been restored to full health, there were many still outside who never made it to the healing water source, both Atlanteans and humans. Most people bore an expression of resigned weariness. Some cried openly. Others stared blankly through the window at the frozen, bloody world.

Standing on a podium, Wade addressed the crowd of five hundred people who had witnessed or fought in the battle with the ghost pirates.

Wade cleared his throat, took a moment to look over our people before he spoke. "We are facing a formidable new evil. An evil that seems...undefeatable." Murmured ascents passed through the crowd. "Many of you were there for the battle with the Hound of the Ocean and the fight with the dragon kings when we reclaimed our beloved island. During those terrible days, we thought our foe was too powerful."

"But the ghost pirates really are immortal," Blaze said

from the back of the room. He glanced at me. "I've never met a foe who didn't burn before."

The murmurs from the assembly grew louder. Wade raised his hand to restore order. "The ghost pirates are *not* immortal. They can be turned to flesh by the combination of all six elemental orbs. We have half in our possession." Several eyes fell to the swirling spheres of color. "What we know of the elemental orbs so far, is that each one chooses an Atlantean to be its protector, and that individual will wield exceptional power. We have witnessed this with Cordelia's increased abilities, and the trees that grew through our courtyard during the battle just now as Ford fought his way to the ship. So you can imagine how powerful all six orbs will be in combination."

The whispers in the crowd took on a new edge. Words and conversations were laced with hope.

Wade offered our people a fragile smile. "There are two hundred and fifty thousand people on Atlantis. We have an army of ten thousand. Which seemed substantial at the time, but in our current quest to locate the orbs within the labyrinthine tunnels beneath the island, now seems far too few."

"With Maya's capacity to understand *The Mermaid Chronicles* compromised, it is imperative we find these orbs as quicky as possible."

The red orb came to hover by my head, casting me in a warming glow. People looked my way, whispering and pointing. Flames appeared on my fingers, whether I wanted them or not. Ford's green orb floated near him, casting him in an equally pleasing green glow and showering him with leaves.

Babette entered the room, her eyes scanning the crowd. The Power of the Sea remained atop its pillar—it was not one for movement—but her eyes radiated with a brighter purpose.

"I hear you're in need of my help," she said.

I narrowed my eyes at her, trying to ignore the irritation prickling my skin.

"I'll catch you up after, Babette, but for now, I'd like to continue my address." Wade turned his attention back to the gathering. "We need your help. Our children are being taken. Their innocence is being stripped from them to power the ghost pirates' ship. If we want to get them back before it's too late, we must move quickly. We must locate the orbs. That means every single inhabitant of this island, who is physically able, must descend into the tunnels alongside the army to search for the orbs. We have no more time to waste."

The crowd murmured their agreement.

"What about the humans? The human children?" Babette asked.

Trust her to stir the pot.

Wade focused his gaze on her. "Both Atlantean children and human children are being abducted. There is no prejudice among the pirates. And on that note, it has heartened me to see all races coming together to face the pirates. That is how it should be."

"But the fountain still doesn't work for us," a human woman piped up.

"Have you seen all the dead bodies outside?" A human male asked. "Most of them are human."

"And I bear that pain with you," Wade said. "My own son is aboard that ship, having his innocence stripped away.

He was already injured, suffering from a concussion. You are all aware the fountain doesn't work for him. So whatever state he returns to us in...will be who he remains." His voice broke on the last few words.

I longed to hold my husband, to take him in my arms, to give him the comfort that I so desperately sought myself, but a crowd of people separated us and all we could do was hold each other's gaze.

Wade directed the crowd away from the hall and into Rob's care where he would assign them a group number, a tunnel number, and ensured they logged in and out so we could keep a record of their whereabouts in case of a collapse.

When the crowd had dispersed, Wade poured himself two fingers of an amber liquid into a glass from a decanter near the cold hearth and slumped into a chair. Babette and I remained. A sickly dawn light poured in through the frozen windows, only highlighting the exhaustion on our faces.

"Shouldn't we be joining the search?" Babette eyed his glass.

Wade took a long sip of his drink. "I've been up all night. More than one night. If it's all the same to you, I'm going to take a minute."

I turned to Babette, my new red orb giving me confidence. "Your father and one of his troops are going door to door assigning people to search groups as we speak. We'll have more people looking for the orbs than ever before."

Babette eyed my orb as critically as she'd eyed Wade's drink. "And what are the orbs, exactly?"

Wade and I filled her in on everything that had happened

during the days she'd been on the mainland. She took it all in with a blank face, but I could see her cogs turning.

"We need you here," I said. "Until all the orbs are found, and we can face the ghost pirates once and for all. You are the protector of the Power of the Sea. You must remain here."

"I get it, Cordy. You don't need to spell it out," she said. "I've brought back more humans. They're all in the hospital."

A tense silence wound between us. After being awake for I don't know how many hours straight, an argument with Babette was the last thing I needed. So I said nothing and stole a sip of my husband's drink.

"If Maya is unable to interpret the prophecies, I ought to go and read the book," she said.

"Maya is next on my list," I said. "She gave birth last night. I was giving her space. Perhaps if you could join a search team. I'll let you know if I need you."

Babette gave me a curt nod, turned on her heel, and left the room. Wade downed his drink and followed her. After I coaxed my fiery orb to a position near the Power of the Sea, I left it there and made my way through the snowy palace gardens to Maya's house.

When Trent let me in, he led me through to the living room where she sat huddled by a fire with baby Coral in her lap. The other two children were in the kitchen where Trent had been making pancakes. *The Mermaid Chronicles* lay on the coffee table beside her, its cover looking unusually dull, its pages dead and unturning. Maya stared at the fire, didn't look at me when I sat next to her.

"There's a new prophecy," she said. "But it's got nothing to do with the ghost pirates."

CHAPTER SEVENTEEN

I clutched the armrests as I took in Maya's words. "What does it say?"

Before replying, she placed a kiss on Coral's head, then raised her eyes to mine. *"Old enemies die hard."*

My chest turned to ice and my stomach churned. Words got stuck in my throat as I contemplated the ominous prophecy. The possibilities were endless, but deep down, I knew who the prophecy referred to.

"It doesn't have to be him." Maya said, reading my thoughts. "There have been so many battles, Cordy. So many enemies, not just in our time, but throughout the eternity of Atlantean history." She gestured toward the book, indicating the large section detailing our people's past struggles. "It could be anything. Hell, it could even be Vorago himself deciding we're no longer worthy of the island he created for us."

"Vorago was never our enemy," I muttered, attempting to work some feeling back into my numb body. So not the point.

I sighed, massaging the weariness from my face. "So there's no prophecy concerning the pirates at all?"

"The book is still blind. Or I'm still blind. I'm not sure which." The baby gurgled in her arms, and she rocked it gently back to sleep. "It's as if that period of time is lost to me forever."

I stared at the fire, attempting to ignore the fear licking through my veins. My hands trembled and sprouted ten small flames.

"It's not him, Cordy."

"I might be."

"I won't let it be."

"It would make sense."

"It makes *no* sense. He is in prison." Maya released her hand to touch my shoulder.

"Is he? The High Council made that prison for him. The old High Council. Gal specifically. Who knows what happened to it when they died?"

"There is nothing in the book to suggest what you're saying."

"Doesn't mean it's not him."

Maya sighed.

"I love you, Maya, but we can't trust your relationship with the book right now. Anything could be coming."

"Exactly."

A heavy silence hung between us. I interlaced my fingers in my lap, squeezing them together until they hurt. Something real. Something solid. Something to hold on to.

"What do you want to do?" Maya asked.

I chewed on my lip, stared at the crackling flames in the

fire. "There's nothing we *can* do. I assume this new prophecy has appeared because we will be successful in our battle against the ghost pirates. Then he'll come for me. Which means we get our children back. Which means I must keep hunting for the orbs."

"That's a lot of assumptions," Maya said.

"It feels right."

She remained silent as I stood and kissed her forehead, then passed a hand over the baby's cheek. "Let me know if anything changes."

"Of course."

"And don't go outside," I said on my way to the door. "There's a curfew in place. Stay at home or join a team in the tunnels. No going in the courtyards. Especially the kids."

Maya clutched the baby to her chest a little tighter.

I made my way outside, closing the door softly behind me, bracing myself for the cold. Maya's house lay nestled in the rear gardens of the palace and there was no need for me to walk past the courtyard and subject myself to the aftermath of the battle, but this was my island, my people, and I needed to bear witness to their bravery.

As I trudged through the palace gardens, now blanketed in fresh snow, a desolate wind plucked the ends of my hair, teased the hem of my coat, and snuck down the back of my shirt. Shivering, I crossed my arms and hunched my shoulders. I didn't think I'd ever get used to the cold. And it wasn't just cold outside, but in the palace too. Despite the new radiators and the fires roaring in every hearth, the royal suite remained eerily frigid, devoid of Gal's happy laughter, empty of his presence. I could barely stand to go in there.

In the courtyard, the trees that had sprouted when Ford attacked the ship remained, their roots firmly entrenched in the cracked marble, their branches bare and truncated, as if the battle and the elements had stolen their lives. A few soldiers carried stretchers of the dead toward the beach. Pyres awaited on the sandy shores, a solemn Atlantean tradition to commemorate lives lost and celebrate each individual. It wouldn't be long before my flames were needed to ignite the kindling. Wade would say a few words, and then we would send the burning pyres into the ocean, where Atlanteans found their final resting place.

I weaved a path among the soldiers and bodies, offering a few words to those tasked with the grim duty of dealing with the dead. Then I happened upon one lifeless form that stole my breath. Kneeling in the bloody slush next to the man, I swept the snow off his face and discovered terrible burns and spider bites across his cheeks and the length of his neck. The venom had caused bursting red pustules, bleeding eyes, and bloated cheeks. Dan. The father of Mini Cordelia.

I smothered an involuntary sob as I closed his eyelids. This death weighed heavy on me. No matter what Mini Cordelia endured on the ship of cobwebs and dust, when she returned—if she returned—nothing would ever be the same for her. No child should lose a parent so young.

A soldier approached and helped me to my feet. My knees were damp from kneeling in the slush. He offered me a tissue. I hadn't realized I'd been crying. Frozen tears marked my cheeks. I mumbled my thanks and wiped them away, balling the tissue into my fist before disintegrating it with one of my flames.

"We'll call you when we need you to light the pyres," the soldier said.

I acknowledged his words and moved away. There was nothing more I could do here. I found myself facing the door to Dylan's bar. A place I'd previously found so comforting and warm, despite the seawolf rug that filled the area in front of the fireplace. It was said they guarded Vorago's trident, the very trident he used to create Atlantis, but no one had any proof of that, and it seemed more of a legend than anything else. Yet the seawolf rug existed, so part of the story must have been true.

I stepped into the dimly lit bar to find it completely empty, apart from Dylan perched on a stool by the bar, taking measured sips from a glass and staring at the fire.

"Where's Babette?" I asked.

Dylan transferred his gaze to me. "She's back?"

"A few hours ago. Rob messaged her asking her to return."

"I haven't seen her." He refilled his glass.

Shaking the snow out of my hair, I slid onto the stool next to him and poured my own drink.

"There was another battle," I said.

"I was there."

"I didn't see you. Were you hurt?"

He shook his head.

"Dan is dead."

"Dan?"

"Mini Cordelia's father."

"Oh, shit."

We both took a sip of our drinks. I coughed, spluttered,

slapped my chest as the liquid went down the wrong way. I struggled for air, but my chest tightened into a vise. Warmth spread over my skin. An uncomfortable warmth that was nothing like my flames. My vision blurred. The flames danced mockingly in the fire, taunting me with images of my past.

"Cordelia?"

I slipped off the stool, shrugged out of my thick coat, placed my hands on my knees. I still couldn't breathe.

Dylan ran around the other side of the bar, grabbed a flask from a shelf hidden from view, and thrust it in my direction. "Drink."

I brought the fountain's water to my lips, dribbled some into my mouth, but it did nothing to change the pain in my chest, the fire on my skin, the blurriness in my vision.

Dylan came back around the bar and placed his hands on my shoulders. "You're having a panic attack."

I forced a nod, tried to remember the anxiety-relief techniques my father had taught me. Couldn't latch on to anything. Could only ride out the wave. Dylan steered me to one of the couches by the fire and pushed me to a seated position. I drew my knees into my chest, laced my hands around my legs, and rocked myself. Burying my face on my knees, I whispered reassurances to myself. I told myself everything was going to be okay. But everything wasn't okay. My people were dying. My son had been abducted. And an old enemy wanted revenge.

I forced air into my stubborn lungs, willing my heart to slow and my trembling legs to steady.

"There you go." Dylan sat on the arm of the couch, rubbing my back with tender strokes.

I gulped another breath, willing my heart to stop pounding and my legs to stop shaking and the feeling of hopelessness and desperation to leave me the hell alone. *Gal.*

"I want my son back," I said through my tears.

Dylan said nothing. Words didn't help.

I wiped my tears away, but more came to replace them. There was no point pretending to be strong. I wasn't anymore. I was falling apart. This was it. This was the moment when I broke.

"I wished for you and Mom and Dad every day for five years," Dylan said quietly. "I had panic attacks too. Nerida helped me."

My memories settled on the mermaid who had saved Dylan from the jaws of Zale and taught him the merfolk ways. She had helped us in our quest to find Atlantis, getting herself caught and locked up in a lab in the process. We had rescued her, only for her to die during the battle with the dragon kings.

"I hate it," I said. "I hate all of it."

Dylan planted my drink in front of me and I took a large gulp. The warmth of the alcohol slid down my throat and settled in my stomach, blunting the worst of the anxiety.

"I don't know how you coped for so long," I said, touching the hand that rested on my shoulder.

"I wasn't alone," he said. "One day at a time."

"One day at a time." Even a day seemed insurmountable.

My twin brother slipped onto the couch beside me, cradling his own drink in his lap. Together, we watched the fire and sipped our drinks. We stayed that way for an hour, sometimes talking, telling each other stories from when we had been apart. Other times we were silent, watching the flames, sipping our drinks. I couldn't remember a time when my brother and I had shared such a moment.

"I miss him too." Dylan's hand shook as he refilled his glass. "I think he's my favorite person on Atlantis. No offense."

"None taken," I said. "He's my favorite person too."

"He was getting so good at martial arts."

"But not good enough."

"Nothing can defeat a ghost pirate."

"Dylan, I can't do this. I can't talk about him like he's gone."

"I'm sorry."

A fierce wind stirred outside, rattling the glass in the windows, howling down the chimney breast, pushing its way through the cracks in the door. It chilled the room, dueled with the fire, and brought icy crystals to frost my cheeks. I summoned a flame onto my hand, but even that was extinguished. I tried to summon the flames once more, but this time they would not bend to my will. My emotions were depleted. I had no strength left.

Dylan stood. "I hope the pirates aren't back."

I stood with him. We watched, and we waited, both our eyes fixed on the door. The wind continued its furious assault, and we strained to hear any signs of life beyond the bar's walls.

"It feels like the whole island is ripping apart at the seams," I said.

"Maybe another tunnel collapsed."

We braced ourselves. Shouts sounded from outside, but it was only the wind bargaining to be let inside. An icy air filled the room, billowing our clothing, chilling our skin. Shutters slammed shut, then flung open once more. The cabinets inside the bar mimicked the action. Glasses rattled in their overhead racks and a couple of bottles from the top shelf fell and smashed on the floor.

"What the hell is going on?" I yelled as the wind snatched the drink from my hand and threw it onto the seawolf rug.

"What's that?" Dylan asked.

I followed his gaze to the fireplace. The flames danced wildly in the chimney. But they were no longer ordinary flames. They were a bright yellow, the yellow of sunflowers, of golden beaches, of soothing sunsets and everything in between. It wasn't just the fire, but the hearth too, and the room we stood in. A yellow glow touched every surface.

A moment later, a bright yellow orb flew out of the chimney breast and made a beeline for Dylan. Dylan raised both palms, backing away from the swirling orb, pleading with it not to come any closer.

I smiled. "It's an orb. And it's yours."

Dylan shot me a look. "I don't want it."

"You don't have a choice. It's chosen you as its guardian."

Dylan frowned. "Which one is it?"

"Judging by the color, I'd say Air and Flight."

His frown deepened into a scowl. "Shouldn't that go to Blaze, or Ember, or you know, someone who can actually fly? And I hate wind." He lowered his hands, and the orb made a few circles around his head, granting Dylan a halo of light that smoothed away his hard edges. He looked at me. "Seriously, I don't want it."

"We'll need you and it when the time comes," I said.

"That's fine," he said. "I can do that, but for now, take it away. Put it in the great hall. I don't need a pet. I can't even keep a girlfriend, how am I supposed to protect a magical orb?"

"We can walk it over together."

"Does that mean there are only two orbs left to find?"

A shiver of anticipation ran through me. Only minutes ago, I'd been consumed by loss. Now, with the appearance of another orb, hope bloomed.

"It does," I replied. "Why don't you see what happens when you touch it?"

"I don't want to touch it. Didn't you see those big-ass trees that grew out of the courtyard? I don't want to grow wings, or something. I'm no Icarus."

"Dylan. Come on. It chose you for a reason. And when the final battle comes, you're going to have to touch it to wield its power."

He glanced at me, scrunched his face, slitted one eye, and poked the glowing orb. Wind rushed around the room, whipping our hair and clothes. Without warning, Dylan left the floor and slammed against the ceiling, where he remained suspended as the orb circled him.

"Get me down!" Dylan yelled.

"I think that's up to you."

Dylan looked from me to the orb and extended his hand. The yellow orb floated into his palm, and then Dylan descended to the ground as if he were being lowered by the clouds themselves. With the wind gone, a subtle rustling sound lingered in the room. It felt like the orb was whispering.

"Yeah...that's so not staying here," Dylan said as he smoothed his hair into place.

"I wonder what else it can do."

"So don't need to find out. I like my feet firmly on the ground."

I smiled at my brother, took in the bewilderment on his face, the permanent pain that hovered in his eyes. "There's something else I need to tell you."

Dylan's expression hardened. Something resembling an exhausted weariness joined the pain in his eyes. "What is it?"

"There's a new prophecy in the book. *Old enemies die hard.*"

He searched my face. I waited for the realization to settle on him.

"Is it him?" he whispered.

"I think so."

My brother kneeled on the floor and wept. I cradled him in my arms as the glowing orb circled us both. We were both so broken. Neither of us had anything left to give. And yet the prophecies continued.

CHAPTER EIGHTEEN

I kept the name of my oldest enemy firmly locked inside as I made my way to Tunnel HQ, but the images of our last confrontation intruded. Although I bore no physical wounds from that encounter as the fountain had healed my scars, the emotional fallout festered inside and compounded the anxiety I already struggled with. An anxiety that originated the day half my family was taken from me. It came with panic attacks and a crippling fear of water. He'd been responsible for all the trauma in my past. My mother. My brother. And almost killing Wade.

The frigid bite of the weather outside did little to thaw my anxiety as Dylan and I climbed the palace steps, the orb hovering between us, its radiant yellow glow bathing the battleground in a warm hue that made it look more palatable. But death was still death.

When we stopped by the great hall, the yellow orb seemed to understand Dylan wanted it to remain, and it floated toward the Power of the Sea, joining the other two magical spheres in a glowing orbit.

"Are you going to help find the other orbs?" I asked.

"I will," Dylan replied, stealing a quick drink from the decanter. His eyes already bore the signs of exhaustion, and his words slurred. I doubted he'd be much use, but the distraction might help. God knew we both needed one.

After passing through security at the entrance to the underground system, we descended the tunnel steps together. Dylan was assigned a group, and shortly after, disappeared down a passageway. Wade emerged, covered in dust and cement, using his fingers to remove the debris from his hair.

I rushed over to him. "Are you okay?"

"Another collapse," he said, drawing me close. "The deeper we go, the more unstable it gets. I really hope we find the remaining orbs soon."

"And we still don't know what happened to the yellow one," Rob said as he stared at the map on his desk. "Zoomed out of here so fast it made me dizzy."

"It's Dylan's," I said. "It came to the bar."

"At least that's one mystery solved," Rob said, then reported the information over his radio for the soldiers in the tunnel to hear. "Babette found it."

Of course she did.

"Have you come to help search?" Wade asked.

"I thought we could go together."

Wade took my hand with one of his, then grabbed a flask from the table with the other. He peered over Rob's shoulder to look at the map. "We'll take tunnel twenty."

"It hasn't been secured yet," Rob said. "And it's right next to the one that collapsed."

"Exactly," Wade replied.

Rob snapped his head up and shot us a penetrating look, scanning our faces, lingering on Wade's muscular frame, and finally settling on my hands. "Be careful."

After securing the strap of the flask around his neck, Wade gestured to the tunnel. We proceeded along the well-lit passage until we arrived at a fork. After a few quick turns, the gradient descended dramatically, and the air grew heavy with damp and moisture. We reached the end of the lanterns.

"Light 'em up, baby." Wade pointed to my hands.

"You're relying on me for light?" I arched an eyebrow. "Me, whose emotions are all over the place and might end up burning you alive?"

Wade smiled. "I trust you."

"That makes one of us," I muttered as I closed my eyes and summoned my flames. Only half an hour ago they had resisted my command, but now, in the dark tunnel with the reassuring presence of my husband, they obeyed my will. When I opened my eyes, a flame burned from each fingertip.

"That's useful for dealing with spiders too."

"Have you come across many of them?"

Wade's eyes tightened, then flashed selachii black. "We lost someone earlier today."

"They didn't have a flask?"

"It was a human. We've sent them all home. I can't have more of them dying and widening the unease between us."

"They're going to hate sitting at home twiddling their fingers, waiting for us to rescue their children."

"I won't have more of them hurt."

"I understand," I said. "But it doesn't make the situation between our races any easier."

Wade exhaled, fanning his hair away from his face. "I was trying to help them."

"I know." Unable to touch him with my fiery hands, I pressed a kiss to his lips. "Come on, let's carry on."

We ventured deeper into the tunnel, the walls closing in, the ceiling descending, and the terrain growing more treacherous. Regular tremors rumbled under our feet and soon my hair was as caked in dust as Wade's. The oppressive darkness became a weighted, physical thing, my flames the only light capable of dispelling the menacing shadows. And it resurrected the memories of teeth and blood and terror and loss. I halted, squeezed my eyes closed, took a breath.

"Cordy?" Wade came back for me and swept an arm around my waist. "What is it?"

"Everything," I said as I exhaled.

He pulled me closer, his touch gentle yet firm, his fingers threading through my hair. If only all my problems could be smoothed away by a loving touch. "I got you."

I still couldn't bring myself to utter Zale's name. Voicing it would give him too much power, and perhaps even manifest his presence. If I didn't say it, maybe it wouldn't be true. A foolish notion, but one I clung to.

"We're going to get him back," Wade whispered into my hair.

I wished I could believe him.

The ground rumbled once more, causing rocks to rain from the ceiling and throwing us apart. My flames flickered, threatening to go out, but I willed them to remain. The tunnel groaned, the noise escalating to an ear-piercing crescendo. My stomach dropped as the walls trembled, and pebbles and rocks rolled past our feet. My flames flickered off and on, a strobing action that illuminated the horror of the tunnel in bursts of light. A pounding reverberated through the walls, or beneath the ground, I couldn't tell which. Something was coming. Wade glanced back up the tunnel. The light of my dismal flames highlighted a boulder speeding down the passageway, heading straight for us.

"We need to run," Wade yelled, yanking my elbow, spinning me to face the darkness, and propelling me forward.

With one hand in front to light my way, and the other behind to help Wade navigate the passage, I sped through the tunnel. Rocks fell beside us, grazing our shoulders, landing on our toes, opening cuts on our cheeks, but we ran, and all the time the boulder behind us gained speed.

Wade's hand remained on my back, and he yelled at me to keep running, to never give up, and that he loved me. With my heart racing, I ran, ignoring the way the uneven ground grabbed for my feet. Ahead, I sensed an opening—a widening of the tunnel. I stepped into the darkness and the ground disappeared beneath me.

I screamed.

Adrenaline spiked through my veins, causing fireballs to shoot from my hands, revealing only an abyss of darkness. Wade grabbed my arm as I plummeted and swung me to the side. Below me, my flames exposed the dim outline of an enormous chasm. As I cycled my legs uselessly in the air, I screamed for Gal.

I sensed a wall approaching and instinctively reached out, my fingers finding purchase on the rough rocks as I swung from Wade's grip. Balancing precariously on a narrow ledge, my flames still burning bright in the dark, I clung to the side of the cavern.

Wade roared as the boulder crashed into him, almost knocking him out of the tunnel and into the abyss. He braced his back and prevented the boulder from escaping until he found his balance, then tiptoed onto the ledge next to me.

The boulder groaned and protested. It shifted to the lip of the tunnel, teetered there for a moment, and disappeared into the chasm beneath us. I counted twenty seconds before I heard a distant crash.

"You okay?" Wade asked beside me.

"I think so." Tremors shook my limbs as I clung to my perilous position.

"Can you climb onto me?"

"Aren't you hurt?"

"I'll be fine. I need you to climb onto me, then we can get back into the tunnel."

"I'll have to extinguish my flames."

Wade nodded and I doused my flames, plunging us into total darkness. Or so I thought. Even without my fiery light, I noticed a faint purple glow several feet below me.

"What's that?"

"Just climb, Cordelia."

I groped along the ledge, inching my way forward until my fingers touched Wade's warmth. I clambered onto his back and wrapped my arms around his neck.

Slowly, he edged his way back into the tunnel and set me

on my feet. I summoned my flames once more. A nasty burn covered his hand and wrist.

"Did I do that?"

"It'll be okay in a minute." He attempted to remove the stopper from the flask, but his hands trembled violently.

Shaking the flames out of one hand, I reached for the flask, careful to avoid his burns, removed the stopper, and held it to his lips. He drank deeply, then offered me a sip. Our wounds healed instantly, but it didn't stop my heart pounding or the guilt from constricting my throat.

"I'm sorry," I said.

"It's okay."

I searched his face, his blue eyes that always flashed selachii black when he was emotional, and saw nothing but love. His brow furrowed as I examined him, my gaze roaming not just his face, but the strength in his body. My love for him was overwhelming, a pressure in my chest that couldn't be contained.

"I hate it when I hurt you."

Our eyes locked. With a tender touch, he lifted my chin, angling my face toward his. Anticipation hung heavy in the air, a palpable tension that sent shivers down my spine. And then, his lips, like a whisper from a forgotten dream, met mine. His mouth was soft against mine, a gentle brush that took my mind to other places, that created a longing in me I had suppressed since our son had been taken. He deepened the kiss, his tongue parting my mouth. As our lips moved in unison, I felt the rhythm of his heartbeat echoing mine. I surrendered myself to him, melting into his body, careful to keep my flames at bay. The tunnel around us dissolved, and I was left only in the presence of Wade.

My flames dimmed, and I raked my fingers through his hair, crushing my mouth against his, needing to feel every inch of him pressed against me. The hard curve of his thigh separated my legs. His corded arms curled around me, holding me against the solid wall of his broad chest, where our hearts sang to each other. As his lips found my neck and drifted to the hollow of my throat, I clutched his shoulders, pulling myself tight against him. Then he was still, simply holding me close.

"I needed that," he whispered.

"Me too," I replied softly, our breaths mingling in the chilly underground air.

He pulled away. I reignited my flames so we could stare at each other in the darkness.

Wade glanced at my hands, then my face. "You know your hair was on fire when we were running?"

I blinked, my flames dancing in the darkness. "It was? I didn't notice."

His eyes brightened with amusement. "That orb of yours is definitely giving you some interesting powerups."

"I'll have to have a word with it."

He chuckled, then looked into the yawning chasm below. "What did you see?"

"Down there." I pointed into the darkness.

Crouching on our hands and knees, we peered over the edge of the tunnel. A pulsing purple light emanated from twenty feet below, casting an eerie glow.

"It must be another orb," I said.

"I hope so." Wade gave me a quick kiss. "I didn't think it would be this easy. I feared it was going to take us years."

I examined the distance between us and the mesmerizing light. "I don't think this is easy."

Wade laughed. "We could use Jordan's climbing equipment right about now."

"Or Dylan and his Air and Flight orb."

Wade lifted both eyebrows. "He can fly now?"

"Sort of."

"Climbing equipment might be safer."

"Probably. But how do we get back to Tunnel HQ? Pretty sure that boulder was a sign of a tunnel collapse."

Wade's eyes tracked the ceiling. "I think we're going to have to dig ourselves out."

"But we don't know what's above us. We might cause a massive sinkhole. Destroy homes...people...and speaking of collapsing tunnels, why is the fountain allowing it? Why is the Power of the Sea permitting such destruction? They're both supposed to keep our island in a state of magical paradise. At least that was my understanding. So why are all these tunnels collapsing and hurting people? Is it the orbs?"

"I don't think it has anything to do with the orbs," Wade said, still inspecting our enormous prison. "I think it's because of the unrest between the shifters and the humans. It will only keep the land in harmony when the people are at peace too."

I threw my hands in the air, flames and all. "What are we supposed to do about that?"

"We figure it out."

"How?"

"I don't know yet. I expect we're going to have to appoint a human to the senate. Maybe another to the High Council too."

"The High Council chooses its members, not the other way around."

"We'll have to see. Our priority is the orbs, then we can see about the senate. For now, I reckon you could throw a few fireballs around, and we might get some idea of the scope of this place."

I froze, locking my muscles in place. The crackle of my flames muted other sounds. "I think a spider just crawled over my leg."

"You're okay. I don't think one of the white ones could make it down this far."

With a determined flick of my wrist, I sent a small fireball skirting the length of my legs, burning away any insects that dared to approach. I didn't know if it was a white spider, or if I might have been bitten, but I took another sip from the flask to be sure.

"I'm okay."

Wade placed a hand on my back. "You're not okay. Not really. Neither of us are."

I swallowed hard. "If we don't get him back..." I couldn't finish the thought out loud. "He has to come back."

"I know."

We stared into the darkness together, using the light of my flames to examine the underground cavern. The purple stone glowed, pulsing with vibrancy, as if calling to us.

"We might not need Dylan or Jordan's climbing equipment." I leaned further over the edge. "I think I can get the orb from here."

"How?"

"I was with Ford when we discovered the green orb of Rock and Earth. I was...frustrated...lost control of my flames for a moment, sent a fireball down the tunnel. But it burned away the cement keeping the stone in place. Ford merely plucked it out of the wall. It's like they want to be found."

"They do. Maya told me. The orbs are like companions, in a way. They want to be with their chosen guardian, so they try to be found."

"I could send a fireball down there now. Release the orb. It could find its chosen Atlantean."

Wade pulled at his jaw as he inspected the wall beneath us. "You might burn the ground out from under us."

I glanced at the flask strapped to his side. "We have the fountain."

"It's dangerous." Wade's lips thinned as he looked at me, then at the purple light below. "Gal needs both his parents when he gets back."

I ignored all the warning bells sirening in my head and said, "We need to get him back first."

"What's gotten into you?"

"I don't know what else to do." Possibilities cycled through my mind. Find climbing equipment. Ask Dylan or Blaze for help. But we had to make our way out of the cavern first, and I was pretty sure the tunnel at our backs was no longer an option. "We've been in dangerous situations before."

"But none of our own doing."

"We're going to have to burn our way out of here anyway."

Keeping his fingers away from my flames, Wade gripped my hand. "I love you."

"Don't do that."

"Do what?"

"Tell me you love me."

"But I do."

"You know what I mean."

Wade tightened his grip on my hand. "No one is going to die here today."

"You don't know that."

"Cordelia Blue, I *love* you." He held my chin again, forcing me to look at him. "I love everything about you. I love how fiercely *you* love. Me. Gal. And all our friends. Your love is a beacon that has guided me through our dark times and eased the burdens of ruling Atlantis. Nothing matters to me more than you and our son. Our Family. You've taught me to love with an unwavering fierceness, with tenderness and compassion. My love for you knows no limits, no boundaries, and has no end. It is a love that burns with an intensity I never knew existed within me. *I love you*. That will never change. And I will never stop telling you that. Okay?"

I wiped a tear from my cheek. "Okay."

"Now let those fireballs rip."

With renewed determination, I aimed my hands at the pulsing light below and unleashed a torrent of fire, the flames dancing and swirling as they descended into the depths of the underground cavern.

CHAPTER NINETEEN

Fire blazed a brilliant path through the colossal cavern, leaving trails of flames in its wake. As I unleashed my fiery power, the flames surged, dancing along my arms, coursing down my waist, and enveloping my legs, until I stood aglow with their fiery embrace. Wade instinctively retreated, pressing himself against the tunnel wall as the inferno consumed my entire being. Yet, my flames never brought me harm; I was immune to my own incendiary abilities.

After a few minutes, I drew the flames back inside, leaving only one hand alight. Together, Wade and I peered over the edge. The purple stone radiated with newfound vibrancy, transitioning through delicate lavender shades to the deepest violet, but it remained firmly lodged in the wall. My fire had destroyed much of the wall beneath us, burning away substantial chunks of stone and leaving jagged, treacherous ledges in its wake.

"Maybe we could climb down there," I said.

"But how would we get back up?"

"If I use more fire, I'm worried we'll collapse this ledge—" Before I could finish my sentence, a chunk of rock dislodged from the ceiling above our heads, letting in a rush of daylight, and fell into the chasm below. Water surged through the opening, pouring into the cavern, creating the most beautiful underwater waterfall I'd ever seen.

"Jesus!" Wade muttered.

"We need to get to that stone."

"We've got time. This cavern is huge. It's going to take forever to fill."

"Not if we're under Lake Echomere. And what if there's another stone in here somewhere?"

Wade nudged my arm. "Good point, burn away."

I thrust my hands over the edge, ignited my fingers, and hurled fireballs at the stone. This time, the cement and rock fell away, revealing the embedded stone. It slipped from the wall's grasp, zooming out and shooting toward the ceiling. Passing us by, it halted abruptly, floated back down. It approached, scrutinizing us, as if pondering if one of us was its rightful guardian.

The orb flashed a deep violet; the light pulsing into the cavern, highlighting everything in hues of purple. It buzzed, spun in circles, and finally darted away.

"I guess it doesn't belong to either of us," Wade said.

The orb flew to the ceiling, into the waterfall, and disappeared.

"Someone is about to get a rather large shock," I said.

"And we need to figure out how to get out of here."

We pulled each other to our feet, and I surveyed the

tunnel behind us. A brief investigation revealed the passage was blocked, and retreating the way we had come was no longer an option.

"How do we get out of here?" I asked.

Wade stared at the thundering water. "I think we're going to have to use the waterfall."

"How?"

"We wait for the chasm to fill up a bit."

I stared at him. "You expect us to jump into an unknown abyss and hope we have a watery landing? And then swim *up* the waterfall? We are not in a video game."

"Says the girl who burned the wall away from under us."

Before we could continue the discussion, the purple orb reappeared, descended the waterfall, and halted in front of us. It buzzed, spun, vibrated, and almost seemed to squeak. An air of urgency possessed the glowing sphere.

"I don't think it's able to find its guardian," Wade said.

My heart sank. "It must belong to a child on the ship."

The orb zoomed in circles with such speed it became a blur of purple light.

"I guess it's stuck with us until we can get out of here," Wade said. "We might as well get comfortable."

Sitting, Wade cautiously circled his fingers around my wrist, avoiding my flames, to pull me down beside him. We sat with our feet dangling over the edge of the tunnel and watched the purple orb.

"I don't think you need your flames anymore," Wade said. "The orb will provide enough light."

I shook my fingers to extinguish the flames, and sure enough, the entire cavern glowed a brilliant purple. The entire expanse was now visible, with other tunnels branching into the abyss. I hoped no one else was venturing down those. Leaning over the edge to inspect the walls on our side of the chasm, I spotted more crumbling tunnel entrances.

I pointed them out to Wade. "I think we can make it back through another tunnel."

He crossed his legs. "We still have to wait for the water to fill."

Another chunk of ceiling fell from above, crashing into the unseen water below with a resounding roar.

"I don't think we're going to have to wait too long."

"Long enough," Wade said, his gaze filled with such longing that desire instantly stirred.

I arched an eyebrow at him. "Our son is missing. There are venomous spiders down here, not to mention a purple orb watching our every move, and you want to have...sex?"

"Did you have something else in mind?"

"No, but—"

"I love you, Cordelia Blue." Wade pulled me onto his lap.

I shifted my body so I was facing him, my legs wrapped around his waist. Gently, he lay back, bringing me with him so I straddled him. His arousal throbbed between my legs, pulsing with desire.

Wade's hand grazed my cheek, cupping it gently, his fingers tracing my freckles. In the glow of the purple orb, I stared at him, then moved my lips to his and devoured his mouth. Instinct took over. I ground against him, allowing desire to build. Wade unbuttoned my shirt, freeing my breasts and cupping them in his warm hands, his thumbs teasing my nipples. I gasped as the tingling sensations coursed through me. Within seconds, we were both naked, navigating the hard ground beneath us, and he repositioned me on top of him. I took him inside me, gasping with pleasure. He tangled his fingers in my hair, yanked on the ends in the way I loved, and planted bruising kisses against my throat. The orgasm built deep inside me, forming in my center, intensifying until I cried out Wade's name. It spread out in glorious waves, taking my entire body hostage, sending shuddering tremors through my limbs. I clenched my muscles around Wade, drawing him deeper as he thrust into me, drawing out the pleasurable sensations. Wade roared when his pleasure peaked, his grip on my hips tightening, his fingers digging into my skin. Spent, I collapsed against him, and he lowered us to the ground so we could catch our breath.

After a few minutes, I rolled off him, positioned myself beside him, and took his hand. "Stress sex, huh?"

"Love sex."

"Both."

"Pass me the flask, will you?" he asked. "Had a few rocks digging into my back."

We both took sips from the fountain water. I reached for my clothes when I felt a splash on my leg. Sitting up, I found the water level had risen and was now only a few feet beneath our tunnel entrance.

"Looks like we might be able to get out soon," I said.

Wade propped himself on hands and knees and peered over the lip of the tunnel. He frowned.

"What is it?"

"If those tunnels fill up, it could flood the palace, the city..."

"Does it matter? Merfolk and selachii can live underwater."

"Humans can't."

The purple orb swirled around us, paused above the rising water level as if to evaluate the situation alongside us.

"We don't have to wait for the water level to get higher." Wade pushed himself to his feet. "We can climb across that ledge there to that tunnel over there, and if we fall, well, we've got the water."

We dressed hurriedly while the purple orb observed. Wade went first, stepping on the narrow ledge and gripping the tiniest of handholds above his head. I followed him, mirroring the places he put his hands and feet, trying not to look at the raging water below and what it was hiding. This cavern had never been discovered before. All manner of things could have been lurking at the bottom, now dislodged and floating to the top. But we'd have to send merfolk and selachii down here to explore the flooded tunnels in search of the last orb.

We made it the twenty or so feet across the narrow ledge. Wade helped me into the new tunnel. Things moved in the darkness. A heavy dampness hung in the air.

"I don't think anyone has been down here," Wade said, casting a furtive glance at the crumbling walls.

As we plunged deeper into the tunnel's abyss, a soft, ethe-real glow emanated from the floating purple orb, casting eerie shadows on our faces. The tunnel's incline grew steeper, forcing us into a near-vertical climb, our hands pushing off the slick surface.

An hour passed, our steps echoing through the tunnel, the purple orb steadfastly trailing us. Finally, we emerged into a brilliantly lit passageway, both of us heaving a sigh of relief. A few minutes later, we stumbled on Tunnel HQ, where Rob barked orders into his radio.

He placed a hand over his chest when he saw us. "I was getting worried."

"Tunnel collapse," Wade said. "Lake Echomere is now becoming Underground Lake Echomere."

Rob raised a brow, then spotted the orb. "You found one!"

"It can't find its guardian," I said. "We'll take it to the great hall to be with the others."

Rob's expression darkened as he grasped the implications. "We'll keep looking for the last one."

I touched his hand as I walked by. I wondered who the orb belonged to, thinking perhaps it might be Gal.

As Wade and I climbed the steps that led out of the tunnel network, the orb trailed our movements. After a few turns, I opened the door to the great hall and the orb darted inside, spun around its counterparts, circled the Power of the Sea, and settled into a position orbiting the larger sphere. I took a moment to walk among them, marveling at their individual beauty. The purple orb, I presumed, was for Spirit and Soul, a special orb destined for a special guardian. When I reached my fire orb, it pulsed in response, sending a few tender flames in my direction. I extended my hand, and it floated into my palm.

"I don't know if it's possible," I told it. "But I'd really like it if you could make it that my ability didn't burn or hurt my family or friends. Those who I hold dear to me."

The orb vibrated, shifting through opaque orange, nebulous crimson, before settling into its familiar scarlet hue, streaked through with other reds.

I turned to Wade. "Are you up for a little experiment?"

"I just returned our flask to Rob."

"The fountain is only down there." I pointed out the window.

Wade nodded and stepped closer. I summoned a single flame to my forefinger. Tentatively, Wade extended his hand and passed it through my flame.

He smiled. "Not even warm."

"It worked," I said. "Now I never have to worry about burning you again."

"Yeah, when you gave birth to Gal, that was *not* a fun experience."

We both sobered at the mention of his name. Wade offered his hand, and with one more glance at the orbs, we left the magical spheres behind. Before I closed the door, I glanced out the window at the courtyard below. Angelica was standing by the fountain engaged in a heated discussion with someone. I couldn't see the other person from my vantage point. Perhaps it was another member of her clan.

"Let's make sure she's okay," Wade said. "Then we both need to rest awhile."

I followed Wade outside, down the palace steps, and as I drew near the arguing pair, there was something about the second individual that seemed ominously familiar. A sense of unease landed on my shoulders.

The male wore only a pair of black shorts, despite the current temperature of the island, and didn't seem affected by the weather either. His skin was covered in tattoos, menacing swirls of whirlpools and inescapable vortexes. And then it hit me.

I grabbed Wade's hand as the ice landed in my chest. Ice and fire. Fear and anger.

"It's Caol."

CHAPTER TWENTY

Traced down the steps, my flames roaring to life. Wade shouted after me, close on my heels. Babette cornered me as I reached the arguing pair.

Risking a serious injury, Babette yanked my shoulder. "You look like you're about to murder someone."

I pointed at Caol, my fingers flaring with fire.

The bastard selachii turned from Angelica and stared at me, a wide grin spreading across his face. "How nice to see you again, Cordelia."

His voice was just as I remembered it. Smooth. Lyrical. And laced with menace.

Wade caught up with me, frowned at Babette until she released me, then placed a gentle hand on my shoulder.

"You're not welcome here," Wade said to Caol.

"Atlantis is a haven for all the ocean shifters, or so I've been led to believe."

"Not all of them, no," Wade said.

Babette stepped forward. "Now hang on a minute—"

"This has got nothing to do with you, Babette," Wade snapped, his tone unusually tense.

With my hands fisted, my flames roaring, I faced Caol. "How did you get your legs back?" The High Council had imprisoned Caol and Zale, trapped them in a whirling vortex jail created by Gal when their treacherous behavior was revealed. While all the merfolk and selachii were granted the use of their legs and the ability to shift between human and ocean form once more, Caol and Zale had been denied that privilege.

Caol jutted his chin at Angelica. "This lovely lady heard me calling from the water channel. Couldn't swim up too far considering it was frozen solid, but she brought me a refreshing sip from the fountain. And voila, my legs came back." He bowed with an imperial flourish.

Angelica looked between Caol and the rest of us, her eyes uncertain. "I thought I was doing the right thing."

"And that you did, my dear," Caol said. "I can't remember the last time I walked. Feels great to have my land legs back, even if it is a little frosty here. Not what I was expecting." He performed an exaggerated stretch, showing off his corded muscles. He was nothing but muscle, almost rivaling Wade for strength.

"How did you escape?" Wade asked.

"Zale found a way out for us."

The name spoken aloud struck terror into my core.

"Where *is* Zale?" Wade asked, his hand tightening on my shoulder.

Caol's gazed drifted between my husband and me, his

eyes widening, his eyes lighting up. "Ohhhh, so he hasn't made an appearance yet?"

Yet.

Wade gritted his teeth. "Where. Is. He. Caol?"

Caol shrugged. "No idea. Haven't seen him in years. After he escaped, we went our separate ways. But I am surprised he hasn't shown up here. He had nothing but revenge on his mind."

Angelica stiffened, her hands flying to her mouth.

"You're Caol?" Babette said. "I thought you'd be bigger."

I smothered a smile.

Caol's grin flatlined, and his eyes narrowed. "Careful there, sweetheart. You don't want to tango with me. I am a great white after all."

"I'm not a big fan of the water, to be honest, unless I'm sailing on top of it." Babette eyed him coolly. "I'll take my chances."

"You can leave now," Wade said.

Caol shook his head. "No, I don't think so. I could use a break from the ocean. Been a little waterlogged for the last eight years. Grew sick of coconut magic. Think I'll have me a little respite. A little vacay and some downtime. I think I'll stay put for now."

"You. Are. Not. Welcome. Here." I pushed the words through my teeth. My fingers itched with warmth, and I resisted the urge to engulf him with my fiery power.

Caol glanced at my hands, took a step back. "Aren't you the powerful one now? Both of you." His eyes flicked to Wade.

"So you'd do well to mind our words," Wade said.

"You can't exile a shifter from Atlantis. That's a decision for the High Council," Caol said.

"I'm on the High Council," Babette said.

Caol gave her an appraising look. "A human? Interesting. Allow me to present my case—"

"Not now," Babette said.

"Babette, you can't seriously be considering allowing him to stay," I said.

"It's not up to me," she replied. "Or you, or Wade. It's a decision for all of us. I'm tired of knee-jerk reactions. Tired of people storming off and doing whatever the hell they please—"

"Just like you stormed off to the mainland?"

"People are dying there." She glared at me. "I needed some space. I didn't go on some...journey of revenge or redemption or whatever."

"Ladies," Caol raised both hands. "I'm deeply honored, but please don't fight over me."

A small fireball escaped my hand, streaked past Caol, singed his shorts, and ended up hissing in the fountain.

Caol tutted. "Cordelia Blue, that's not every welcoming, is it?"

"It's Waters now." I didn't know why I felt compelled to tell him that.

"Aw, you guys got married, how sweet. Star-crossed lovers from different races defying all the odds."

Wade punched him. No warning, no build up to it, just raised a fist, leaped at the shorter selachii, and punched his jaw. Caol's head snapped back, blood spurting from his mouth, as well as a couple of teeth. The force of the blow knocked him off his feet. He slipped in the snow, falling against the fountain, knocking his head, and landed draped over the lip. He coughed, straightened, his teeth growing back as he moved. "Now, now, Wade, that wasn't very nice. Considering how well I looked after your mother during her time in the water."

"My mother is dead." Wade swung again, but Babette stepped between them.

She raised both arms. "Stop."

Wade shook out his hand. "You are aware of his past, are you not? He can't stay here."

"I don't think you'll want me to leave," Caol said, crossing his arms.

"What are you talking about?" I asked.

"Put your flames out first, fire mermaid."

I clenched my jaw as a few choice words tumbled through my head. How dare he tell me what to do. But I sensed he had information, something he was enjoying keeping from me. With considered effort, I extinguished my flames, taking comfort in the thought that I could summon them once more in an instant.

"Why would we want you to stay?" Wade asked.

Caol hiked a thumb at Angelica, who'd remained silent during the conversation so far. "This lovely orcana leader has told me of your dilemma with the ghost pirates, the orbs you need that will make them mortal once more. I happen to have one of those orbs."

My heart skipped a beat, then thundered in my chest. My ears rung with the incredulity of his words. "An orb chose *you* as its guardian?"

"Oh no, I wouldn't say that," Caol said. "But we've come to an understanding."

"Where is it?" Wade asked.

"Allow me to stay, and I'll consider telling you."

"He could be lying," I said.

"I could be," Caol said. "But do you want to take that risk?"

My flames roared to life.

"If you kill me, you'll never find the orb," Caol said.

"If I kill you, you'll be out of our lives forever."

"No one is killing anyone," Babette said.

"Thank you so much, oh wise council member." Caol bowed deeply.

"I don't take kindly to mockery," Babette snapped. "I'm the only thing standing between you and certain death. Spare a minute for that thought."

Caol covered his bare chest with both hands. "My deepest apologies. You're quite right."

"You cannot be falling for that crap," I said to Babette.

I felt the pulse of a telepathic thought. All ocean shifters were able to communicate telepathically, sometimes privately, sometimes in groups, and most of the time only when in water. But occasionally, if a bond was strong enough and the distance short enough, telepathic thoughts could be expressed on land too.

"*We'll put the guard on him,*" Wade's thought entered my head. "*He will never be out of our sight.*"

"*It's not enough.*"

"*It's the only thing we can do if we want to protect the orb.*"

Caol's eyes narrowed as the silence stretched on.

"Don't even think about it." Caol backed away from us.

"Think about what?" Babette asked.

"Putting guards on him," Wade said.

"No, no thanks." Caol turned and ran. He sped across the courtyard, leaped when he reached the cliff edge, and dove into the water below.

Without a word, Wade ran after him, mimicked his leap, and disappeared over the edge. The last time they'd gone head-to-head, Wade had almost died. But that was before Wade had inhaled the Power of the Sea. He was much stronger now, granted a Herculean strength that would be a formidable match for Caol. The tables had turned. But Wade would want him alive to discover the location of the last orb, and Caol wouldn't come without a fight.

"I need to get Rob," I said, preparing to dash up the steps.

Angelica put a hand on my arm. "Wait."

"It doesn't matter now, Angelica. What's done is done. You didn't know."

She shook her head. "It's not about Caol."

I came back down the steps to meet her on equal footing. "Then who? What?"

"It's about Zale."

CHAPTER TWENTY-ONE

Blinking rapidly, Angelica fiddled with one of her rings, her breath gusting ice. Snow clung to her hair.

"What about Zale?" I asked.

Babette hurried up the steps, calling over her shoulder. "I'll get my father."

I nodded at her, then turned my attention back to the newest inhabitant of Atlantis. "What's going on?"

Guilt flashed through her icy eyes. "Frost was dying."

"I remember."

"You would do anything to get your son back, right?"

My mind swirled with possibilities. Anything? My automatic response was 'yes.' But what did she mean by 'anything'? Could I put an entire island and its inhabitants at risk in exchange for my son's life? Yes, I could do that. Wade would never allow it, but I could do that.

"What did you do, Angelica?"

Snow fell, thick and quick, covering the ground as easily as she had hidden her lies.

"Frost wasn't going to make it."

"So you brought him here, to the Fountain of Youth."

"Yes." She kept her gaze trained on my face, but didn't quite meet my eyes. "But I didn't know about the fountain. I didn't know it existed, let alone that it could heal Frost and the rest of my people. Not until *he* told me."

"Zale told you about the fountain?" The friend she had referred to before. She had tried to tell me, but I had waved away her concerns.

"In exchange for a favor."

"What kind of favor?"

She swallowed. Her once graceful stature now appeared fragile and diminished, as though admitting the truth had drained away her poise. "He asked me to put a rock in the fountain."

"A rock?"

"It was black and hard and streaked with glints of ice."

I'd never heard of such a rock. "What does it do?"

"He didn't tell me. I assumed it blinded the book and Maya's ability to interpret the prophecies."

I stared at her, my head crowded with thoughts, each one vying for attention. Once upon a time we had put the Power of the Sea into the dying fountain when we'd first reclaimed Atlantis. It had brought the fountain back to life and healed our island. I'd never tried putting another jewel or magic key into the water; there had never been any need.

But this was a rock given to Angelica by Zale. It was not intended for the benefit of the island, but to aid his own sinister intentions. His image still haunted my nightmares, even after all these years. I had underestimated him as a threat. All the planning I had done to keep Gal and our family safe…never included Zale. He would do anything to see me brought to my knees and make it as painful as possible. And what better way than stealing the very thing I loved the most.

Fire danced briefly on my fingertips before I snuffed it out. Struggling to compose myself, I hid my hands from view. The weight of unease settled on me, accompanied by an anxious energy that raced through my veins. "He tried to kill my mother. He tried to kill my brother. For five years, he took them from me. For five years, I thought they were dead."

Angelica shrank. "I'm so sorry. I didn't know."

"Because you were only trying to save your nephew."

"I was forced to make hard decisions. Impossible decisions. I knew when Zale handed me that rock his intentions weren't pure. Deep down, I knew." She took a breath and collected herself. "But I didn't want Frost to die. As a mother, and a leader, I'm sure you can understand. So I made the wrong decision, but for the right reason, I think. I let my heart rule my head. The orcana is close to extinction as it is. I couldn't bear to lose another. Especially Frost."

"I do understand that. But mark my words, Zale doesn't make a move without a reason. I was responsible for sending him to prison. A prison the High Council designed to be inescapable. And if he's out now, he will seek revenge."

Angelica lowered her head. "It's because of you he spent time with the Denizens of the Deep?"

Old enemies die hard.

"A prophecy has spoken of revenge."

Angelica blanched. "Oh no."

"Zale will never change," I told her. "He's only out for himself. In all the time you've been thinking about the rock and what it may have caused, did you ever ask yourself why?"

Angelica's skin markings pulsed with an icy vibrance. "I buried that question deep."

"I know he can be charming, I know he can be bigger than life, I also know he is somehow responsible for unleashing the ghost pirates on us. He wouldn't dare risk facing me again, not with the power I now wield, and so he sent the pirates to do his dirty work and steal the very thing I love most."

"I will do anything to make amends for what I've caused."

I could be angry. I could be furious. I could burn her to a crisp with my flames. But I couldn't blame her. She'd done what she'd done out of love, and that I understood. She wasn't the first person to be deceived by Zale. And he would have found his way here with or without her help.

"Can you find the rock you put in the fountain?"

Angelica walked to the far side of the fountain, her bare feet leaving prints in the fresh snow, and moved her hand into the water. Moments later, she retrieved a black rock, darker than midnight and streaked with veins of ice, and handed it to me. "It's smaller now."

I gripped it in my hand. There was nothing remarkable about it. It was just a rock, but it was darker than nightmares. "What happens now?"

"I don't know," she replied.

The sound of splashing water diverted my attention.

Wade erupted from the waves and landed on the rocks. He ran toward me, slipping in the snow.

"Did you find him?"

Wade's expression hardened. "He got away. Rob and some of the army joined us, but he slipped through our grasp."

"He won't go far," I said. "He wants to torture me with his presence. And he's not the only one."

Wade tilted his head. "What's going on?"

I told him about Zale and showed him the black rock.

Wade's knees buckled, and he fell in the snow. Both Angelica and I rushed to him.

"I'm so sorry." Angelica repeated the words as she attempted to help him up.

"Leave us," I snapped at her as I sank to the snow to cradle my husband.

Angelica backed away, across the courtyard, and disappeared down the beach path.

"You can't fall apart on me," I said. "You're supposed to be the strong one."

Wade sat in the snow, even though he was half-naked from his swim and shivering. Hunched shoulders, trembling hands, haunted selachii eyes. I'd never seen him look so powerless. "Sometimes I wonder if it was worth it."

I weaved my arms around his shoulders, trying to keep him warm. "What?"

He clenched and unclenched a fist. "Everything."

I gripped his shoulders, holding on to him, unsure if I was giving him comfort or seeking it. "Don't say that."

"We've both lost family, almost died more times than I

can count...The ice demons, the dragon kings, the submersible, the eels, Atlantis, Stephanie...it's all too much. How much more can we endure?"

"You sound like me."

"They say what doesn't kill you makes you stronger." He shook his head. "But it can also break you irreparably."

To hear him speak of the bleak doubts that crossed my mind every day left me profoundly unsettled. I was the pessimistic one. Or realistic, as I liked to think. Wade was the one who never gave up, who always saw the silver linings, who relied on my love for him to carry him through. But now he was as broken as me and I didn't know how to help him. "We can't give up."

"I know. But I don't know how to keep going either."

"We have each other."

He clutched my hand. "I couldn't do this without you."

"Me neither."

"Don't you ever leave me."

"Why would I leave you?"

He locked his eyes on mine. We both knew we would never leave each other by choice; only death could separate us.

"What do we do about Zale?" I asked.

Wade pressed his forehead against mine. "If you're right about him being behind the ghost pirates, he won't reveal himself yet. He'll wait to see the outcome. And if the pirates fail. Then he'll come."

"So we're safe for now."

"I never thought I'd say this," Wade said, "But Gal is probably better off on that ship where Zale can't get to him."

"We've still got Caol creeping around, and if we want that last orb, we need to find him."

Wade picked up the black rock from the ground and crushed it in his fist, obsidian fragments crumbling to the snow. He covered his face with his hand, smothering a wretched sob that tore my heart into pieces.

Ford appeared on the steps with ten other soldiers and approached us in the icy courtyard. "I've been briefed on the current situation. You've been assigned a unit to accompany you at all times. Stay together, stay inside, and let the rest of the army handle Caol."

Ford helped Wade to his feet, and we followed him inside the palace. The security presence had doubled, the tunnel entrance guarded by a force of eight. Every entrance and exit had at least two guards standing by. Rob had broken out the guns. A long time ago, we'd decided there would be no guns on Atlantis. Our army had trained in the traditional shifter land weapons of spears and tridents, knives and poison. But when Rob came to Atlantis several years ago, he'd used his military experience to teach Atlanteans about guns too. They'd been locked away in the armory. But now every soldier carried one.

"We need Caol alive," I told Ford. "If he really has the last orb, we need him alive. And we need the lookout stations manned in case Zale decides to visit."

"Understood," Ford replied as Wade and I entered our suite and closed the door behind us.

I led Wade to the bathroom, placed him under a warm shower and washed his hair, scrubbing his back as the hot water cascaded over him. We had no words of hope to offer;

all we could do was move from one minute to the next, guarding the pain in our hearts and praying for Gal's safe return.

When we were both dressed, I guided Wade to an armchair in front of a roaring fire and poured him a strong drink. I sat beside him, and we both watched the dancing flames.

Wade brought the glass to his lips, his hands trembling. "I'm sorry."

"What for?"

"For not being strong enough."

I struggled to meet his gaze. The well of pain he stored there was terrifying to behold. "I don't know what that means anymore. We are who we are. We've been through what we've been through. We have breaking points. That doesn't make us weak. It doesn't make us strong; it just makes us human."

"I feel..." He didn't finish his sentence; perhaps words were too painful. So we sat together, gazing at the fire, sipping our drinks, and holding hands. What else could we do?

After a while, Wade leaned over the small gap between us, searching my face. He swept a hand into my curls and pressed his lips against mine. "Together."

"Together."

After an hour, Wade fell asleep in the chair. I couldn't tear my eyes away from him. He wore only loose sweatpants and a T-shirt, which revealed the curve of his sculpted shoulders, the impenetrable power of his chest, the sinewy strength of his arms. He was the strongest person on the island, yet inside, he felt as shattered as I did. Throughout our years together, and even though we had both experienced trauma, I was the one who fell apart at regular intervals. I relied on him to prop me up, to give me strength when I had none, to help me face the battles when my instinct was to turn the other way. To see him so broken and sad, it tore at the walls of my heart.

It was time for me to step up. Even though my anxiety was as bad as it had ever been, new strength surged within me. I would not let my husband despair; I would not let him experience the same hopelessness that I carried. I would do anything to see him smile again, to hold our son. That sense of determination sent a fiery rage through my veins. Despite the presence of my oldest enemy, I would not let my husband down.

A howling wind stirred me from my thoughts. Gently releasing Wade's hand, I walked to the windows to find the ghost ship sailing over the beach.

CHAPTER TWENTY-TWO

I stormed outside to the wide balcony overlooking the courtyard, my heart pounding like a kettle-drum. With deliberate gentleness, I shut the doors softly behind me, the wooden panels whispering as they met. At this late hour, the courtyard below was empty, people adhering to the curfew and keeping their children safe inside. As I glared at the ghostly ship, anger surged within me, a torrential force threatening to consume everything in its path. My eyes burned, even though I knew my fiery power couldn't harm its intended target.

The ship creaked and groaned as it glided over the court-yard, drawing closer to the palace. Pirates stood sentry on both port and starboard sides; their luminous white whips dangling from the ship and writhing in excitement as they sought their prey. The kids remained tied to the balustrade. As the ship sailed by the palace, I caught sight of Gal. He was tethered to the mast, his arms laced tightly behind his back. His head lolled to the side and his skin was whiter than the pirates' bones. Unconscious. How much of his innocence had they stolen? Was his concussion swelling his brain to a dangerous size?

Some of the other kids were awake, their faces not quite as pale, a little color remaining in their cheeks. Of those who were conscious, their eyes were wide, but all of them remained silent, even when a treacherous whip lashed close, or a white spider scuttled over the deck near their feet.

How dare this ship steal our children. How dare it come back again and again each night seeking more victims. How dare the pirates leach the innocence from their lives.

Rage boiled in the pit of my stomach, not building gradually but roaring to life, taking my fiery power along with it. Fireball after fireball erupted from my hands, an uncontrolled torrent of flames. My ability knew what I wanted, and right now, I wanted those pirates dead and the children safe in my arms.

Flames danced across my body, leaped from my arms, and streaked toward the ship, but they passed through the pirates, the mast, the rigging, and the sails. My fire was useless, but I couldn't stop. The pain inside me needed to be released, and fire was the only way I knew how.

The fireballs continued their relentless assault, scorching the beach, shattering windows, setting the bar roof ablaze, burning the tree stumps Ford had created into non-existence, and creating flaming craters in the courtyard. The fountain's lip cracked and began to leak, a symbol of the chaos I'd unleashed.

I looked at my fiery hands, at the flames consuming my entire body, and willed them to leave me. But they wouldn't, or couldn't, and continued to hurl themselves at the ground and buildings in the vicinity. The glass in the doors behind me shattered, and the children on the ship screamed, while the pirates laughed wickedly, their poisonous whips cracking.

Suddenly, strong arms enveloped me, Wade's arms, pinning my hands to my sides. He whispered into my ear, telling me he loved me, that everything would be okay. I no longer feared burning him, and my flames spread to his body too, consuming us both.

"Cordelia, you can control this."

Ignoring the searing pain that cut through my body, I closed my eyes, held my breath, and willed my flames to cease. After a minute, the air around me cooled. I opened my eyes. My flames had been extinguished, but infernos spread throughout the city below.

"What have I done?"

The ship sailed by, the conscious children staring at me with open mouths and fear in their eyes, the pirates grinning from their skeleton faces. It headed into the clouds and disappeared into the night.

Wade kept his arms around me, tucked his chin into the crevice of my neck, holding me tight. Below us, soldiers rushed around the courtyard with hoses, battling the fires.

I stared at the destruction. "What kind of queen am I?"

"A queen who cares about her people."

Ford stepped over the shattered glass, joining us on the balcony. "You're wanted in the great hall."

Wordlessly, he led us out of our suite, down the ornate staircase, and into the vast room. The High Council was already in attendance, seated near the fire. All but Babette, who paced behind a couch. Maya cradled the book in her arms. Trent stood behind her with their newborn rucked against his chest, while Blaze perched on the edge of an armchair. Ford was the fourth member.

"What is it?" I asked Maya, rushing to her side. "Is there a new prophecy?"

Wade poured drinks for everyone from the decanter and passed them around. Only Babette declined.

"No," Maya replied. "Nothing new, but I'm no longer blind. I can now see the prophecies as they were intended and understand their implications. And there was one about the ghost pirates, but it didn't appear while I was blinded."

I recounted Angelica's confession, the removal of the black rock, Caol's appearance, and the possibility of him possessing the last orb. All six pairs of eyes swiveled to the glowing orbs and the Power of the Sea.

"You were right about Zale," Maya said. "*Old enemies die hard.*"

"And Caol. They're both old enemies," Wade said.

"And it will not be easy to kill them," I said.

"Hang on a minute," Babette said. "No one needs to kill anyone. I thought we lived in a modern society with law courts and hearings and juries and judges? Yes? We don't go around killing people just because they committed a crime in their past."

Wade and I gaped at her.

"Caol turned my husband into a selachii," Maya's voice rose, and she slammed the book closed.

"That is not an experience I want to repeat," Trent said as he rocked the baby. "Nor would I wish it on anyone else."

"He kept my mother prisoner," Wade said.

"Zale took my brother and mother," I said. "And they both tried to kill me. And Wade. And Trent."

"What a fucking asshole," Blaze said. His words almost elicited a smile.

Babette whirled on him. "I don't need you getting all hot headed too. We need to have a calm and measured discussion about this, not just, *kill everyone.*"

"It's not like that, Babette," Wade said. "Caol and Zale aren't *everyone.* They are two very evil individuals who will never change."

"So we don't even try to offer a rehabilitation program?" Babette asked. "Even the most hardened criminals were offered that, before the war."

I shook my head. "Not the ones on death row. And if Zale and Caol were tried by the same courts, that's where they would be."

Maya's eyes bore into her. "I've seen their destruction, and I know what they're capable of. They need to die."

"I'm surprised at you, Maya," Babette said.

"And I'm surprised at you." Maya stood, her resolve unwavering. "You haven't always been part of this world, Babette. And while I appreciate what you've done for Atlantis, for everyone in this room, you don't know Zale and Caol. You don't understand the destruction and terror they caused. If you did, you'd side with us. There are seven of us in this room. The king and queen, and four members of the High Council, and my husband, a member of the senate. No one here makes decisions lightly. No one here is allowed to get carried away with emotion, but trust me when I say Zale and Caol need to die."

"Is that something you want? Or something you read in the book?" Babette asked. "Because I've got to say, I can't get on board with ordering executions. That's not how I was raised, and that's not who I am now."

"You go find Caol," I said. "Spend some time with him. Get him to give you the orb. If he doesn't kill you first or turn you into a selachii. We need that orb for the children, Babette. And if he doesn't agree...well, that makes him a monster."

Wade faced her. "You complain the humans don't have the same benefits on this island. You complain there are no other humans on the senate or High Council. You fight with Cordy about every decision she makes and every idea she has. But trust me, Babette, there are six people here telling you this is the right way. Listen to us."

"Do I not get a say anymore?" Babette asked.

Blaze's wings unfurled from his back, filling the area. "Of course you get a say. We all do. But I can guarantee you, you're not going to win this one. That ship has my son. And there is only one person who stands in the way of me getting him back."

"Maybe you're all biased because you all have children who've been taken," Babette said.

"And Zale is behind it," I said.

"But Caol may not be," Babette said.

"Why are you defending him?" Maya asked.

"She likes an underdog," Blaze said. "She likes the down-trodden male who needs her love to get him going again."

"I do not plan on loving Caol." Babette's voice dripped with her signature sarcasm.

Blaze spoke the truth. Babette and Dylan and been together for years. Never progressing their relationship, but never leaving each other either. They were as broken as each other. Drawn to each other's misery. Babette wanted to fix Dylan, and he only wanted to drown his sorrows. And now she wanted to save Caol.

"Why do you care so much, Babette?" I asked. "What does Caol mean to you?"

Her eyes swept over my face. "Persecution."

"But that's what he did to all of us," Wade said, rendering Babette silent for once.

A tense silence seeped into the room. We sipped our drinks and Babette walked to the window.

I approached Maya. "Does the book say...does it say if... we get them back?"

Maya turned to the prophecy section of the book. "No, only that ghost pirates are a plague on Atlantean society and will take many children. That not all of them will survive. Which implies some of them will—"

"Which implies we do get some of them back," Wade said.

"Yes," Maya agreed. "And as we do, Zale will be furious and there will be a reckoning. A fight. But he will die. Because *old enemies die hard*."

Wade and I locked eyes. We had both battled Zale before. It wasn't an experience I wanted to relive. But if it meant my family was safe, I would engage him once more.

And this time I would win. This time he would die. This time I would exorcise him from my nightmares.

"We need to fix the fountain," Babette said, still looking out the window. "Looks like the fires are under control, but the fountain is still broken. The island won't heal if the fountain is broken."

"Would you please go put some of the Power of the Sea in it?" I asked her.

She looked at me, nodded, then walked to the swirling blue orb. She stuck a finger into the nebulous sphere, collected a smaller ball of the magical substance, and carried it out of the room.

Wade and I watched her from the window. She spoke with her father by the fountain, and in the space of a few minutes, they'd performed a patch work job on the stonework to prevent it leaking more. Babette placed the orb into the water. It glowed and caused the water to hiss and effervesce, but the craters I'd caused with my fires remained.

"Maybe Atlantis doesn't like me anymore," I whispered to Wade.

"It's not you. It's everything," he replied. "It senses the discord between its people, and that's what is reflected in our land."

Blaze joined us at the window. "There will be a battle with the pirates when we secure the final orb. Many will be... hurt. I hope the fountain's curative powers are still in working order."

"Why don't we go test that?" I said to Blaze.

I left Ford, Maya, Trent, and Wade inside the great hall

debating strategies of how to find Caol, while Blaze and I ventured outside.

"I can no longer hurt you with my flames," I said. "My orb made me a deal that it wouldn't harm those I love."

Blaze smiled. "But my flames could still burn you."

I offered my hand. "Shall we try it?"

Blaze inhaled through his nose, held it inside for a few seconds, then exhaled gently through his mouth, sending a few fiery sparks flying into the air and a tiny fireball streaking toward me. I caught it in my palm, letting it burn me without flinching. Blaze led me to the fountain, and I dipped my hand into the cool water, watching as the burn vanished. But it didn't disappear completely. It left an aching blister. "Partially working. That's not good."

"Let's hope it's enough to make a difference."

"Cordelia?"

I turned at the sound of my name. Angelica stood on the last of the palace steps, blood pouring from a wound on her side.

Blaze rushed to her side, and she collapsed against him.

I didn't blame Angelica for her actions; I would have done the same for Gal. But my fire didn't care. My hands burst into flames. I stuck them in the fountain, but my fire was one which water didn't affect. The flames continued to burn.

Blaze brought Angelica to the fountain and made her drink. Out of the corner of my eye, I caught sight of her wound closing together, but an ugly ragged scar was left behind, as well as a large area of deep purple bruising.

"What happened?" Blaze asked.

"I went after Caol," she replied. "Cordelia?"

"I can't turn around," I said.

"I'm sorry."

"I don't blame you," I said. "But my emotions are all over the place right now and my fire power doesn't care who it hurts." I didn't know if Angelica was included in the definition of "people I cared about," according to my orb, so I had to play this safe.

"I want to help."

"Going off in search of Caol on your own was a suicide mission. If you really want to help, join a team in the tunnels, in case that bastard selachii is lying about the orb."

"Okay. But Cordelia?"

Taking a breath, I straightened and faced her, but I couldn't help the fireball escaping my hand and whizzing by her cheek. "I'm sorry."

"I'll leave." She turned and dashed up the steps.

Blaze perched on the cracked rim of the fountain, his fiery aura casting dancing shadows in the gloomy night. "I see you have some fire power problems."

I sighed, the faint scent of smoldering embers drifting through the air as I joined him on the ledge. "The Power of the Sea saved my life and graced me with this incredible ability," I said, my gaze fixed on the unstable waters within the broken fountain. "I can single-handedly defeat an entire army, but when things get tough, my emotions always get the best of me. What's the point of having this power?"

Blaze leaned closer, his voice softening. "Cordelia, everyone's emotions can be a hindrance at times. Life's journey is about learning to master them. You're still young, you know, with much left to learn—"

I barked out a laugh. "Tell me about it."

"Sorry, I'm not as good at this as my father."

I turned to face Blaze, his sun-kissed skin seemingly aglow with inner fire, his flared nostrils allowing the fiery energy to escape. He was the son of someone I cherished, and I held an equally fierce affection for Blaze. "You're doing just fine."

"What I'm trying to say is, you're too hard on yourself."

I thrust a hand at the courtyard, gesturing at the aftermath of destruction. "Do you not see the damage I caused?"

Blaze shrugged. "I've seen worse. And on one was hurt."

"I wish I could find a way to bind my ability."

Blaze shook his head. "We would never have defeated the hound without your fire."

"Or yours."

"And it worked when you needed it. Both with the hound, and with the dragon kings."

"I guess it did."

Blaze stood, his wings cocooning us from the icy chill. "What you mustn't forget is that you are not your power, and your power is not you. You two are a team, and it will know when to step up."

"I think it's been stepping up a little too much lately."

Blaze chuckled softly. "Perhaps. But you'll find your balance."

"I need to put out a formal apology. The palace will house anyone who needs it until the fountain is working properly."

"That's the gracious queen I know and love so well," Blaze said with a warm smile.

"Thank you, Blaze."

"Think nothing of it," he said, and made his way up the steps. "I need to check on Raina. With Ember taken…"

"I understand. Tell her I'll visit soon."

I watched Blaze's silhouette, his wings gliding gracefully above his head, until he disappeared from sight.

Snow fell silently. Too silently, its delicate flakes drifting down from the heavens, cloaking the world in an eerie stillness. An alarm bell rang in my mind. My senses heightened as I spun around, my skin electrifying with deadly anticipation. The world seemed to hold its breath alongside me as I scanned the courtyard, my eyes searching for signs of movement. The cold air crackled with an electrifying tension, wrapping around me like a vice, squeezing the air from my lungs.

And then, there he was—a drenched figure emerging from the obsidian shadows, his silhouette distorted by the falling snow, his face twisted into furious determination. Each step he took toward me was laden with unspoken menace, his footsteps slamming across the broken cobbles.

CHAPTER TWENTY-THREE

Caol, the embodiment of all my fears and hatred, barreled toward me like a vengeful storm. His malevolent sneer contorted his face into a grotesque mask of malice, and his eyes, as dark and merciless as the great white he was, bore into my soul. I stood my ground, my heart pounding, bracing myself for the impending clash.

Silence enveloped us as he closed the distance, an eerie anticipation hanging in the frosty air. Caol's gaze remained locked onto mine, a silent challenge. When he was only a few feet from me, I flicked my hands and my fire swept along my arms.

Caol didn't pause but removed a gleaming knife from his belt. The blade glinted malevolently in the pale light of dawn. I fixated on the deadly weapon, knowing this was a fight to the death. But I needed none of the combat skills Ford had taught me.

Suddenly, a voice echoed through the courtyard, breaking the silence like shattering glass. "Cordelia!"

I kept my focus on Caol, my hands trembling as I channeled my fiery power. This was where it was going to end. One way or another.

Snarling, Caol pumped his arms and legs as he barreled toward me and brandished the knife.

"Stay back!" But I knew he wouldn't. A searing fireball erupted from my outstretched palms, hurtling toward Caol with unrelenting force. Flames engulfed him instantly, searing away his hair, eyebrows, and eyelashes. He staggered, his body a grotesque spectacle of agony. He remained silent. Maybe the fire had stolen his tongue.

Through the fiery veil, he stared at me, his hatred palpable, until his eyelids melted onto his face. He unleashed a brief, tortured scream before his vocal cords were consumed. The knife clattered to the ground, glowing red with heat. Caol sank to his knees, then rolled in the snow, but my flames showed no mercy.

"Cordelia!"

My attention remained on Caol. He'd caused so much devastation in my past, I had to ensure he didn't come back from this.

His flailing movements ceased, and he lay in the snow, burning brightly as the bruising light of dawn appeared. The reek of burning flesh filled the courtyard, mingling with the loosening of his bowels, and a sense of grim satisfaction tugged at the corners of my mouth.

"Cordelia!" Maya reached me, spun me around, my flames not daring to hurt her. Trent was close on her heels, clutching the baby Coral, and followed by Ford. "What have you done?"

"He was going to kill me." But the truth of it was, my motives were far more complex. Caol's death was a culmination of years of torment and lust for revenge.

Maya shook her head, then turned to her husband. "Help me get him into the fountain."

The two of them approached the flaming mass, pushed their limbs into the fire, then recoiled when the flames scorched their skin. There was no saving Caol. We watched my fire burn, his figure unmoving, the stench of his flesh filling the air. Caol was dead.

Maya turned to face me, an accusation on her face. "What did you do?"

I shook the flames away from my arms and hands. "What needed to be done."

Ford approached and stood next to me, a gentle touch on my arm.

Maya shook her head, tears tracking down her cheeks. "How are we going to get our children back now?"

"He could have been lying about the orb."

"And what if he wasn't?" Maya's voice cracked. "What if he stashed it somewhere, never to be found, and now we must watch the innocence drain from our children, night after night? How could you, Cordelia?"

Trent stepped in; his face just as angry. "This isn't just about you. Many of us have children on that ship. But you made a selfish decision without thinking about anyone else."

Maya turned and dashed up the steps. Trent gave me a lingering look, his lips a grim line.

"He had a knife." I indicated the melting metal half buried in the snow.

Trent didn't reply, but followed his wife.

"Cordelia," Ford said.

I whirled on him. "Don't you start! Caol deserved to die. Everyone knows that. He almost killed me. And Wade. And he was lording the last orb over us. We'll find another way. The orbs want to be found. It will let us know where it is. I know it. Caol *deserved* to die."

Shoving his hands in his pockets, Ford lowered his head, kicked at the snow, then finally met my burning eyes. "There's nothing I can say here to make this situation better. You know what you've done, and you'll have to find a way to atone for that."

I jabbed a finger at him. "I'm going to find the fucking orb."

"I hope you do. I hope *someone* does."

"Fuck you," I hissed before turning and storming up the steps.

Old enemies die hard. But Caol had died so easily, his previously terrifying power no match for the flames I wielded.

Wade was waiting for me at the top of the steps.

"I killed Caol."

"I know."

"He deserved to die."

"I know."

"Maya and Trent are furious."

"I know that too."

"What do you think?" I asked.

"I'm glad he's dead."

I sighed, my shoulders deflating. "Thank you."

"But we still need to find the orb."

"I know."

Babette came out of the palace, followed by Blaze and Dylan.

"How could you?" she screeched at me.

"How could I not?" I countered. "He had a knife."

Babette laughed. "There are a million ways you could have dealt with that. You've been training with Ford for two years. If you can't make decisions with your head, decisions that affect everyone on Atlantis, maybe you shouldn't be here at all." She turned on her heel and marched away.

Blaze gave me a look. "I'll try to calm her down."

Why was he not furious with me? His kid was on that ship too.

Dylan came down the steps and threw his arms around me. "Thank you."

I tightened the embrace and wept on his shoulder, unexpected tears pouring out of me. "Maybe Babette is right."

"Not about this."

"But how are we going to find the orb?"

"We'll find it," Dylan said.

People emerged in the courtyard, stared at the crumbling fountain and the craters my fire had created. Their voices rose in a cacophony of anger and confusion, condemning my actions.

"What have you done?"

"What is Atlantis now?"

"I thought this place was supposed to be a haven."

I turned to face my people, both Atlanteans and humans, united in their disappointment and fear. The weight of their judgment bore down on me like a leaden crown.

"I took care of one of our biggest threats," I told them, my voice ringing with a feeble attempt at justification.

"But our children are still missing," Laura said, mother of Mini Cordelia, her eyes red from tears. "And my husband is dead."

"We'll put out a statement later," Wade addressed the gathering crowd.

"You can take your statements and shove them up your ass!" a man yelled, his anger echoing the sentiments of many. "It doesn't change the state of the fountain, the courtyard, the entire island. Crops are failing. The rivers, if not frozen, are polluted. And not to mention the kids. Thank Vorago I haven't got one of my own yet."

"I'm sorry you feel that way," Wade said, his words falling on deaf ears. He took my arm and led me into the palace. I turned to watch Dylan descend the steps, making his way to his bar. People accosted him on the path, but he shrugged them off, gesticulating angrily, set his jaw, and marched away.

Wade and I didn't speak until we reached our private rooms. Once there, I stood in front of the fire, but the flames did nothing to ease the chill on my skin or the guilt constricting my throat.

"I didn't have a choice," I said.

"Did you want one?"

"Not really."

"So we must deal with the aftermath."

I met his pain-filled eyes. "I'm sorry."

"I know you are."

"I seem to be saying that a lot lately. And now our people hate us too."

"People are fickle."

"They used to love us." I stared at the closed doors of our suite. "I'm going to ask Maya for a way to bind my powers. Then I can't make rash decisions ever again."

Wade caught my wrist, his touch gentle yet firm. "That's not the way to manage your emotions. If they don't express themselves in fire, they'll spill out in other ways. Besides, we will need your power when we find the last orb."

The unspoken "if" hung between us.

A chill seeped into the room, exacerbated by the shattered doors on the balcony and the unrepaired window. The once-healing fountain now refused to mend the island, and the situation was deteriorating rapidly.

I stepped onto the balcony to find the crowd below had doubled in size. When they spotted me, the insults grew in volume and some hurled rotten fruit and stones at me. I retreated inside, gritting my teeth, and curled into the chair by the fire.

"We need to put out that statement," Wade said. "This situation needs to be diffused as soon as possible."

"I don't know what to say."

"I'll have Ford compose something and then we'll deliver it over the island's Wi-Fi."

I nodded. Wade opened the door to the suite to find Ford standing guard with three other soldiers. A whispered conversation ensued, and all the while, ice ran through my veins. The aftermath of spent adrenaline shook my limbs, made my hands tremble, my lips prickle, and my scalp tingle with an uncomfortable sensation.

My breath caught in my throat, refusing to fill my lungs. Panic washed over me as I gasped for air, each breath colder and more suffocating than the last. I pushed myself out of the chair, collapsed to all fours, the reality of what I had done pressing down on me. I had killed Caol, and in doing so, I had sealed our son's fate.

"Wade!"

His arms wrapped around me, providing a lifeline amidst the suffocating darkness. He cocooned me against him, rocking me gently, spreading sweet kisses over my neck and cheeks as I cried.

"What have I done?" I choked out between tears. "What have I done?"

CHAPTER TWENTY-FOUR

The noise outside our broken window grew throughout the day. Neither Wade nor I dared to make an appearance on the balcony. Ford remained planted outside the door to our suite and Rob had the unenviable task of marshaling several squads of soldiers to confront the raucous assembly.

"I've never seen them act like this before," Wade said.

"Atlantis thrived under the mantle of sovereignty for thousands of years, and it's only taken eight years for us to screw it all up," I said. "Not you. Me."

"Atlantis never had humans on it before."

"And it never had me."

"Don't be so hard on yourself."

I faced my husband. "I know the statistics for couples who stay together when a child is abducted. I also know how deep our love for each other is. But I acted rashly, I followed my heart, and I can understand if you never forgive me."

"I haven't given up hope." Wade placed his hand across his heart. "The orb is here somewhere. And I will always love you. No matter what. Please stop doubting that."

I bowed my head. Although Wade and I were both descended from royal lines and had equal right to the throne, I had never felt like I truly deserved it. He had been raised in the world of ocean shifters and water deities. I had been ignorant of it all and never felt that my true place was on Atlantis. He had always been the better politician, the better at democracy and defusing the flames of our people. The better at showing his love. He was the one true king.

I whipped around at a sudden onslaught of noise, flames igniting on my fingers. Bricks and stones flew through the fractured window. Ford burst into the room, accompanied by a unit of ten soldiers. They escorted us to a temporary wing beyond the reach of the agitated mob.

There was fresh coffee on a table, a platter of food, and a tray of chocolates. I deserved none of it. Although comfortable and well decorated by the palace staff, the suite carried a strange and unfamiliar air. I couldn't relax.

People streamed into the rear gardens. We had intentionally left these gardens open, wanting our people to feel welcome, to have access to us. However, now with the fountain's flow disrupted and animosity poisoning the air, our priority was safety. Not just for us, but our people too. Angry crowds were dangerous, often crushing unsuspecting members under their feet.

Ford, stalwart and resolute, stood guard with his unit, a human shield against the seething anger beyond. Inside, tensions thrummed in the air. Outside, rabble-rousers were being pushed back by units securing the palace perimeter, constructing towering fences to ward off the imminent threat.

Another unit was dispatched to guard the Power of the Sea and the orbs. They had always resided in the great hall; a vast room open to anyone who wanted to experience the power of our island. And while I knew none of the orbs would go willingly, I worried someone would try to steal them.

Each night the ship came. Half the crowd retreated during the hours of darkness to protect their children, but those who remained were subjected to the lashing whips trawling for innocence. Many were injured. A few died. The fountain strained under the effort to heal. The flasks that had been used during the tunnel searches—some still full of working fountain water—were passed among the crowd. But it didn't deter them. In fact, their injuries, and each devastating return of the ghost ship, seemed to fuel their anger.

On the third night, an intruder breached the palace, made it up the stairs, and to the doors of our suite. The sounds of a scuffle woke Wade and me, but the guards in our room prevented us from venturing outside. They wouldn't even let us within six feet of the windows that overlooked the gardens.

Ford burst into the room a few minutes later, a large gash across his forehead, panting for breath. The culprit had been accosted and removed. He'd had a knife. Murder on his mind.

The thought that one of my own people wanted to kill me filled me with deep sadness. How had I failed them so badly? And now Ford was injured too. At least he had a flask of fresh fountain water left over from the tunnel searches. But soon that would run out too.

On the fourth day, the crowds continued to surround the palace, growing, seething, becoming a vicious unit. Not all demanded justice; many were scared and seeking answers. Answers I couldn't give them.

"We have to face them," Wade told Ford.

Ford took one look out the window and grimaced. "It's not safe."

"We'll do it over the island's Wi-Fi," I said. "We can make an address and air it to every home. Put screens outside. Our silence isn't helping."

Ford nodded and went to gather the press crew, ordered them to erect screens in the courtyard, to set up their cameras in our suite. A hushed expectation settled on the restless masses outside while I sat with my sister, composing a speech intended to pacify our citizens. I didn't offer any amendments. I would say whatever they wanted me to say. As long as our people stopped fighting. As long as they stopped cursing Wade's name. He didn't deserve that.

My sister wrote notes on a tablet, her face a mask, but the pain in her eyes gave her true feelings away.

While the camera crew brought their equipment to life, I leaned closer to my sister, placed a hand on her arm. She flinched, stepped away from me.

"I understand if you hate me," I said. "If you can never forgive me."

She pursed her lips, as if considering what to say. "My son is aboard that ship. And I would do anything to get him back. Anything." She sighed. "I know less of this world than you. And I'm not a queen. I can't imagine the pressures that weigh on your shoulders, the difficult decisions you must make. And I know your heart is pure. I know you wouldn't hurt me, or anyone else intentionally. But your anxiety, your grief, your anger, it got in the way this time."

"I know."

"I love you," Raina said. "But I'm furious with you too."

We stared at each other, the heaviness of her sentiments filling the gap between us.

"Will the speech work?"

"We can only hope."

A staff member arrived with a printed version of the speech, and another set up the teleprompt. I scanned the words. "This doesn't even sound like me."

"Read it anyway," Raina said.

Wade approached, kissed my cheek, and led me to the camera. "They're ready."

I clutched his hand.

"I'll stand with you," he said.

Someone came at me with a makeup brush, but I ducked out of the way. The people of Atlantis didn't care what I looked like, and wearing makeup would only emphasize the gulf between my privileged position and the grief of others.

I knotted my fingers together to stop them trembling and faced the camera, my gaze fixed on the teleprompter.

"Today I stand before you with a heavy heart, burdened by the weight of a grievous mistake I have made. I come to you not as Queen Cordelia, but as a humble soul seeking forgiveness and a path to redemption."

I glanced at Wade, who offered an encouraging nod. The rest of the room remained deathly silent as the twenty or so people involved in recording the speech held their collective breath.

"Recently, our beloved Atlantis faced a grave threat—the ghost pirates who abducted our precious children. In our quest to retrieve the last magical orb that could defeat these wretched invaders, I, regrettably, took a life. I killed Caol Ortega, a selachii, a creature who had inflicted upon me untold trauma in my past. In my anger and pain, I believed his death was the only way to secure our future and protect our children."

My pulse thrummed in my ears. Sweat broke out on my skin. I recognized the signs of a bubbling panic attack, but I pressed on.

"I cannot deny that Caol's actions tormented me deeply, and the scars of my past have festered far too long. But I now understand my actions were rash and reckless. The power I possess, the gift of fire magic, was never meant to be used for vengeance or harm. I vow never to wield it in such a manner again."

I clutched Wade's hand, and he squeezed back.

"I stand before you today, not seeking excuses, but baring my soul in the hope that you can find it in your hearts to forgive me. I was blinded by my pain and anger, and in doing so, I failed not only myself but each one of you. Atlantis is not just a kingdom but a family, and in my reckless pursuit, I tarnished our unity."

A bitter taste lingered in my mouth. While I believed every word, baring my soul in such a public manner was an excruciating ordeal. Would it be enough, or would they choose to exile me?

"Let it be known that my beloved husband, Wade, bears none of the blame for my actions. He has been my rock, my source of strength, and a true royal in his heart. He has always sought the best for Atlantis and our people."

Wade kissed my cheek, a silent testament to his unwavering support, a beacon of unity for our people.

"Now, we must find a way forward, a united front to face the challenges that lie ahead. Our abducted children, our future, depend on our ability to come together once more. The last magical orb may elude us, but our resolve, our unity, and our love for our children are unbreakable."

"I ask for your forgiveness, not as your queen, but as a fellow Atlantean who is ready to learn from her mistakes and grow. Let us heal together, let us rise above the shadows of the past, and let our strength as a united people guide us toward the brighter future that awaits us."

The faintest of roars reached me from outside the palace walls. Was it working?

"Thank you, my dear citizens, for your patience, your understanding, and your enduring faith in Atlantis. Together, we shall face the challenges that lie ahead and bring our abducted children back home, where they belong, in the heart of our beloved kingdom."

I beat my chest and left my hand over my heart.

"Cut," the cameraman announced, extinguishing the red light. The crew began dismantling their equipment, leaving us in suspense as an indistinct roar from outside the palace walls washed over us. Was it approval or condemnation?

"You're needed in the great hall," Ford said to Wade and I. "A meeting of the senate and High Council."

We followed Ford out of the suite, flanked by ten soldiers on either side, their polished boots reverberating through the marble tiles, weapons holstered securely to their belts. As we passed the rooms belonging to my parents, my mother emerged.

"Cordelia!" She fought her way through the guards until I told them to stand down. Then she swept me into her arms. How I needed the forgiving and loving touch of a parent right now. But I couldn't rely on her to right my wrongs, this was something I had to face alone.

She rubbed my arms as we descended the stairs, as if trying to erase the chill on my skin. I leaned into her maternal comfort, but for the first time in my life, her presence brought me no solace.

Before we opened the thick wood doors leading to the great hall, Angelica approached me with a guard of her own.

"Cordelia," she called my name, her voice carrying a mixture of urgency and concern. "Can I talk to you a minute?"

I nodded at the guards to allow the beautiful orcana to pass.

"It's about Caol. The orb," she said. "I don't know when or how he found the orb, but I have a feeling I know where it is."

"Go on," Wade said.

"When I followed him, when he turned shark and bit me, it was in the underground tunnels, the ones way down deep. He didn't have the use of his legs before he came to Atlantis, and so he could only swim in the channels, which were frozen at the time, apart from the tunnels underground. If he was hiding the orb, it must be down there. It was in those tunnels he attacked me."

"Thank you," I said, my mind racing with possibilities. I turned to Ford. "Tell Rob to focus his search on the flooded tunnels. Send selachii and mermaids in their ocean forms."

Ford barked the orders into his radio.

Angelica stared at me a moment longer. "Your speech was perfect. If I didn't feel you were my queen before, I certainly do now."

I swallowed to prevent emotion clogging my throat. "Thank you."

"No. Thank you. Thank you for taking us in. From giving us a home when all I did was betray your trust."

"You didn't know."

"I should have."

An unspoken understanding passed between us, then after offering me a fragile smile, she turned and left, her skin markings pulsing with purpose.

Wade put a hand on the door. "You ready?"

After smoothing my dress, I nodded.

When we entered the great hall, the rest of the senate was already present. Trent, Marina, and Jordan. Wade's cousin had been absent for much of the past few days, first searching for Mini Cordelia in the distant villages, then helping Rob in the tunnels. Maya, Blaze, and Babette, the other three members of the High Council besides Ford, were seated near the fire.

"Early results are showing a positive reaction," Blaze said as I stepped further into the room.

I skimmed the faces of the people gathered. I loved each and every one of them.

Maya wouldn't meet my eyes. "I called this meeting to discuss how we find the last orb, now that Caol is dead."

I stepped forward, my hands trembling. I was far more nervous now than when I had spoken to the camera. It was these people gathered here who I cared about most, who I would do anything for. I hated that I had caused them pain.

"I owe you all an apology," I said. "I'm not going to deliver a fancy speech written by my sister or the palace staff. You all heard what I said on camera."

Maya met my eyes, finally. It was a start.

"If I'm honest, I don't regret killing Caol, but I do regret making it harder for us to find the last orb. And I'm sorry for that. I'm sorry that I have caused you all pain. But know that I suffer along with you. My child is also onboard that evil ship and I will not stop fighting until he is in my arms again. Until we have all the children back. My power is a devastating one, but it will be needed when the time comes. I don't expect you to forgive me, or even trust me, but please know I will never act so rashly again."

Blaze nodded at me, a silent affirmation.

"Thank you," Trent said. "That means a lot."

My mother came to my side and kissed my cheek, wiped the tears from my face.

Babette faced me. "You did good."

Jordan and Marina came to stand by my side, while Wade took my hand. Only Maya was left.

"I hope in time you can forgive me, that we can repair our friendship," I said to her.

She marched purposefully across the floor and enveloped me in a fierce hug. "Please promise me we're going to get them back."

I would make no such promise, but I returned her hug with equal force.

When I pulled away, I addressed the gathering once more. "I have an idea how to find the orb." I told them of Angelica's suspicions. "The tunnels beneath our city are collapsing at an alarming rate. I propose we evacuate the city to the north, or to the beach, and then I burn the hell out of the caverns. I've released two orbs already by burning them out of the stone."

"But you could cause a catastrophic collapse," Babette said.

"And the fountain isn't working properly either," Ford said.

"I understand that," I said. "Which is why we must evacuate. Then it shouldn't matter how much I burn. But if my fire is hot enough, if my flames reach far enough, that orb will be released from wherever Caol stashed it, or wherever it remains hidden."

A tense silence weaved through the gathering, the only sound the fire crackling in the hearth.

"I vote yes," Wade said.

"Me too," Blaze said. "Hell, I'll help."

"Yes," Jordan and Marina said at the same time.

"If you're sure." My mother touched my shoulders.

"Yes," Trent said.

Ford settled his gaze on me. "Absolutely."

"For once, I'm agreeing with you, Cordelia. Yes," Babette said.

"Maya?" I asked.

"Yes."

The doors were flung open, and Dylan marched into the room. "No one is making any daring moves to rescue my nephew without me. I say burn the fucking place down."

CHAPTER TWENTY-FIVE

It took two days to evacuate the city. During that time, an eerie silence enveloped the palace, broken only by the hushed whispers of soldiers and the sound of heavy boots against the cobblestone streets. The army had reluctantly abandoned the futile search for the last orb in the labyrinthine tunnels, shifting their focus to the desperate evacuation effort. They went from door to door, imploring the residents to pack only the essentials for a few days and make the arduous journey north.

Electric carts, a rare commodity, were in short supply, and the frozen water channels rendered them useless. The only choice remaining was to trek on foot. Atlanteans, swathed in layers of warm winter gear, shouldered their backpacks or pulled suitcases, their children's small hands clutched tightly in their own, as they embarked on their journey. Several groups ventured westward to the farmland, while others headed north toward the mountain villages. A brave few chose the path that led to the distant forests beyond the formidable mountains.

I ventured to the palace balcony; my heart heavy with the responsibility that lay ahead. A few groups strolled through the barren courtyard, their faces a mix of determination and despair. Dylan extended a rare kindness by offering them a free shot or a warm cider for the long road ahead. Several faces in the crowd turned toward me, some offering waves and shouts of encouragement, while others simply stared, their expressions hard to read. I prayed that my efforts had been enough to win their trust. The people of Atlantis were placing their faith in me, and I was determined not to let them down.

As the last of our people streamed out of the city, the ominous ghost ship reappeared on both nights, casting a sinister shadow over the mass exodus. The first night caught us unprepared, with many still on the road after dusk, and a few innocent children were snatched. The second night, the survivors sought refuge in villages along the way, and no new victims were taken. Each report of these horrifying encounters only fueled the fire within me, reinforcing my unwavering resolve to find the elusive last orb.

When the last person evacuated the city, Dylan left the bar and joined us in the palace. Babette organized the transfer of the patients in the hospital to the north, most of them traveling in the solar-powered electric carts driven by the remaining soldiers. Only the High Council and the senate remained, with the addition of my father and Maya and Trent's children. We gathered in the great hall, the vast room echoing the emptiness of my beloved city.

The four radiant orbs hovered in a gentle orbit around the Power of the Sea, their ethereal glow casting dancing shadows on the walls. I took a deep breath, steeling myself for what lay ahead.

"It's time for you all to go," I said, tucking my hands behind my neck so my loved ones wouldn't see them tremble. "I have no idea the destruction my fire will cause when I burn through the tunnels. With the fountain malfunctioning, it's too risky for you to remain here."

Maya was the first to hug me goodbye. "Good luck, Cordy. I believe in you."

My throat tightened as I asked, "Is there anything new in the book?"

She shook her head. "I'll let you know if anything appears." She took Trent's hand and led her three children out of the room, away from the city.

Jordan and Marina were next. Marina gave me a quick peck on the cheek.

Jordan and I met eyes. So much had passed between us over the years. Once, he had been my enemy. And now, although not a friend exactly, he was someone I trusted. "We'll be in the mountain village if you need us."

"I should stay and protect both you and Wade," Ford said.

I shook my head. "Your unwavering loyalty to us over the years and goes without question, but now I must insist that you stay safe. It is my turn to look after you."

He nodded and stepped away.

Then it was my parents, both with tears in their eyes.

"This is the hardest thing I've ever done," Mom said.

I smiled. "I doubt that."

"Truly," she said, placing her hand over my heart. "Of all the battles, of all the fights with Zale, leaving you to deal with this on your own…"

I covered her hand with both of mine. "I won't be alone. I have you and my people supporting me from afar. And Wade and Blaze will be with me."

It was my father's turn. "I'm so proud of you. I admire you every day."

I gritted my teeth so the thickening in my throat didn't turn into a more emotional display.

"I'm proud to be your father."

I thew my old Navy baseball cap at him, which I had stolen from him anyway. "Keep it safe."

"Always." With a brief but fierce hug, he turned away and marched out of the room.

"Don't mind him," Mom said. "He's seen you prepare for battle too many times."

"I know."

Mom left after one more hug, holding my eyes until she walked through the doors.

"I'm not leaving," Dylan said.

There were only four of us left in the room. Wade, Blaze, my twin brother, and me. The weight of our impending mission pressed upon us.

"It's not safe for you here," I said to my twin.

Dylan jutted his chin at the glowing orbs. "I can fly, remember?"

"Is that what you call it?" I said, keeping my tone light. "I seem to recall you being thrown against the ceiling and then falling to the ground."

His hands fisted. "I'm not leaving."

"We can't guarantee your safety," Wade said. "If you can't fly, if you get caught in a fire...our focus is on finding the orb."

I turned to my husband. "Which is why you must leave too."

He gaped at me. "No."

"Yes."

"I'm not leaving you."

I placed a hand on his chest, much like my mother had done to me moments ago. "You feel safe because my flames can no longer hurt you. But that's only when they are attached to my body. If you get caught in a blaze, you will burn. And I know you are strong, but your skin is not fire retardant. And you don't have wings like Blaze to fly away. You must leave."

"I don't want to," Wade said, his voice barely above a whisper.

"I know." I kissed his cheek. "But if anything goes wrong, Gal needs one of us alive."

"Don't say that," Wade said.

"For fuck's sake, Cordy." Dylan said. "You're going to make me cry."

Tears welled in my eyes as I looked at my brother, his determination burning brightly in his gaze. The yellow orb, a beacon of hope and understanding, hovered at his side like a loyal companion, radiating an otherworldly warmth. It was as if the very essence of his courage had taken form in that orb.

"He needs his uncle too," I said.

"Which is why I'm staying," Dylan said. He nodded at his yellow orb, and it floated to his side. "It knows what I want. It knows how to help. For once in my life, I'm going to be brave and I'm going to kick some ghost pirate ass."

I swallowed hard, struggling to find the words to make him leave. "I can't stop you. But I don't agree with you."

"I don't care," Dylan said, his tone unyielding.

There was nothing more I could say to convince him to go. Turning to my husband, I took his hand, flames already burning as I led him toward the door. "Please go far from here. Look after our people. I'll join you as soon as I can."

He cupped my face with both hands. "I don't want to leave you."

I held onto his forearms. "I know. Hopefully, it won't take too long."

"We've always fought our battles together before."

"We're not fighting this time," I said. "We're seeking. And when we find the orb, I'm going to need you to come back and fight the ghost pirates with me."

"I know I should go, but I don't know how to leave you."

Raising myself to tiptoes, I pressed my lips against his, pouring all my love and fear into that kiss. "I love you," I said. "Now please go before I change my mind."

Wade squeezed my hand once, a silent promise, and then left.

When I turned back to face Dylan and Blaze, I found my brother floating near the ceiling with a huge grin on his face, and Blaze regarding him with an amused expression.

"I feel like Peter Pan," Dylan said, waving his arms at me.

"You look like him too," I said.

Dylan floated back to the ground as I walked back across the room to meet them.

"So," Blaze said, splaying a hand. "Any idea how we're going to do this...exactly?"

We'd spent so long searching for Atlantis, years bringing it back to life and showing the love it deserved, and now we faced the heart-wrenching task of destroying it.

I glanced at my fiery red orb, its intensity matching the turmoil in my heart. "I'm going to ask my magical sphere to *bring it on.*"

"And me," Dylan said.

"We're going to go back to the cavern where Wade and I found the orb of Spirit and Soul."

Dylan raised an eyebrow. "The cavern that's now underwater?"

"Yep. It's the deepest part of the tunnels I can think of. Then we blow it up from the inside."

Dylan gulped as Blaze unfurled his wings. Although dragon kings were capable of flight, their wings were better suited for swimming. All the same, the power of his wings lifted him a couple of feet into the air. Perhaps it was nerves.

"I may need an assist if things get hairy." I looked at Blaze. "Think you can fly me out of there if necessary?"

"Absolutely."

"Right...Yeah..." Dylan stammered. "Let's go...Like now. If we're going to do this thing, I need to go now, before I chicken out." The yellow glow of Dylan's orb cast his face in a sickly sheen.

With a deep breath, I called for my red orb to follow, and

the three of us began our solemn journey out of the great hall, across the foyer, and toward the door leading to the treacherous tunnels. There were no guards today, for everyone had evacuated, and by the time we reached the underwater cavern, I hoped the rest of the High Council and senate would be out of harm's way as well.

By the glow of the two orbs and the fire on my hands, we navigated our way through the dark and winding tunnels, slipping over loose shale. After half an hour, we came to a blockage where the tunnel had collapsed—a grim reminder of when Wade and I had braved these very passages. With Blaze's fiery breath added to my own powers, we blasted the rocks with scorching torrents until they were reduced to ash and continued.

Sweat poured down our faces as we ventured deeper into the bowels of the earth, and dirt and soot clung to our skin. After tripping a couple times, Dylan used his new abilities to hover in the air, often knocking his head on the ceiling, but grinning with delight all the same.

"Oh my God, you're like a kid at Christmas," I said to him.

His smile broadened. "Wait until I show Gal."

I thrust a fiery finger in his direction. "No. Nope. You are not taking him flying when he gets back."

"Spoil sport," he muttered, kicking off the ceiling.

The sound of water soon competed with the crackle of flames on my hands. A couple of steps later and my feet were drenched. The once dry passageway had become submerged, its depths filled by the cascading waters of Lake Echomere after the cavern's cataclysmic collapse.

"We're going to have to swim," Blaze said.

We shared a silent moment, all three of us locked in place, staring at one another.

"Thank you for being here with me," I said. "I would have been terrified to do it alone."

"Twins for life," Dylan said, and high-fived my fiery hand.

"Always got your back, my queen," Blaze said. "And to be honest, it helps to be doing something. Not sitting around like everyone else."

"I hear that," I said.

I stepped into the watery embrace, dove beneath the surface, and transformed into my mermaid form. My scarlet tail flicked out behind me while my flames continued to light the path ahead. Although my flames couldn't burn the water itself, they could burn other material in the water if it was flammable, so I had to be careful what I touched.

Sensing the tunnel's opening ahead, I felt the vastness of the cavern spread out around me. Not just ahead, but beneath and overhead too. Looking up, I noticed a faint glimmer of light piercing through the gentle current where the ceiling had crumbled.

Blaze joined me on my left, his powerful wings creating ripples in the water. Dylan flicked his green merman tail to draw level with my right. His orb remained by his side, as did mine.

"Let's go as deep as we can," I communicated telepathically. "Then we'll unleash our powers when we reach the bottom."

We all dove simultaneously, our tails propelling us

through the inky depths. If it weren't for my flames or the glow of the orbs, we'd be in complete darkness.

It took a full ten minutes to reach the cavern floor. I shuddered to think what might have become of Wade and me if either of us had fallen.

The three of us hovered at the bottom, using our telepathy to communicate.

"You two fire together," Dylan said. "I'll call on air to create pockets in the water, so the flames burn more easily."

"And to make the flames bigger," Blaze said.

Before I could chicken out or overthink the danger of the situation, I counted to three, pushing the countdown to the other two telepathically. On three, Blaze roared, conjuring flames from the depths of his throat, while I hurled fireballs from my hand. My red orb radiated a kaleidoscope of different reds as I directed a relentless stream of fire at the cavern's floor. Dylan's yellow orb matched its intensity as he parted the water at the bottom, allowing an airy space for the flames to breathe.

It was hard to see through the flames and the smoke that soaked into the water and clogged my gills, affecting my concentration and the force of my fire. Dylan created air pockets around our gills, and once again, I focused my attention on the ground.

The stream of fire burned through the water, chiseling into the rock, and carving craters and tunnels into the depths. Chunks of rock bobbed around us, colliding with our bodies, melting and igniting as the water's temperature rose. Amidst the searing flames and the thick veil of smoke that permeated the water, my concentration wavered, and the temperature soared. I hadn't considered that. Foolish. Although my own flames couldn't hurt me, anything that caught fire consequently could burn me, and Dylan and Blaze. Even the pockets of air heated to such a degree that our eyebrows were singed.

Forced to alter our strategy, we redirected our flames toward the cavern's walls. As we ascended through the water, Blaze and I unleashed torrents of fire in all directions, collapsing walls, destabilizing tunnels, and triggering a cascade of falling boulders from above. Dylan kept pace with us, giving us respite with his air bubbles.

My head finally broke the surface, the cacophonous sound of rocks splashing above and walls disintegrating on either side. The water level surged, elevating us toward the gaping hole in the cavern's roof. We had an exit. I hoped.

Just as I was about to break free from the water's grasp, a boulder hurtled toward me, striking my shoulder with bone-crushing force. I released a strangled cry as I spiraled helplessly in the water, my arm broken, and the flames on that hand extinguished. Dylan sent me an air bubble to support me in the water while I struggled to get my breath back.

"We must go deeper to avoid the rocks," Blaze said, nudging me down.

Despite the light of my flames and the two glowing orbs, it was dark underwater. The relentless onslaught of rocks persisted, plummeting toward the abyss with frightening speed. The pain in my shoulder was a white-hot agony that I could only bear by gritting my teeth and screaming a series of curse words in my mind. Blaze held my good arm as I struggled. After a moment, I ignited my hand once more and pushed my flames outward. I had no direction in mind. I wanted the cavern destroyed. I wanted the orb to be found. I wanted my son back.

"Shit," Dylan muttered, and pointed below.

I followed his gaze to the fiery orange glow emanating from the depths below us, intensifying with each passing second.

"Volcano," Blaze said.

The word filled me with both excitement and dread. A volcano would burn this place to hell and reveal the orb. But the three of us might never escape. At that moment, I accepted my fate. Somehow, I knew I was never going to make it out of this alive. But that was okay. The orb would be found, and Gal would have Wade.

Dylan locked his gaze on me. No words passed between us. We were together. Memories of the day I lost him to Zale flitted through my mind like unwelcome specters, haunting me with echoes. His scream. His fear. His desperation. There was none of that now. He was going to die for my son, and he was glad to do it. We had each other in our final moments.

I turned to Blaze. He had a child of his own. But the resignation sat firmly on his features. No panic. No anxiety. So like his father. He reached out, and I grasped his hand, forming an unspoken alliance. Then I took Dylan's, and the three of us waited for death.

As the lava surged toward us, devouring everything in its path, we felt the searing heat of the brutal attack melting rocks, and the end of our island.

The yellow orb nudged Dylan, floated around his head, pressed against this chin, lighting his face in an insistent glow.

As the lava came for us, Dylan's eyes flew wide, and he smiled.

Suddenly, the water was gone. I found myself encased in a giant air bubble with Dylan and Blaze.

"Get ready," Dylan said. "We might make it out of this."

I braced myself for impact as the lava made contact with our miraculous bubble. Dylan stared at the angry orange fire, or the bottom of the bubble, I wasn't sure. I heard his thoughts, concentrating hard on keeping us enclosed, the yellow orb brightening with each passing second. Our ascent began, propelling us upward through the roiling inferno toward the gaping hole in the cavern's ceiling. The world outside was a blur of fire and tumult, but in that moment, the spark of hope burned fiercely within me.

As we hurtled through the air, I caught sight of another glowing object. A sphere gleaming with an icy white light, nearly obscured by the perfectly formed clouds and the blue, blue sky.

High above the emptying lake, we zoomed across to the distant shore toward the foothills which led to the mountains. In an instant, we approached the distant shoreline and collided with a jagged point. The fragile bubble burst into a shower of shimmering fragments, and we fell our separate ways.

Blaze flapped his wings. Dylan hovered in the air, then zoomed after me as I plummeted to earth at an alarming rate. The white orb performed frantic circles around the lake, zooming in all directions, perhaps unable to find its guardian.

A hard point dug into my broken shoulder as I landed. Then I rolled, banging a hip, busting up my side, knocking my head, and then finally came to rest against a soft cushion of air. Dylan.

He landed beside me. "I got you covered, sis."

I groaned. Pain swept through my limbs, through every cell in my body. A pain I couldn't contain. I closed my eyes and allowed the world to go dark.

CHAPTER TWENTY-SIX

"Is it working?"

"When will she wake up?"

"Will there be any permanent damage?"

The air was thick with uncertainty, and my eyelids felt like lead. I opened my eyes to find a sea of faces crowding around me. The lights were bright. The smiles tentative.

"Wade?" My throat felt raw, as if I had swallowed fire.

"Here." His face came into view. Stooping, he kissed my cheek. "You're in the hospital. You had a nasty fall. Dylan and Blaze got you to safety."

My eyelids fluttered closed for a moment, and then I remembered the volcanic eruption. "Is the island gone?"

Wade shook his head, his fingers brushing a strand of hair away from my forehead. "The island stands, as do the palace and the city. But Lake Echomere has become a pool of lava and metamorphic rock."

"Everything hurts."

"You broke a few bones." My mother's voice. "We put the

fountain water in your IV line, and it's helped cure the worst of the injuries, but you still need to heal. Rest and heal."

I tried to nod, but a thundering pain pounded in my head when I moved.

"Let's sit you up a bit." Maya pressed a button on the bed and raised me into a sitting position.

"Is there anything new?" I asked her.

She shook her head.

"The orbs? Are they safe?"

"All of them," Blaze said with a smile. "We have all of them. Apart from Babette."

"What's wrong with Babette?" I asked. "Has she deserted us? Gone back to the mainland?"

Although I didn't think she'd shirk her duties when Atlantis was the only viable land for her to bring injured humans to, part of me knew the island wasn't really her home, that she felt more comfortable out there, chasing the remnants of the human world. I'd never fully trusted her to remain loyal. Perhaps that was why the fountain was in such disarray. It sensed the doubt deep inside me, knew that I didn't feel as united with her as I should. Despite the many heroic acts she'd undertaken and the many times she'd risked her life for my people — Wade...me—I didn't think I'd put our past behind us. Which was childish on my part, an old high school feud that meant nothing in the real world, and yet, I couldn't quite move on. Perhaps my resentment was solidified when Shane, a previous selachii High Council member, made her the guardian of the Power of the Sea—the most powerful item on the island. My issue. Not hers. I knew that. But knowing didn't erase it.

Knowing didn't take the hurt away. Knowing didn't heal the fountain.

"She wouldn't leave us at a time like this," Wade said.

"And where is Dylan?" I asked.

"Looking for her," Mom said.

Babette and he had been in a relationship for years. Albeit a tumultuous one. But if anyone understood Babette and could predict her actions, it was him. He would know how to find her.

"No one has seen her," Trent said. "Not since she evacuated the hospital."

"Is it only Dylan looking for her?"

"Rob too," Wade said. "He's taken a couple of units to scour the island. We hope she wasn't—"

"Burned alive," I muttered, covering my face with my hands.

"It's not your fault," Blaze said. "If she was in the vicinity. It's not your fault."

"It was my fire."

"And mine," Blaze said.

"I caused the volcano."

"Both of us did," Blaze said.

My head pounded. "If she was caught in the...incident... we'll never know."

Maya approached the bed. "She knows better than to put herself in harm's way."

"Exactly," Trent said. "She's not stupid. And she was last sighted far to the west in the farmlands with her patients. In all likelihood, she's fine."

"But where is she, then?" I asked. "We can't defeat the pirates without her, or my brother. She is the guardian of the Power of the Sea. He, the guardian of Air and Flight. We need them."

"Doc says you can't leave the hospital for a few days," Wade said. "Not until you're properly recovered. We'll find her."

"We can't just sit around and do nothing." I threw the covers off. "Have you tried combining them yet?"

"We were waiting for you," Wade said. "The red orb hasn't left your side. And we don't have Dylan and Babette."

It was only then I noticed the red tinge in the room. As if sensing my need to see it, the orb floated from behind my bed and came to rest near my shoulder.

"We should still try," I said, scanning the room for my clothes. They'd probably burned in the eruption. "We need to move. We need to get to the courtyard."

Wade laid a gentle hand on my chest. "You need to rest."

"And eat something." The doc entered the room carrying a tray of food. A young woman, one of the first humans on Atlantis, who Babette had trained as a doctor. "Chicken soup and a soft roll."

"We need to get our children back." We were so close. We had the orbs.

"We will," Maya said. "But we need you strong. We're going to need your power. When the orbs are combined, the powers they granted their guardians will diminish. You had your fire power before matching with your orb, so you're kind of like our only decent weapon."

"Hey!" Wade flicked a hand at her.

"Yeah, *hey*," Blaze said.

"Okay, three weapons," Maya said. "Against pirates and venomous spiders and poisonous whips. And with the fountain not working properly, we can't guarantee those who fight will be healed."

"Fair point," Trent said.

I attempted to sit up, but the pain in my head sent me reeling back onto the mattress.

"You have a concussion," Wade said. "It was pretty serious. The fountain made it not so serious."

"It hurts," I said, reaching for his hand.

"I'll put more painkillers in the IV." The doc moved to the side of the bed and emptied a syringe into my drip.

My family and friends gathered around me, keeping a vigil while I rested. It was then I noted the burns littering Blaze's face and arms. "You got hurt."

"Just a scratch," Blaze said. "The fountain took away the worst of it."

"I'm sorry." My fire had caused so much destruction, and now a volcano served as a permanent reminder of our quest for the orbs, the ghost pirates, and our missing children. I squeezed my eyes closed in an attempt to block it all out. Just for a moment. Just long enough so I could breathe.

"Time to leave," the doc said to the room. "Cordelia needs to rest."

One by one they filed out of the room, some squeezing my hand, others offering me a quick hug. Only Wade remained.

"I thought I'd lost you."

"Never," I said.

"Promise?"

I saw the haunted look in his eyes. The look that had appeared when Angelica had revealed her relationship with Zale. A look I feared would never leave his face. How worried he must have been while I lay here unconscious, not knowing if I was going to wake up. "I'll do my best."

He crawled onto the bed and lay by my side, his fingers tracing soothing patterns on my arm, and he placed sweet kisses on my cheek.

"When can we go?" I asked.

"I'm not ready," he said. "I just got you back."

I touched his chin, made him look at me. "We can't ignore it."

"You're not going anywhere until we get the all-clear from the doc." His tone hardened. "I know you wield an enormous power. But it's connected to your emotions and your physical health. You need to rest. We need to launch an attack when our chances are strongest."

"I don't want any more kids to be taken."

Wade's lips pressed into a grim line.

"What is it?" I asked.

"We've lost thirty more."

"Thirty?" I sat bolt upright, forgetting about the pain in my head until it was too late. "How long have I been out?"

"Five days."

"*Five days?*" I swung my legs over the side of the bed once more, only to be hit by a dizzy spell that threatened to send me crashing to the floor.

Wade pulled me back onto the bed, using one strong arm

to restrain me against the mattress. "It's morning. We can't do anything until nighttime anyway. The ship only comes at night. Every night. Sometimes more than once."

"Fuck!"

"We're close."

"I don't feel comfortable in my own skin," I said, scratching at my hand where the IV line entered. "I can't sit here and wait."

Wade ran a hand through my hair, tugged on the ends in the way I loved. "We don't have a choice."

"I hate not being in control."

"I know."

I sighed and allowed him to help me eat the cooling soup. "How are the...people? Have they forgiven me?"

"Mostly," Wade replied, wiping my chin with a napkin. "There are still rumblings, especially when the volcano erupted, but I think you've won back their hearts."

"When I rescue the kids, perhaps that will put things right."

"We."

"What?"

"*We.*" His gaze was fierce. "We fight together, remember?"

I cupped his face and brushed my thumb over his cheek. "Always."

The door swung open, interrupting our moment. Angelica poked her head in. "Can I come in?"

I gestured for her to enter. "Is everything okay?"

Her eyes were tight, her jaw tense, her skin markings so pale they were barely visible. "How are you feeling?"

"I'm recovering," I replied. "But by the look on your face, you didn't come here to ask me how I am. What is it?"

She sighed, then stepped closer to the bed. "A shark's been spotted off the coast of the island."

"Half the population is selachii," Wade said.

Angelica's expression darkened. "A shark I recognize."

The blood in my veins turned to ice. Wade gripped my hand.

"Why isn't there anything in the book?" I asked.

"There is," Wade said. "*Old enemies die hard.*"

I looked at Angelica. "Are you sure it's Zale?"

She nodded. "I'd recognize that dorsal fin anywhere. And it's huge."

"He *is* a great white," Wade said.

Angelica shook her head. "Not anymore."

"What else could he be?" I asked as my heart fluttered uncomfortably.

"He spent time with the Denizens of the Deep—"

"Who?" Wade asked.

"The gods of the deep," Angelica replied. "They haven't concerned themselves with the world above for quite some time, but they continue to exist, and they have powers that rival Vorago, Cascadia, and Tempest."

"Holy shit," Wade exhaled.

"What's your point, Angelica?" I asked.

"He won their trust, and not only did they give him the blinding rock, they gave him an increased strength and size."

"Like Wade?"

"Bigger than Wade," she said. "He's megalodon size."

My chest seized. I had faced Zale underwater more than

once and had been lucky to escape with my life. And that was when he was a regular great white. There was no way I could battle a megalodon on my own. Not without my fire orb. And even then, it was risky.

"He doesn't have legs," Wade said. "He can't transform and come ashore. Even if he could reach the fountain, it's not powerful enough to grant him the ability of transformation right now."

"And the water channels are frozen."

"Not entirely," Wade said. "The volcano melted most of the snow. Most of the water is currently an icy slush."

"Gal." I spoke his name aloud, seized by the worry if Zale got a hold of him.

"Is actually in the one place Zale can't hurt him," Wade said.

"Until we defeat the ghost pirates," Angelica reminded us.

"Pirates first," Wade said. "Then we'll deal with Zale."

"What if he has Babette? What if that's why she's missing?" I asked. "He could have Dylan now too."

I loved my brother dearly and admired the new confidence he'd found as the guardian of the Air and Flight orb, but Zale was the one monster from his past who could drive terror into his heart, who would immobilize him with fear. If they fought one-on-one...no. I attempted to shake the morbid images out of my head, but all I could see was blood.

Wade stood, making for the door. "I'll let Rob know. With Babette unable to transform, we didn't think to search for her in the water. I'll tell him now."

"I'll help you," Angelica said. "Zale trusts me. I could cause a distraction or a diversion or something. He'll never see it coming. It's the least I can do...considering..."

I reached out and took her hand. "Thank you. We're going to need all the help we can get."

It took three days for the doctor to give me the all-clear, even though her own child had been abducted. Three days of staring out the window at the frosty gray world. A world of melting ice and sludgy ash and fire repairs. The fountain had cured the worst of the destruction, filling in hazardous craters, securing teetering boulders and even including a safety railing around the new lava lake. Some of the worst destroyed homes had also been improved, but for the week I lay in a hospital bed, both unconscious and conscious, Atlanteans spent their time making repairs to the water channels and pathways and homes and the hospital itself that the fountain hadn't touched. The army searched for Dylan and Babette. Both on the island and beneath. Angelica swam the coastline, calling for Zale, trying to coax him out of hiding. A member of the High Council or senate always sat with the orbs in the great hall. The smaller spheres remained in a glowing orbit around the Power of the Sea. All but one. Dylan took his orb of Air and Flight when he went searching for Babette. I prayed it was still in his possession.

Wade spent the evenings with me, reporting on the progress and saying how proud he was of his people learning new trades, when previously we'd relied on the fountain to fix the smallest of issues. Perhaps we could learn something from the humans after all.

The army made a sweep of the tunnels, or what was left of them, securing those that were most unstable and searching for nests of white spiders that had burrowed deep. Only one was found and destroyed, and our people breathed easier knowing our island wasn't home to venomous arachnids. But the ship came every night, and during each attack more spiders found their way to the ground, scattering wide. The army repeated their job of flushing them out on a daily basis.

While Wade was away, another member of my family sat with me. Often my parents. Although Maya was nursing her newborn, she visited often, the baby in one arm, *The Mermaid Chronicles* in another. We spent hours chatting about the past, more hours plotting the battle, and even more time watching the pages of the book, hoping new information would be delivered concerning the whereabouts of Dylan and Babette. But the pages remained stubbornly inactive. *Ghostly vengeance seeks innocence on Atlantis* and *old enemies die hard*, being the last two prophecies. The former appearing when the rock was removed from the fountain, and we both understood what it referred to. But there was nothing new, nothing we could pin our hopes on. Maya read to me the full prophecies concerning our enemies. Until now she'd only given me highlights, explained the most important parts of what was heading our way, but while we waited for me to recover, she told me some prophecies gave longer accounts.

"*The echoes of long-standing enemies will resonate through the ages,*" she read. "*Refusing to be silenced. Those who have harbored hatred for generations will cling to their vendettas, making peace a challenging endeavor. To mend the rifts that divide the ocean's denizens, old wounds must be healed, and reconciliation must triumph over the echoes of ancient strife."*

"So Zale is behind the ghost pirates," I said.

"It seems that way," Maya said. "But I think there's more to this prophecy."

"How so?"

"Forgiveness. Acceptance. Moving forward."

"I will never forgive Zale." I gritted my teeth. "And I have moved forward."

"Only because you thought he was in prison." Maya shot me a sympathetic look. "Not because you really felt it."

I studied her profile, the adorable bump in her nose, the delicate curve of her chin, the stretch of her lips that offered so many smiles.

"He took half my family away," I said.

"I know."

"How do I move on from that?"

"To be honest, I don't know," she said. "But while it's still eating you inside, I don't think you'll truly heal."

"I need therapy."

"It's not a bad idea."

"As soon as we destroy the pirates. And Zale."

Maya took my hand, gave it a gentle squeeze.

"Should I not want revenge?" I asked.

She lifted a shoulder, then settled the baby in her other arm. "I guess it's only normal. I can't say part of me wasn't glad when you killed Caol, after everything he did to Trent, but I didn't spend my nights wishing he was dead. And besides..."

The baby snuffled and Maya brought her hungry lips to her breast.

"Besides?"

"It doesn't matter."

"Is there something you're not telling me?"

She met my gaze. "Only that the prophecy has several interpretations. We shouldn't make assumptions."

"*Old enemies die hard*," I said. "How can there be more than one interpretation? Zale won't fucking die. He won't leave us alone, and he'll keep coming back until I delete him from existence."

"See? This is why I'm the oracle, not you."

"His death is going to be so fucking hard."

"Not on your own, Cordy." Maya said. "Remember, he's a megalodon now."

"Don't remind me," I muttered. "What are they? The other interpretations?"

"I can't tell you that."

I rolled my eyes. "Because you might change our fate."

"Exactly," she said. "You need to do whatever it is you're going to do. If I give you new information and you change your path, then it could alter your fate for the worse."

"But aren't we supposed to make new, informed decisions based on the information it provides?"

"Yes and no," Maya said. "There's a balance."

"I hate that book."

"It's saved us more than once."

The doctor entered the room. She checked my vitals,

stuck a bright light in my eyes, examined my injuries, then declared I was free to leave.

My heart raced. I had been waiting to battle the ghost pirates ever since they had arrived, but now the time was finally here, now that we had equipped ourselves with the necessary weapons, fear flooded my veins.

CHAPTER TWENTY-SEVEN

I trudged through a desolate and haunting world that bore no resemblance to the place I once called home. The air retained its icy grip, and snowflakes danced hesitantly in the overcast sky. Most of the snow on the ground had melted, mingling with the ash and soot, transforming the once-pristine island into a dismal, sludgy wasteland. I walked out of the hospital, through the courtyard, noting the aftermath of destruction; the ragged hole in the roof of Dylan's cherished bar, cobblestone paths upended like unsightly veins on the island's battered skin, and a once-majestic fountain now concealed beneath layers of grime. The mermaid statues had collapsed into the water, which was barely blue anymore. Bubbles effervesced on the surface, a sign of its struggle to maintain equilibrium.

When I entered the palace, I found the rear gardens no longer existed. The quaint cottages nestled among the woods, including Maya and Trent's, had vanished, devoured by the relentless tide of the volcano. The rear lawns and residences were buried beneath two feet of ash. Thankfully, because of the evacuation, no one had been hurt. Those inhabitants affected had been moved into the palace, which seemed to be the one structure unaffected on the entire island. I took that as a sign of hope.

I entered the great hall to find Maya waiting for me. My orb flew from my shoulder to join the others. All the spheres were present except Dylan's orb of Flight and Air.

"What is it you wanted to try?" Maya asked as I ventured closer.

"Combining the orbs," I replied.

Shaking her head, she rose to meet me, carrying the book open to the pages dedicated to the orbs. "They won't combine unless they're all present. And each of their guardians must instruct them to do so."

I gazed at the orbs of Spirt and Soul and Snow and Ice. They had not found their guardians, which led me to believe they belonged to a child trapped on the ghost ship.

"We need to try," I said. "Because when we have all the orbs, and all the adults are here, and that ship attacks again, how on earth will the guardians on board know what is expected of them? We can't get close enough to the ship without those whips lashing us down. And with the fountain not working, we can't afford to get too close. So you tell me, how are we going to do this?"

"Don't get mad at me, Cordy," Maya said, splaying a hand across the book. "I can only tell you what the book says."

"But the book has been wrong before, right?"

"Has it?"

I searched my memories for a time when the book had failed us but came up blank. It had only been Maya's interpretations that were slightly off, or my own sheer stubbornness that led me down a different path. The book had always guided us correctly.

"I still want to try."

"And I support that," Maya said. "Any way you want."

With renewed resolve, I turned my attention to the orbs. "I'm going to start with the Power of the Sea and my orb of Fire and Heat."

"Good call."

As the red orb hovered by my shoulder, I approached the Power of the Sea. "I want you to push yourself into there," I told my magical companion, pointing at the swirling blue orb.

The red orb responded with a vibrant display of colors. Deep scarlet veins pulsed within its core, while pale crimson danced around its circumference. It radiated heat, warming my face and sending tiny sparks cascading toward me. I laughed as they tickled my cheeks.

"You have a really weird relationship with fire," Maya said.

"And you have a really weird relationship with that book."

"Point taken."

Lighting the flames on one hand, I turned back to my orb and encouraged it toward the Power of the Sea. The red sphere floated toward the blue orb, paused before it made contact, then disappeared inside.

"It worked!" Maya said, dropping the book and clasping her hands together.

"Careful with that," I said. She dropped to her knees and recovered the book.

Inside the combined orbs, the smaller red sphere pulsed, casting a kaleidoscope of colors that filled the room with hues of blue, purple, and red. Sparks, water droplets and bubbles emanated from the amalgamated spheres, their radiance growing in intensity, and filling the room with the smells of not just the ocean, but bonfires too.

"Try another one," Maya said.

I glanced at the newest sphere, the orb of Snow and Ice. Its icy whiteness made me shiver just looking at it. I raised my hand as I approached it, fire crackling with anticipation. Upon contact, a searing pain shot through my palm as the icy orb resisted my touch, leaving a deep burn in its wake. I flinched and yelped. Despite the fire on my hands, the orb was too cold to touch.

I drew my hand away and extinguished my flames, allowing Maya to inspect my palm. "That looks painful."

"It is," I said. "On top of the headache I still have too."

Maya glared at the white orb. "That wasn't very nice."

"It's only protecting itself. If anyone could access the power of these orbs..." I shook my head.

"Can you imagine if Zale gained legs and found his way here?"

"Exactly."

"Is it worth trying another one?" Maya asked.

I examined the remaining orbs, contemplating which one held the least potential for harm. The purple sphere of Spirit and Soul caught my attention. Maya winced as I approached it.

"What?" I asked.

"Careful with that one."

"Why?"

She turned a page in the book and read. "*It is not merely physical prowess that the orbs unlock; they unlock the depths of one's soul, endowing them with the wisdom of ages past and an unbreakable bond with the mystical world below. The Spirit & Soul orb, with its purple aura, grants a profound connection to the very essence of life, and unlocks the depths of emotion and empathy, empowering its bearer to heal the wounds of heart and soul.*"

"So it might heal my emotional wounds?"

"Only if you're its guardian. Which you're not," Maya said. "And as you're not, it could do the opposite."

I removed my hand. I had a fragile grasp on my anxiety and depression, and I didn't intend to be catapulted over the edge. I turned to the green orb of Rock and Earth instead. Unable to think of anything it could do to hurt me, I touched a finger to the sphere.

"That's weird."

"What's weird?" Maya asked.

"I can't stick my finger in it. All the other orbs are nebulous. They have structure, but you can still put your finger inside. Not this one."

Maya approached and tentatively tapped the green orb. "It's hard."

I pushed harder, using both hands and my body weight, but the orb remained fixed in the air. "And it won't budge."

"Can you go join your queen's fire orb inside the Power

of the Sea please?" Maya addressed the stubborn green sphere.

The green orb didn't move. Didn't even pulse with a spectrum of color.

I sighed. "We're going to have to wait."

I slumped into a chair, a sense of despair washing over me. For the seven days I'd spent in the hospital, I couldn't wait to get out and fight. To defeat the ghost pirates, get my son back, and deal with Zale. But now, as I faced the stubborn orbs and the overwhelming obstacles before me, doubt crept in. The island teetered on the brink of chaos, and the weight of responsibility threatened to crush my spirit. People were going to die. Several had already. I didn't know if I had it in me to go through an ordeal like that again.

Fuck it.

I already was going through an ordeal. I was already broken. What was one more fight?

Maya sat next to me. "I miss them too."

"You must be far away from here when the ship arrives," I said.

"I can't let you fight without me."

I gripped both her hands. "You have no powers, no offensive skills. And you have four children to stay alive for. You need to protect them."

Maya dipped her head. "I hate this."

I hugged her. Words wouldn't help the situation. Words were inadequate.

"Take care of Trent for me," Maya said.

"Of course."

As we left the great hall, my fire orb detached itself from

the Power of the Sea and followed me to the door. With a soft command, I instructed it to stay with the others, and it floated back into orbit. Maya left for her secured suite while I made my way to the courtyard to look for Wade.

The sun, in its final descent toward the horizon, painted the sky with hues of crimson and gold as I descended the grand palace steps. Fueled by a sense of creeping dread, I navigated the uneven terrain, taking two steps at a time, avoiding the worn, cracked stones. I wanted to check on the status of the fountain to see if there was anything I could do to repair it before the ghost pirates appeared.

But when I arrived at the fountain, an ominous chorus of screams grated the air, and I ran toward the source. Tripping over the ruined cobbles and dashing past the moldering fountain, I headed for the rocks, my pulse quickening with every step. I scrambled over the boulders to find Angelica climbing up the cliff face, her hands bloody, her eyes wide with terror. Below her, Dylan followed step for step, an unconscious Babette draped over his shoulder.

"I'll get help," I yelled.

I dashed across the courtyard in the other direction, calling for Wade, or Ford, or Blaze, or anyone who could help. All three came running. I led them back to the cliff to see Angelica cresting the top, the wound on her side torn open and bleeding.

"Zale..." she rasped as she staggered to the fountain and collapsed into it. Her skin markings turning an infected purple. "...has one of the orbs."

Blaze flew above the rugged cliffside, his wings slicing through the air, and swept down to the rocks. He plucked

Babette from Dylan's shoulders, carrying her in his arms. As he brought her to the fountain and laid her in the water, Wade and Ford helped Dylan over the edge. He was covered in blood, but I couldn't tell it if was his or someone else's.

"I'm okay," he said, his voice trembling as he ran to the fountain and jumped inside next to Babette. He kneeled beside her, cupping water over her face, onto her mouth, between her lips. "Please, please, please."

Her eyelids fluttered in response, and a faint groan escaped her lips, but she didn't regain consciousness. A red pool seeped out beneath her, turning the fountain a murky color. I waded into the water with my brother, ignoring the chill, and kneeled beside her. Her lips turned an unsettling shade of blue, her face a ghostly white, and her hair was streaked with blood. Deep, painful bruises littered her skin and colored the hollows beneath her eyes.

"What happened?"

"Zale...kidnapped Babette," Dylan said. "He demanded my orb as ransom."

A haunting blue glow filled the surrounding area. The Power of the Sea appeared in the palace's window and made its way across the courtyard, a chugging locomotive, pulling the other orbs along with it. It had never done that before.

"It knows you're home," I told Babette, but she didn't respond.

Dylan locked his eyes on me. "Do something, please."

I wasn't a doctor. If the fountain didn't work, there was nothing I could do. Babette's chest remained motionless. Her lips grew even darker.

"Don't you dare fucking die," I hissed at her. "After all

you've put me through. Trying to get between Wade and me in high school. Lording your humanness over me, your ability to use my ring, the fountain, and that you were chosen to be the Guardian of the Power of the Sea. I didn't understand that at the time. But now I do. Shane knew the last time selachii and mermaids were left to their own devises on Atlantis, it all went to hell. He trusted you to make the right decisions. He knew you would challenge me. You belong here, Babette. You do. You always have. If our relationship hadn't started out so rocky, maybe we would have been closer. And I'm sorry for that. I'm sorry for keeping you at arm's length, for arguing with you, for shooting down your suggestions. I'm sorry for all of it. But I don't want you to die. Please don't die. My brother loves you. Hell, I love you too."

As if in response to my impassioned plea, the Power of the Sea descended in a radiant cascade over Babette's head, bathing her in its ethereal glow.

"Give it to her," Wade said.

"Give her what?" I asked.

"Make her inhale it."

I nodded, remembering how a fraction of the Power of the Sea had once saved both Wade and me when we were in a similar state. It had also granted us our abilities. Now it was Babette's turn to be healed.

Dylan scooped a portion of the nebulous blue energy into his trembling hand, holding it ready for Babette to inhale. It danced in his hand like a wisp of hope. In the few inches of water, Wade supported her head while I pounded on her chest, trying to coax life back into her battered body.

She coughed, gagged, sucked in a huge inhale. A stream

of vivid blue energy flowed into her nostrils, igniting a spark within her. Her arms flailed as she grasped for solid ground, found purchase on the fractured rim of the fountain. With a surge of newfound strength, she pulled herself upright. "What happened?"

"You almost died," Dylan said, laying a gentle kiss on her cheek. "But we got you back."

Above us, the Power of the Sea pulsed in a mesmerizing display, its vibrant blue radiance intertwined with the other orbs, each a beacon of elemental power. Only the yellow sphere of Air and Flight remained conspicuously absent.

"Where is that fucking selachii?" Babette growled as she hoisted herself out of the water.

"We're looking for him," Wade replied, his gaze scanning the courtyard.

Babette stepped over the lip of the fountain and faced me. "I heard everything you said."

"I meant everything I said."

"Do we need to hug or something?" she asked.

We smiled at each other, our newfound understanding a fragile but pleasing thing.

"That's my girls," Dylan said, sweeping Babette into a protective embrace.

She planted a kiss on his lips, cupping his face, wrapping her legs around his waist, not caring that we were all watching. Ford let out a low whistle.

"At least that's one happy ending," I said.

As if in approval of our newfound unity, the Power of the Sea dipped into the fountain, turned it a bright and bubbling blue, casting a dazzling glow across the courtyard.

"I think the fountain is working again," I said.

"It is," Angelica said, crawling out of the water, her side completely healed.

We all took sips. It was the first time in weeks I felt fully restored.

"See what a little unity will do?" Babette winked at me.

Before I could respond, a deafening splash erupted from the water channel at my back, showering us with a slushy, ashy layer of muck.

I turned to see an immense snout emerging from the water channel. It angled toward the sky, growing with each passing second, breaking through the water channel and the banks, throwing ice and sludge and dirt and cobbles around the courtyard. And still it kept coming. Rolling black eyes. Gill slits. Dorsal fin. The most enormous shark I'd ever seen. No, not a shark, a megalodon.

Zale.

Instinctively, I readied my flames. Blaze assumed an offensive position in the sky. Wade stood beside me, ready to charge. Ford called on his green orb while I gestured to mine.

As Zale emerged from the water, he transformed first to his half human and half shark form, and then leaped high, landing on legs.

I gaped at him. How had he gained the use of legs? Not that it mattered. Clearly, I had underestimated him, and the advantage of surprise was all his.

As he landed on the slick, frozen ground, the yellow sphere, once held by Dylan, floated ominously near Zale's head.

"That doesn't belong to you," I said.

Zale smirked. "It does now."

I glanced at Dylan.

"I had to transfer my guardianship in exchange for Babette's life," he told me, pain and guilt etched in his eyes in equal measure.

"I don't care if you transferred it, Dylan, it doesn't belong to that treacherous selachii."

"Now, now Cordelia," Zale growled.

The yellow sphere, as if heeding my command, zoomed back to Dylan. "Well, that was easier than I thought," Dylan muttered.

"Because you are its true guardian," I said.

Zale, undeterred by our defiance, took deliberate steps closer. "Flying is all well and good. But it's the Power of the Sea I have the most need for."

"No," Wade said. "You tried to gain access to it once before, and you were punished. You will be punished this time too."

"I won't let you cause any more harm to these people," Angelica said.

Zale tutted. "Angelica, my love, you have deeply disappointed me. But then you always had a soft heart. But to think, after everything I've done for you, this is how you repay me?"

Angelica bristled. "You have done nothing for me."

"Is Frost not alive and well?"

"That was the fountain, not you."

"Semantics." Zale dismissed with a casual wave of his hand. "I feel as if you owe me."

"I did what you asked. I put the rock in the fountain, and

it blinded the prophecies." Angelica dipped her chin. Her shoulders trembled. "How could you?"

"Because I didn't want them to see me coming. Wasn't that obvious?"

"What did they ever do to you?" Angelica braved a couple of steps closer to the threatening selachii.

Zale's smile flatlined. "More than I care to speak about. But it's in the past now. I escaped that hellish prison. And now I have the Denizens of the Deep on my side. As well as the ghost pirates." He pointed skyward, diverting our attention to the phantom ship sailing silently through the night.

I snapped my head back at Zale, realizing he was creating a distraction. But instead of seizing the Power of the Sea, he disappeared into the water channel, leaving us to confront the looming threat of the ghost ship.

CHAPTER TWENTY-EIGHT

The ship blotted out the moon as it descended to the island. All around us, the restored power of the fountain was repairing the city, cementing the ruined cobbles, rinsing away the ash and soot, filling in dangerous craters, and thawing the frozen channels. My heart soared to see my island restored to its former glory, but it was only a matter of time before it might fall to ruin once more. The ghost pirates. The spiders. The poisonous white whips. They attacked not only our people, but our island too, the poison leaking into the ground, destroying it from the inside out. I prayed the fountain had enough power to deal with it all.

"Here they come." Wade sought my hand.

I glanced at the Power of the Sea and its surrounding smaller orbs. All were present, as well as their guardians, apart from the two imprisoned on the ship.

"Do we know how this is going to work...exactly?" Ford asked, gesturing to his green orb to join him.

"We start now," I said, and explained the experiment I'd

conducted in the great hall with my fiery orb and the Power of the Sea.

Before the ship drew too close, I urged my orb to enter the Power of the Sea once more. It quickly floated inside, repeating its spectacle of blended colors. Ford instructed his green orb to do the same, and then Dylan with his yellow orb. Only the orbs of Spirt and Soul and Snow and Ice remained outside.

"Let's hope they know what to do when it's time."

The sound of marching boots filled the courtyard. Rob and the army had arrived, several troops dashing down the palace steps, others sweeping up from the beach. A little under ten thousand soldiers. Confidence bloomed in my chest. With the fountain working once more, casualties should be minimal, but we couldn't carry out the entire battle by the fountain. Not only could we not all fit, but we would risk damaging the fountain itself. And I had no idea what would happen to the healing water if a poisonous whip flew too close.

The front line consisted of Wade, Ford, Blaze, Trent, Angelica, Babette, Dylan and me. Trent and Angelica possessed no extraordinary abilities, but nothing would make Trent abandon the fight to get his daughter back, and Angelica only had vengeance on her mind. Perhaps redemption too.

An idea flickered at the back of my brain. A memory. Something Maya and I had discussed concerning the latest prophecy; *old enemies die hard.* We'd talked of forgiveness and acceptance. I glanced at Angelica. Perhaps the prophecy had nothing to do with me.

My attention was stolen by the buzzing of the two remaining orbs. They glowed brightly, making the night seem like day, and pulsed with their chosen colors. Their guardians had to be on that ship.

The ship descended. Only a few yards above my head now. The white whips lashed down, seeking life as if they had a mind of their own. Some soldiers fired a few potshots, but it was too soon. Bullets couldn't hurt the pirates yet.

An icy wind tunneled through the courtyard with the docking of the ship. Its hull scraped against the cobble. An anchor was thrown over. They'd never docked before. They must have known, as well as us, that this was the final reckoning.

The anchor was a white stone that shifted with movement; a nest of venomous baby spiders. Revulsion curled in my throat, and I shot a fireball at the anchor, managing to scorch the seething mass. Dislodged, the ship bobbed in the air. I wouldn't make it easy for them to kill us.

Whips lashed down from both sides, ensnaring those who stood too close, flaying their flesh with an unforgiving poison. They were dead before they hit the ground.

"Back!" Rob shouted.

The two orbs buzzed and pulsed, zoomed up to the ship and spun around it in circles. I caught sight of Gal, tethered to the starboard side. Had he been there the entire time? Had they fed him at all? His skin was as pale as an ashray, his hair tangled and knotted, his body limp and unmoving. Was he still alive?

"Wade!"

"I see him."

Una was next to him. Her eyes were open but unfocussed. She didn't flinch when a spider crawled over her face.

"Una!" Trent yelled.

And next to her was Ember, Blaze's son, his small dragon king wings unfurled and broken. Then Mini Cordelia, and several other children. I couldn't tell who was alive.

The pirates threw ladders over the side of the ship and quickly disembarked. They descended in droves, more than could possibly fit on the ship. Lashing their whips, they cackled their evil laughs and encouraged their spiders to explore Atlantis. The pirates swarmed through the courtyard, their bony faces glinting in the moonlight, their matted hair filled with cobwebs and spiders, their skeletal mouths grinning without remorse.

Blaze shot into the sky. "Ember!"

The white orb of Snow and Ice caressed Gal's face. His eyes flew open and he screamed. A scream so full of pain and terror that it took everything I had in me not to release my flames.

The glow of the orb surrounded him, and he calmed, examining the strange spectacle. Oddly, he laughed and jutted his chin toward the other combined orbs.

The orb of Spirit and Soul made a circle around Una's head. She blinked, focused on the radiant purple light, and smiled.

The courtyard turned into a battlefield. The whips swept close, and we had no more room to retreat. Several soldiers went down. Trent received a lash to the arm and dashed to the fountain. Angelica swatted at several spiders insistent on crawling up her legs. Ford stomped on a few, Wade ducked under a whip, Dylan floated in the air and attempted to blow away the frigid wind wreaking havoc with the direction of Blaze's flames.

Babette raised her hands and the water in the fountain began to bubble and hiss. She enticed the water into a funnel, levitating it over the fallen, and dropped it over the wounded. Those who were not dead rose to their feet. The Power of the Sea had clearly seen fit to grant her an ability. And it was about time too.

The frigid wind lifted my hair, tangled my clothes, pushed back our advance, but I refused to back down. My son was *right there*.

The two orbs aboard the ship, after spinning around their guardians once more, zoomed toward the Power of the Sea, and crashed into its center.

"Now!" I screamed.

The guardians in the courtyard gathered close. We held hands and implored the combined mass of orbs to do our bidding.

Extending a tentative hand, Wade touched the swirling mass. When he wasn't hurt, he gathered it in his hand, and hurled it at the ship.

A shock wave shook the island, rumbled under our feet, sent people toppling over, and created a sonic boom.

While I covered my ears, the swirling orb engulfed the pirates and the ship, spun around the courtyard, and turned the dead to life.

A pirate approached, its whip lashing at my feet, spiders cascading from its broken shoulders. "Time to die, my pretty."

"I completely agree." I hurled a fireball at its face and it disintegrated immediately.

Battle sounds raged at my back. The clang of swords, the bang of bullets, the shouts of triumph and also pain. I spun in a circle, making sure my friends were safe, and took off for the ship. Clearing my path of spiders and poisonous whips with my fireballs, I made it to a ladder while Blaze rained fire on the advancing pirates. No longer skeletons. No longer grinning. No longer immortal. They died like anyone else, with screams of tortured agony. And they were not immune to their own whips.

I took the ladder two rungs at a time, heaving myself to the top, throwing fire at anyone in pursuit.

When I swung a leg over the balustrade, I came face to face with who I assumed to be the captain of the dastardly ship.

"I want my son back," I screamed in its face. I followed my words with a fireball and deleted the pirate from existence. How easy they were to kill now. A vengeful need consumed me.

Wade appeared at my side. A quick glance over the deck revealed forty or so children tied to the sides. Many of them in desperate need of the fountain.

I leaned over the edge of the ship. "Babette! Babette! One of those funnels up here!"

She acknowledged my words with a nod and immediately began to create another healing whirlpool.

I turned back to the ship. Wade had already begun releasing the children, unbinding their ropes with a twist of his fingers. I remembered the deal I'd struck with my red orb, that it wouldn't hurt anyone I cared about. But its power had been sucked into the Power of the Sea, had been used to turn the ghost pirates to flesh; I could no longer count on it to do my bidding. I couldn't risk burning the children.

I ran to Gal, threw my arms around him.

"Mom!"

"I love you so much!" I undid his binds, then cupped his face. "I have to help the others."

Babette's funnel burst over the deck, splashing the sails, raining over the children. Those who had slackened sat up, opened their eyes, and called for help. Wade dashed to them all, untying their bonds, telling them to stay hidden until it was over.

"I have to go," I yelled at Wade. "I have to help with the pirates."

He gave me a solemn nod. "I'll finish here."

I ran for the balustrade and leaped over the side of the ship, not thinking about how far I had to fall.

"I got you!" Blaze flew by, grabbed my hand, and swung me to safety.

I landed on my feet, my knees buckling, so I dove with the forward momentum, launching myself back to my feet, only to find myself face to face with a fearsome pirate. A single fireball to his head put him out of his misery.

"Over here!" Angelica's voice.

I scanned the courtyard. Soldiers fought pirates in hand-to-hand combat. With no immunity to their own weapons, the pirates abandoned their whips, instead relying on ancient pistols strapped to their belts that took over a minute to reload. We had this.

Then I spotted the fallen Atlanteans, spiders crawling over their unmoving bodies. Too many dead. More than I had feared.

"Help!"

I ran toward Angelica's voice; leaping over the fallen, ducking under bullets, hurling fireballs at the enemy. I arrived to find Angelica on the ground, a pirate standing on her arm, spiders biting her flesh. Her skin markings were barely visible as her life leached away.

"No!" I threw a fireball, cursing how much smaller they were now that my red orb had been drained of power, and called for Babette.

A funnel of healing water hovered above us, not only curing Angelica or bringing me a restored energy, but healing the pirate too.

I pushed the pirate off Angelica's arm and yanked her to her feet, then hurled another fireball at the pirate. This time he went down and stayed down.

"Thank you, Cordelia," she shouted above the melee.

I gripped her arms. "You must get to safety. There's nothing you can do here."

"I must atone for all the harm I've caused."

"You've done enough."

"I love you, Cordelia. And I love this island." She gave me one last look and took off for the palace steps.

I turned to face the battle. I glimpsed Wade still aboard the ship, Trent with him, cradling the children and keeping them safe. But the courtyard was a mess. While Babette continued to make healing funnels of water and send them to those in need, Blaze threw fireballs from the sky, and Dylan, now grounded without the magic of his orb, had gotten ahold of a rifle and was picking off pirates from the roof of his bar. I had no idea when he'd learned to shoot.

Ford fought in the middle of the crush, stabbing pirates through with his longsword, or sometimes slicing their heads clean off. He reminded me a little of Gal. Not my son, but the one he was named for, the old High Council member who had been more of an uncle to me than anything else. A second father. He'd guided me through life's decisions with a firm hand and never let me squirm away from the difficult things. And he was the toughest and most capable warrior I knew. His statue stood near the fountain, not far from the place he'd died, watching the carnage take place. Ford was so like him: his bravery, his strength, and his unwavering loyalty.

I hurried to his side as a pirate lashed a cutlass against the back of his legs. Ford buckled, but I was there to prop him up and take the offending pirate out. Back-to-back we stood in the moonlit courtyard, both of us breathing heavily as we fought to protect our island, our lives, and our children.

"You good?" I threw the words over my shoulder.

"Good," Ford panted. "You?"

"Let's burn the motherfuckers."

I felt the warmth of his grin.

He swung and I threw fireballs. They streaked through the courtyard, in tune with my will, just like during the battle with the dragon kings. No longer did I need to hurl them at a specific enemy. My fiery power understood the desire forming in my mind. I pictured the ghost pirates in my head, showing it my preferred target, and the fireballs streaked away from me, scoring several simultaneous hits.

"We're making progress," Ford said.

The battle raged on for another hour. Those who were not there occupied my mind. Maya and her children, my parents, Angelica...I prayed they were safe.

Babette continued to move her funnels of healing water over the Atlanteans, sometimes healing a pirate accidentally, but that couldn't be helped. Blaze roared his fire from above, and I threw my flames from the ground. Ford slashed. Trent and Wade protected the children. Dylan, Rob, and the army pressed the pirates back.

Dawn appeared in the sky. A bruising light that brought the reality of day and highlighted the fallen at our feet. Only a few pirates remained. Exhausted, I charged toward the ragged group, who stood back-to-back with their whips back in their hands.

They begged for mercy. They promised they'd never return.

I narrowed my eyes at the murderous group and burned them out of existence.

Ford and I fell against each other, our backs supporting our weight as we took in the aftermath of the battle. Smoke billowed from small craters. Spiders scuttled away. The white whips shriveled and sank into the ground. The fountain healed it all, repaving the paths, fixing the bullet holes, healing the wounded, but the dead remained dead. At least a thousand. We would mourn them all in the Atlantean way.

The fountain continued to heal. Snow melted away, water channels flowed, and the temperature rose. The wind died down to a gentle breeze, bringing the pleasing scent of the ocean, while the cobbles glistened, and the sea produced gentle waves.

My parents came rushing out of the palace, the marble steps glistening and shining. Maya was on their heals, along with my sister and Angelica.

"Mom!"

I turned to see Gal sliding down the rope ladder from the ship, not bothering to use the rungs. I winced, knowing the fountain couldn't heal the friction burns he'd surely receive on his palms. But none of that mattered now. What mattered was that he was safe.

He made it to the courtyard, glanced at the bodies littered across the cobbles, and grimaced.

"It's okay now," I called.

He picked his way to me, tears in his eyes, and then threw his arms around my waist.

I kneeled on the ground, curling my body around his, shedding tears that would never stop.

"I knew you'd save me," he said.

"You had a hand in that." He pulled back and gave me a curious look. "You are the guardian of the orb of Snow and Ice."

"Is that what that thing was?"

As if to prove my point, the Power of the Sea sailed into the courtyard, trailing all five of the orbs. But they were much smaller than before, barely bigger than a marble, both their radiance and power diminished. Despite their smaller size, I didn't regret using them and reducing their power for their guardians. They had brought our children back. Even if it took years for their power to accumulate once more, I didn't think anyone on the island mourned their use.

I stroked the back of Gal's head. "I think it's going to be a long time before we can use their power again."

"That's okay," Gal said. "I've got you."

I laughed and hugged him close. Wade joined us and swept the two of us into his arms.

"How's your head?" I asked my son, putting a hand to his flushed skin.

"A little sore, but much better than before," Gal replied.

"We'll get you checked out in the hospital," Wade said.

Gal groaned, making us both laugh.

Happy reunions ensued, despite the presence of death all around. We moved toward the fountain, a symbolic area that offered hope and longevity and a way through our battles. Under the cover of the fountain's gazebo, we could focus on moving forward and keep the scene of death away from the children.

Mini Cordelia was reunited with her mother and told the news of her father's death. Her face crumbled, but she didn't cry. Mother and daughter clung to each other, whispering promises of hope and new beginnings.

Then came the reunion between my sister, Blaze, and their son, Ember. Raina was unafraid to shed copious tears. She locked eyes with me as she hugged her son and allowed Blaze to shroud them with his wings.

"Thank you," she mouthed.

"I love you," I signed back.

"Look what I can do!" Ember sucked in a huge breath, held it for over ten seconds, then opened his mouth wide. He exhaled, producing a few sparks. It wasn't fire, but it was a start.

Blaze ruffled his son's long hair. "That's my boy."

Una hugged both her parents tightly, a wobbly smile on her lips, the odd tear tracking down her cheek. "I was so scared. But Gal helped."

I smiled at my son.

"He was so brave," Una said. "Always yelling at the pirates. Always hatching a plan to escape."

"You gave each other courage," I told her.

Gal nodded. "I couldn't have done it without you, Una. I was scared too."

Una wrapped her arms around Gal and kissed his cheek, and for once he didn't recoil.

"Una," Maya said. "You have a new sister to meet." Maya offered the swaddled bundle to her eldest child. Little Coral was sound asleep, her mouth puckering as she dreamed.

"She's mine?" Una asked.

"She's all of ours," Maya said, and placed the baby in Una's arms.

"She is pretty cute," Gal said.

"Coral," Una murmured. "I love that name. It's the name for a princess."

Gal's eyes flew wide. "That means she'd have to marry me."

"No way!" Una said. "That's my job."

The kids dissolved in giggles, Ember snorting fire. Laughter and tears filled the courtyard.

"Look, Mom!" Gal broke free of my arms. "That's the most enormous selachii I've ever seen."

My son dashed away from the gazebo, across the court-yard, to a burbling water channel where a dorsal fin was emerging.

"No, Gal!" I screamed his name, hoping that somehow the fate I saw in front of me wouldn't come true.

Old enemies die hard.

Wade and I darted across the courtyard, close on Gal's heals. But he thought it was a game, throwing backward glances and smiles in our direction. He weaved and dodged a path around the cobbles, running to meet what he thought was a hero.

"Gal, stop!" Wade yelled, pumping his arms, gaining on our son.

Blaze took to the sky, fire already bellowing from his mouth.

Zale erupted from the water in full megalodon form. Gal skidded to a halt as he took in the sheer size of the overgrown selachii.

"Mom!" Nothing but terror in his voice.

"Gal!" Flames shot from my hands, streaking through the courtyard, punching holes in walls, searing the hair of a few in the crowd, totally out of control.

Zale's enormous shadow covered the courtyard. Water poured from his body as he emerged from the channel, gnashing his teeth and rolling his black eyes, which settled on my son.

"No!" I screamed, shaking my hands.

Wade and I ran together. But Gal was too close to the water's edge. Gal swiveled toward me, the expression on his face nothing I ever wanted to see again.

"Mom!"

"Gal!"

Wade and I skidded across the cobbles. Wade snagged Gal's arm, encasing him in a protective embrace, but I carried on spinning toward the opening jaws.

Finally, my palms ignited, and I hurled fire at the enormous beast. Fireballs punched through his gills, dented his flesh, took out his teeth, blinded one eye. I roared as I ran toward my oldest nemesis, relishing the blood pouring from his wounds.

"Mom!"

"Cordelia!"

Both my husband and son called for me, but I only had eyes for Zale.

As Wade and Gal slid away from the danger zone, narrowly skimming the area beneath Zale's jaws, I slipped on a cobble and tumbled toward the widening mouth.

There was nothing I could do to stop my momentum. I hurtled toward Zale, throwing my fireballs down his throat. The shadow of his jaws stretched across the courtyard. They closed in slow motion, inch by agonizing inch. I cowered from the violent points, but couldn't avoid his teeth piercing my flesh.

The pain was like nothing I'd ever experienced. Daggers punctured my skin the entire length of my body. Flames snaked along my limbs, but Zale didn't shy away from their fiery touch. He was too big. Bigger than the Hound of the Ocean.

Fire erupted from my palms, my eyes, my pores. A last-ditch attempt to save myself, but I already knew it was too late.

As Zale's jaws tightened around me, I spared a look at my husband and son standing by the bank of the water channel. Wade held Gal in his arms, both of them screaming my name, both of their expressions already tortured with loss.

Old enemies die hard.

It wasn't Zale's death *The Mermaid Chronicles* spoke of, it was mine.

Blood spurted in crimson arcs. Three rows of teeth crunched through my flesh and bones. The pain was a distant thing, something viewed from afar as I was punctured and shaken and bitten to death.

"Cordelia!"

I don't know who screamed my name. Maybe it was Gal. Or Wade. Or Dylan, or any number of my friends and family. There was nothing they could do.

The flames on my hands dwindled as my life poured out of me. Tiny sparks. Nothing that would hurt a shark like Zale. Heat blasted by my feet. Maybe Blaze. Sweet Blaze.

Jaws tightened around me. A splash of water on my arms. My flames burst into life. Had Babette sent a funnel to my aid? But I had no more energy to direct my fire. Not with my body almost torn in two.

Zale took me underwater. He shook my body like I was nothing more than a ragdoll. I recalled the images of Dylan in a similar position all those years ago. What would seeing this do to him now?

We sank into the depths. Music reached my ears, but I couldn't think who would be singing underwater. I tried to twist out of his grasp, but pain lanced through my body, holding me in place.

I drifted through the currents. Wade's desperate thoughts pushed into my head. Urging me to fight. With what? I was too weak. The ocean filled with shouts and screams. Tortured cries of desperation. The jagged pleas filled my head until I couldn't tell them apart.

"Mom! Mom!" Gal's desperate cries reached me telepathically.

"Cordelia!"

I spied Wade's shark shadow, his mouth opening to bite Zale. But Zale did not release me.

We sank.

Through the depths.

Through the darkness.

And then there was nothing.

ATLANTIS' LAMENT

In the depths of the deep blue sea,
Where the coral blooms and the waves run free,
Lived our queen, Cordelia, so fair,
A mermaid's grace, beyond compare.

With her flowing tail and her scarlet hair,
She ruled Atlantis, just and fair,
Her heart was pure, her spirit strong,
In her presence, we all belonged.

(Chorus)
Oh, Cordelia, our mermaid queen,
In your memory, we still dream,
Of the days when you ruled the sea,
Now you're gone, we're lost completely.

But beneath the waves, a darkness grew,
A traitor lurked, a selachii so untrue,

He plotted schemes, with envy's flame,
To steal our queen's eternal name.

Cordelia, she trusted all,
Even as the shadows began to fall,
But betrayal struck, a deadly blow,
Took her life, let our tears flow.

(Chorus)
Oh, Cordelia, our mermaid queen,
In your memory, we still dream,
Of the days when you ruled the sea,
Now you're gone, we're lost completely.

The ocean's depths, they echo your name,
In every heart, your love remains,
Atlanteans weep for what's been done,
A broken kingdom, forever undone.

Now the kingdom mourns, a somber song,
As we swim in the currents, trying to belong,
To the memory of a queen so dear,
Whose absence we'll forever fear.

In the waves, her spirit lives on,
In the moonlit tides, and the early dawn,
We'll honor her, our love so true,
For Cordelia, our hearts renew.

(Chorus)

Oh, Cordelia, our mermaid queen,
In your memory, we still dream,
Of the days when you ruled the sea,
Now you're gone, we're lost completely.

In the depths of Atlantis, our tears we cry,
For our beloved queen, beneath the sky,
Though she's gone, her legacy remains,
In our hearts, in the sea's gentle chains.

ade's world shattered into a million fragments as he carried his wife's broken body along the cobble path and into the courtyard. Gal clung to his legs, sniffing and seeping tears. When they reached the fountain, Wade lay Cordelia's lifeless form in the water, trickling the healing liquid into her mouth. Hope clutched at his heart as the useless organ pounded against his ribs. He held her above the water level, kissing her forehead, her cheeks, her eyelids, as if his love could breathe life back into her.

"Wake up, Cordelia!"

But she had always been stubborn. Her eyelids did not flutter. Her chest did not rise. Her skin remained colorless. The red orb, now no bigger than a marble, hovered in the air beside her, a silent testament to their broken dreams.

Time stretched on, a cruel and unyielding force. Whispers spread among the people gathered. Someone sobbed. It was too soon for that. The water would cure her. But even as he thought the words, he knew it was too late. Seconds turned into agonizing minutes. Someone coughed.

Reality, cruel and unforgiving, clawed its way into Wade's soul. Cordelia did not wake. Her body was beyond repair. Her wounds devastatingly gruesome. Her life...cut short.

Wade clenched his fists and roared at the indifferent sky. The tiny red orb drifted to Blaze's side, perhaps seeking solace from the only other being on the island who could produce fire. Did it belong to him now?

"Mom?" Gal questioned, then swiveled his sad gaze to Wade.

Struggling to find words, Wade scooped Gal into his arms and held him tightly. "She's gone."

Together they cried. The surrounding silence stretched on. The water in the fountain trickled from its spouts, and his dead wife floated in the water, her head supported by Maya.

Wade could hardly bear to look at the faces of his friends and subjects as they gathered around the fountain, their expressions a haunting reflection of his own anguish, but he caught Dylan's eye. Cordelia's twin brother stood frozen, his features twisted into a mask of horror, his skin paler than the marble steps. But Wade had no words of comfort to offer, for his own grief threatened to consume him. Gal sobbed in his arms.

Cordelia's screams of pain replayed in his head on an endless loop. He'd tried to wrestle Zale off her, but when one dark eye rolled toward Gal, who had clung to Zale's pectoral fin, Wade was forced to back off and protect his son. The murderous selachii released his wife's body and swam into a dark abyss.

There was no snow on the island anymore; the fountain had restored the weather. Pointless. Nothing could thaw the sorrow and desperation in his heart. He sat on the rim of the fountain with Gal in his arms and stared at Cordelia's bright red hair. The hair he'd loved to bury his face in, to wrap his fist around...the lips he never bored of kissing, the freckles that charmed his soul...never again. None of it. Ever.

The news of Cordelia's sacrifice spread like wildfire, causing an unusual scudding of gray clouds to shroud the island. Mournful sobs echoed in the courtyard. Maybe his own.

Dylan approached, his steps slow and hesitant, his eyes filled with anguish. "Wade," he said, his voice barely a whisper. "I'm so sorry. I should have held onto my orb. I should have done...something."

Wade turned to his brother-in-law; his grief mirrored in Dylan's eyes. "It wasn't your fault, Dylan. Zale was a monster, and he caught us off guard. There was nothing any of us could have done."

"I'll make sure Zale pays for what he's done," Dylan said.

"Help me with Gal," Wade said, glancing at his son, who clutched his mother's lifeless hand.

Together, they pried Gal away from Cordelia's body. Tears streamed down his son's face as he clung to Wade.

"I want Mom back." Gal's lower lip quivered.

"I know, buddy. I do too." Wade's voice broke. There were no more words. None that would take away his pain, none that would bring back his wife, none that would vanquish the sadness in his son's eyes.

IN THE DAYS THAT FOLLOWED, Wade went through the motions of ruling the island, but every decision he made felt hollow, every decree an empty echo of the past. The numbness that shrouded him seeped into his skin a little deeper every day.

With his focus on Gal and attempting to avoid the crushing weight of grief, Wade had no brain space to plan a funeral. Not one that Cordelia deserved. Her parents took over. They arranged a solemn ceremony attended by all the ocean shifters of Atlantis. Cordelia's body was placed in a carved seashell casket adorned with pearls and sea flowers. The mourners gathered on the beach to pay their last respects.

Wade, Gal, and Dylan stood at the forefront of the gathering. Blaze, Maya, and Trent hovered around the casket. Cordelia's parents and sister cried openly. So much grief. Too much grief. This wasn't supposed to happen.

With concerted effort, Wade cleared his throat, attempting to find the words that could encapsulate the essence of Cordelia's spirit. He blinked, stared at the rolling waves.

"Cordelia Blue was the love of my life." He dipped his head, swallowing back the tears, then faced his audience once more. "She was my queen. And she was your queen too."

"Hear, hear!" someone yelled from the crowd.

Wade pushed his hair off his face, fiddled with his wedding ring. He would never take it off. He would never love another. So what was the point? He looked at his son.

"Cordelia not only possessed the extraordinary ability to wield fire, but she contained a depthless passion and love in her heart. Not only for me, but for all of you too. She loved this island. All she ever wanted was for everyone to be happy. And safe. As I stand here before you, seeing that humans and ocean shifters have come together to mourn her loss, I know she is smiling down on us, relieved that we are all united once more."

There was nothing else to say. His heart was now as empty as Lake Echomere. He had nothing left to give.

Gal, clutching his hand, tried to say something, but burst into tears before he could utter more than a few words.

As they pushed Cordelia's casket into the waves, a profound emptiness engulfed Wade. He had lost his soul-mate, his love, and the mother of his child. Atlantis had lost its queen, and Gal had lost his mother. The island had become a cold and desolate place. A sinking feeling settled inside Wade. One he couldn't control. One that was all-consuming. One he gave himself to. He didn't care anymore.

Blaze ignited Cordelia's pyre. The flames took quickly as she floated out to sea, burning with a bright intensity as if they too felt the sense of loss.

Wade remained on the beach with Gal and Dylan and Cordelia's family. They watched the casket until it met the horizon, and then they watched some more. A storm rolled in.

Angelica approached. "I'm leaving. Taking my clan home. We'll never return."

"You're welcome here any time." The words came automatically.

Angelica's lips pressed into a thin line, her eyes burdened with guilt. "I'm so sorry. Her death is my fault."

Wade focused on her face. "Zale was always going to come for her."

Angelica didn't say anything else. Her clan gathered in the shallows and then slipped beneath the waves.

Wade returned to the palace. His footsteps echoed through the dimly lit corridors of the once-vibrant mansion, each footfall resonating with the weight of his grief. His private chambers, once a sanctuary of love and warmth shared with Cordelia, now felt empty and cold. The memory of her smile, her laughter, her touch, lingered in every corner.

Gal followed him, his eyes red from crying, his small form a constant reminder of what had been taken from them.

Wade sat on the edge of their bed, his head in his hands, tears streaming down his face. Gal climbed onto his lap, wrapping his arms around his neck.

"Why didn't Mom burn him?" he asked, his voice trembling.

Wade held his son tightly, struggling to find words. "The power of the orb was diminished... and Zale is...too strong."

"But she took out the dragon kings before."

"Not without help," Wade said. "Her powers are unpredictable when she's scared. She'd never leave us if...she tried. She really tried."

Gal buried his face in Wade's shoulder, his small body

shaking with sobs. Wade stroked his son's hair, attempting to provide an element of comfort, though he knew no words could ease the pain they both felt.

"What do we do now? Are we going to kill Zale?"

"I think he's too strong for me too," Wade said.

"But we can't just let him get away."

"Gal, I can't think about this right now."

Gal slipped off his lap and trudged to his own bedroom, leaving Wade alone with his thoughts and an unbearable emptiness. How could nothing weigh so much?

THE NEXT DAY Cordelia's parents came to collect Gal. The day after that, it was Maya and Trent with their four children. Then it was Raina and Blaze with Ember. Dylan made an appearance. Then his own sister. Even his cousin Jordan. He barely saw Gal. Only to share a silent breakfast and tuck him in at night.

Days passed. Which turned into weeks. And then months. He stopped going outside. He never swam. Never shifted into his selachii form. He rarely left his suite. The loss of Cordelia left him adrift, a king without a queen, a heart without its beat.

"You can't go on like this."

"You should get some fresh air."

"Atlantis needs its king."

"You have to try."

Even his father returned to offer help. But Wade and his

father had never been close; he wasn't going to start listening to him now.

It was Gal who almost broke through. "Can you tell me a story about Mom?"

Wade found himself lost to memories. He recalled the first time he'd laid eyes on Cordelia Blue, when they were thirteen years old and competing for times in the pool. He'd fallen in love with her then. A foolish notion at so young an age, but his love never wavered, it only grew. And for some reason, she loved him back.

He couldn't tell Gal any of that. The memories were too painful. All he could do was try to exist. But it would never be enough. The world had lost its color, and he, its king, had lost his queen, leaving behind only a heart that beat on, shattered and incomplete.

THE END

Read on for a sneak peek of Vendetta, the fifth book in *The Mermaid Chronicles*...

THANK YOU!

Thank you so much for making it all the way to the end. I hope you have enjoyed **Ghost Pirates** and aren't feeling too bereft! If you enjoyed the story, leaving a review is the best possible present for an author! You can do it here:

https://geni.us/GhostPirates

Cordelia's story has been in my head for years, and all the time I've known what would happen to her. But writing it brought with it a heartbreak I wasn't expecting! Even though Cordelia is merely a character, she possesses such bravery and love that I so wish she was real.

If you're interested in my other books, you can read the first chapter of all of them on my website at **www.marisa-noelle.com**, or buy from any bookshop. Please sign up to my mailing list to get the latest news, free stories, novellas, and chapters from all my other books. Every month I hold a competition and three lucky readers get an **e-book completely free**!

You will receive all eleven origin story novellas set in The Unadjusteds universe FREE!!!

Read on for the first chapter of *Vendetta*, the next instalment of *The Mermaid Chronicles*...

ACKNOWLEDGMENTS

Well, folks, they say it takes a village to raise a child, but I'm here to tell you, it takes a whole circus to birth a book! So, grab your popcorn, because I've got some shout-outs and thank-yous that are more entertaining than a juggling act on a unicycle!

First up, my writing group, The Rebel Alliance. You guys are like the Jedi Masters of encouragement, and I couldn't have done this without you. You've had my back for so long that I'm pretty sure you have a permanent imprint of my book cover on it!

And speaking of covers, Fay, you're the Picasso of book design. Seriously, the cover is so gorgeous it's practically doing the cha-cha on its own. Bravo!

Now, let's talk about Team Swag. We navigate the treacherous waters of publishing together, and boy, do we make a splash! We hold each other's hands like we're crossing the street, and when it comes to sharing knowledge, we're like the Avengers of advice-giving. What a fantastic bunch of writers and friends!

Neil, my rock, my Steady Eddie. You stole my heart in a single night and have been guarding it like a precious gem ever since. I love you more than a mermaid loves the ocean (and that's saying something).

To my kids, Riley, Lucas, and Quinn, thanks for being the wind beneath my writerly wings. Just promise me you won't be embarrassed if I show up at your school fairs with a stack of books. You're my plot problem-solving superheroes, and you always rescue me!

Mom, you're the eagle-eyed proofreader of my dreams, even if we occasionally find a typo or two. Let's just blame it on Dad when that happens, shall we?

To my early supporters, you're the MVPs of my writing journey. Sasha, Michelle, Nikki, Adrian, Darcy, Hetty, Louise, you've given me advice and feedback that's worth its weight in gold doubloons!

Twitter, oh Twitter, (and you will always be Twitter) you've been my trusty sidekick in this adventure. The writing community there has made rejections feel like mosquito bites at a barbecue - annoying but manageable. You all know who you are, and I couldn't have asked for better virtual friends. Thank you!

And then there's Booktok! What a wild and wonderful place I've stumbled into. You've made me buy so many crowns I'm starting to feel like royalty. Thanks for supporting my journey, engaging with me, and even buying my books. You're the crown jewels of my author life!

A big shout-out to my A-level English teacher, Michael Fox, who taught me to think for myself and defend my ideas. You're the reason I can write more than a grocery list!

Last but not least, a standing ovation for my readers. You are the true stars of this show, and I wouldn't be here without you. Stick around, because there are more books in my circus tent, and I promise they'll be worth the price of admission.

Oh, and if you fancy learning more about my books and want to be in with the chance to win exclusive giveaways, sign up to me website below!

(www.marisanoelle.com)

Read on for the first chapter of *Vendetta*, the next instalment of *The Mermaid Chronicles*...

Marisa Noelle is the author behind a treasure trove of middle-grade and young adult novels that dance through the realms of science-fiction, fantasy, horror, dystopian, and mental health. From unraveling mysteries to diving deep into the human psyche, she's your go-to wordsmith for adventures that'll tickle your imagination.

Marisa's literary exploits include "The Shadow Keepers," a spine-tingling tale to keep you up all night, and "The Unraveling of Luna Forester," a masterpiece that snagged the prestigious First Place Incipere Award, rocked the Write-Blend Finalist stage, waltzed as a BBYNA Semi-Finalist, and took its place on the Bookshelf Finalist shelf. With dystopian being one of her favorite genres, you can expect fast-paced thrills from the world of "The Unadjusteds Trilogy," a roller-coaster ride featuring "The Unadjusteds," "The Rise of the Altereds," and "The Reckoning," perfect for fans of Divergent, Pretties & The Hunger Games. And don't forget to dive into "The Mermaid Chronicles," a series that will plunge you into the depths of "Secrets of the Deep," lead you on a wild "Quest for Atlantis," challenge you to "Fight for Freedom," send shivers down your spine with "Ghost Pirates," and leave you craving "Vendetta."

When Marisa's not weaving literary spells, she's helping mold the future of MG and YA authors as a mentor for the Write Mentor program.

With passports stamped on both sides of the Atlantic, she draws inspiration from the rich tapestry of the USA and UK for her storytelling.

When not writing, Marisa likes to imagine herself as a mermaid, and can often be found in the local pool...or lake... or ocean. Despite her undeniable bookworm credentials since she was knee-high to a grasshopper, the author gig took Marisa by surprise. You see, she had a secret past as a bit of a science geek during her school days. But hey, science and storytelling make a surprisingly magical concoction! Currently, Marisa calls Woking, UK, her home sweet home, where she resides with her trusty squad, including her husband, three amazing kids, and a furry four-legged friend named Copper.

Marisa loves to hear from her readers. You can find and connect with her at the links below.

Twitter & Instagram: **@MarisaNoelle77**
Tiktok: **@MarisaNoelle12**
Website: **www.MarisaNoelle.com**

Turn the page for a sneak peek of book five of
The Mermaid Chronicles – Vendetta...

THE MERMAID CHRONICLES
BOOK FIVE
VENDETTA
MARISA NOELLE

OLD ENEMIES DIE HARD...

For twelve years, Gal has nursed a burning desire for revenge. As the anniversary of his mother's death approaches, he leaves Atlantis, determined to track down Zale, the ruthless shark shapeshifter who robbed his mother's life. But as he sets sail on his dangerous quest, he discovers his two closest friends have stowed away on his vessel. It's too late to turn back now.

Their pursuit of the elusive selachii propels them to the unforgiving Antarctic, where a brutal storm threatens to drown them. Gal's reclusive grandfather comes to their rescue, regaling them with stories of his parents' epic love and unveiling hidden family secrets. Yet, Gal is convinced that love is a treacherous path, one he dares not tread for fear of the pain it may bring.

Locked in a battle with his own emotions, Gal's quest leads him to distant horizons in pursuit of his nemesis. But only by trusting in the unbreakable bonds of friendship can he unlock the secrets of a magical ice flute and unearth the lost trident of Atlantis—the sole weapon capable of ending Zale's reign of terror.

Caught between revenge and an unexpected love, Gal faces an impossible choice. Will he give up vengeance for the chance at love, or will he dive headfirst into the abyss of retribution?

VENDETTA

CHAPTER ONE

Enough was enough. I was sick of the book. It had killed my mother, and I refused to be trapped by its ominous prophecies any longer.

I moved through the palace, my footsteps echoing in the grand halls, my eyes fixed on the ornate doors leading to the great hall. Preoccupied with what lay beyond those doors, I flung them open, the heavy wood slamming shut behind me. The Power of the Sea, a magical blue orb that fueled Atlantis and granted the Fountain of Youth its healing properties, hovered atop a marble column, surrounded by five other elemental orbs, each marginally larger than a marble. They had remained unchanged for twelve years, their potent properties combined to defeat the ghost pirates when I was just a boy. But my focus wasn't on the orbs or the Power of the Sea; it was on the ancient tome that rested on its own pillar—*The Mermaid Chronicles*. The book held the history of ocean shifters and prophetic visions that entwined the fate of

Atlantis with my family. And I hated it with every fiber of my being.

Last night I'd heard Maya mention the pages were turning once more, which meant a new prophecy was forming. The book had remained still for years, ever since my mother's death, but now something was coming. As the Prince of Atlantis, there was no doubt it would involve me or a member of my family. I'd grown used to the ignorant bliss over the past few years, training with Ford, helping Uncle Dylan in his bar, spending time in my room with my books, ignoring my father. It wasn't really a state of bliss, to be fair, but at least I was left alone without a treacherous threat looming on the horizon, the abilities Ford had trained me in unused, untested. And I had no intention of allowing that to change.

I stared at the book, its pages glowing ominously. Nope. I would not allow this book to change my life again. I walked around the glass case, flipped it open, and touched the ancient cover. Two mermaids circling around a depiction of the orbs.

My heart raced as I flicked through the pages, half-expecting an alarm to sound and summon the palace guards. But there was silence, broken only by the rustle of ancient parchment beneath my fingertips.

Although Maya, Atlantis' oracle and main interpreter of the ancient language used within the pages of *The Mermaid Chronicles*, had translated most of the book and loaded it onto the island's Wi-Fi, my knowledge of our world's history was limited to what I'd learned in school. Which I had left three years ago, jobless, directionless, but forced to fulfill my princely duties.

Only the four members of the High Council could read the ancient language within the book. Yet now, an inexplicable force enabled me to read the cryptic markings, the words transforming into English in my mind. I glanced over my shoulder, suddenly fearful there was an elaborate trick or joke at play, but there was nothing unusual in the room. A chill swept through my veins. There was no doubt that my sudden ability to read the book had something to do with the new prophecy that had not yet fully formed within its pages.

I slammed the book closed, tugged it out of its case, and strode toward the cold hearth. After making sure the doors were closed, I built a fire, even though the weather had not yet turned. I watched the flames dance, wondering what it felt like for my mother to wield fire. I would never know. Being the guardian of the orb of Snow and Ice, fire had always been an enigma to me. And considering we only had two weeks of cold weather per year on Atlantis, thanks to the orcana visit several years ago, I never had the opportunity to explore my connection with the colder climate. Nor did I particularly care. The orbs were tiny, practically useless, their power leached from them several years ago. Some speculated it would take a lifetime for them to regain their power. Whatever.

I flipped the book open once more, couldn't ignore the words floating off the page and seeping into my brain.

Celestial Abyss...
Vorago's Trident...

Parting the sea...

Ignoring the provocative words, I tore the page from the book, crumpled it into a ball, and threw it into the fire. It didn't immediately take, as if magically protected. I foolishly hadn't considered that. Gritting my teeth and muttering several curse words under my breath, I tore out five more, ripped them to shreds, and threw them into the fire too.

The fire hissed and spat, as if angry with my actions. A cold wind swept through the open windows, toying with my collar, slipping down the back of my shirt, and the book glowed a little brighter.

Abandoning the cover to a couch, I tore more pages, huge chunks. The cover dimmed, its golden glow fading, as I ripped and shredded and crumpled and burned. Not all the pages took. Some of them stubbornly remained, so I poked and pushed them deeper into the flames until they acquiesced to my will.

Celestial Abyss...
Vorago's Trident...
Parting the sea...

I blocked out the words, refusing to let them penetrate my thoughts, guarding my heart against the potential for future trials. I would not entertain anything that infernal book had to say.

As I held the last chunk of pages in my hand, the door swung open and Maya entered the room, Una trailing a few paces behind her.

"It's a little warm for a fire, isn't it?" She smiled, not yet aware of my actions, of what I had done to her precious book.

Her eyes moved from the fire to my hands, to the dimming cover I'd tossed on one of the couches. She gaped at me, a fury I'd never associated with her burning in her eyes. Her skin leached of color as she marched across the room and ripped the remaining pages from my hands.

"What have you done?" she demanded. Una stood by her shoulder; her face as shocked as her mother's.

I turned to face my mother's best friend. "What I should have done a long time ago."

Maya's face turned from bone white to beet red. "How. Dare. You."

Una retreated a few paces, her expression torn, her gaze wavering between us.

"That book has brought nothing but trouble," I said, jabbing my finger in the air. "Nothing but death and destruction and war."

Clutching the remaining pages against her chest, Maya shook her head, took a deep breath. "That book didn't cause any of those things. It *warned* us of those things."

"That book killed my mother."

Maya's face softened. I looked away.

"It didn't kill your mother. Zale killed your mother."

"Do not speak his name to me," I snarled. Maya had taken a breath to calm herself, but no amount of air would still my anger. "And you didn't interpret the prophecy well enough to prevent her death."

Maya flinched as if I'd slapped her. "That's not fair."

"Isn't it?" I took a step forward, attempting to intimidate

her. "You were busy having your fourth child, your eye wasn't on the ball—"

"I was blinded by the blinding rock."

Una raised her hand. "Gal—"

I silenced her with a look, then turned back to Maya. "Is that your excuse?"

Maya pushed her shoulders down. "You're right. I did let the island down. Your mother. You."

"Mom—"

"It's okay, Una," Maya said, then looked at me. "I ask myself everyday if there's something more I could have done. Your mother was my best friend and I miss her constantly. I mourn her every day. And I will mourn her tomorrow even more during the remembrance ceremony. But I also must live my life. She wouldn't want me or you or your father to wallow in grief. She would want us to live our lives."

"She would want revenge."

Maya tilted her head, relaxed her grip on the pages in her hands. "Perhaps she would. And if the opportunity presents itself, perhaps we can seek justice for her murder. But without *The Mermaid Chronicles*, we're fighting in the dark."

"We were fighting in the dark anyway."

Maya sighed. "Actually, we weren't fighting at all."

"You said there was a new prophecy coming."

"Prophecies aren't always bad."

"I guess we'll never know."

"No, I guess not."

We stared at each other in a silent stalemate. The fire crackled in the hearth, burning through the last of the pages.

All but the few Maya had ripped out of my hands; a selection of paragraphs about the creation of Atlantis. Nothing useful.

"I'll have to inform the senate, the High Council, and your father, of course."

"Of course," I said.

"They're going to be furious."

"Like you."

"Una was next in line to be the oracle." Maya glanced at her daughter. "And you've taken that away from her."

My hands fisted at my side. Like being the prophet of doom was anything to aspire to. "I'm sure the two of you will figure it out."

"I see." Maya's lips pressed into a thin line. She said nothing more, but turned and walked out of the room, the last few pages tucked under her arm.

Una stared at me, her short blonde hair reminding me of an angry hedgehog, her bright blue eyes filled with...I don't know what, but it was nothing I wanted to look at.

"Don't you start," I told her.

"I wasn't going to say anything." She walked toward me, laid a hand on my shoulder, which I immediately shrugged off.

"I don't need your sympathy."

"I'm only trying to be a friend. I know how hard this is on you. Tomorrow...twelve years—"

"I don't need your friendship either."

She took a step back, her eyes filling. Why did girls always have to cry?

"We grew up together."

"So?"

"You don't have to be alone."

"I'm not."

She sighed. "You can't live the rest of your life like this."

"Like what?" I didn't know why I was still there, still listening to her spout words I wasn't interested in. Maybe there was an ounce of good manners still left in me. Or perhaps an iota of guilt for taking away her future career. And let's face it, it was more than a career, it was a calling, passed through the females in her family for generations.

"I wish I could help you."

I laughed. "I don't need help."

"No, you've made that patently obvious." She gave me a sad smile. "And I do understand why you did what you did, but know this: your actions have consequences for the entire island."

She left, her footsteps echoing her retreat, sealing my fate in the wake of my defiance. The room was left in silence, the remnants of *The Mermaid Chronicles* consumed by flames, a bitter taste of rebellion on my tongue.

To carry on reading, click here:
https://geni.us/MermaidVendetta